Spells of Mist & Spirit

of

Book Five

Spells of Mist and Spirit
Tarot Academy, Book Five
Copyright © 2021 by Sarah Piper
SarahPiperBooks.com

Published by Two Gnomes Media

Cover design by Faera Lane

v6

E-book ISBN: 978-1-948455-50-3
Paperback ISBN: 978-1-948455-24-4
Audiobook ISBN: 978-1-977300-85-0

GET CONNECTED!

I love connecting with readers! There are a few different ways you can keep in touch:

Email: sarah@sarahpiperbooks.com

TikTok: @sarahpiperbooks

Facebook group: Sarah Piper's Sassy Witches

Twitter: @sarahpiperbooks

Newsletter: Never miss a new release or a sale! Sign up for the VIP Readers Club:
sarahpiperbooks.com/readers-club

ONE

ANSEL

Before the man was unceremoniously dumped inside the cave, I didn't think it was possible for a mage's soul to be more broken than mine.

Especially not the soul of one of my Arcana brothers.

Especially not *his* soul.

Cass was supposed to be our leader. The strongest of all of us. Unbreakable.

But he *is* broken. I know it as surely I know all the shades of blue in Stevie's eyes.

How could I not? I'm the one who shattered him. That's how it feels, anyway. I may not have any control over the one they call the Black Sun, but he's still connected to me. I can see—and feel—everything he does. His every word, every action, every thought weighs heavy on *my* conscience. The blood he's spilled is on *my* hands. When the Dark Arcana split me in two, *this* part of me—the true part —kept the conscience, the heart, the soul.

That… that *thing*… He took the malice and cruelty. The darkness I've been carrying my entire life finally made manifest. And then he amplified it.

I wish I could say it wasn't my fault, but it is. And now I watch, helpless and invisible in the shadows of the misty cave, as the Black Sun and his master look upon my Arcana brother like he's a prized buck they've just shot and dragged out of the woods.

They can't see me. Like the rest of the mage and witch souls they've exiled, I exist between realms. Here, yet not here. Alive, yet not.

From the looks of things, Cass may soon join the rest of us.

"Truthfully, I was hoping the professor would put up more of a fight," my dark counterpart says, lips curling back over his teeth. The Wand of Flame and Fury pulses bright in his hand, and he prods Cass's slumped body with it. "Guess he's just as feeble as the others. How he's managed to survive his own pathetic life even *this* long is a mystery."

"But he *has* survived, and you're fortunate that's the case." Dark Judgment places a hand on the shoulder of his star pupil. "You have great passion for this work, my Sun. An admirable quality, but you must rein in your fire until it is time to fully unleash your power."

The Black Sun glares at him, a spark of defiance igniting in his eyes. I feel it rising in my own chest—his unchecked desire to dominate.

To burn.

Not long ago, he looked upon Judgment with reverence and awe, but that's no longer the case. The Wand has given him a thirst for power that only destruction and death can sate, and right now, the other Dark Arcana are all that stand in his way.

He doesn't want to share.

None of them do.

"What the darkness has unleashed will never again be caged, *druid*." He tightens his grip on the Wand, a fierce wave of possessiveness roiling through his body.

Judgment releases his shoulder and smiles—the beaming grin of a proud father, his razor-sharp fangs tipped in blood. "Good man, my Sun. Another test passed."

"A test?"

"Yes. You are more than ready for what awaits. Our Magician will be quite pleased with your rapid progress."

At this, my chest constricts with a mirroring flicker of the Black Sun's only vulnerability.

My vulnerability.

That desperate, endless quest for validation and recognition from a father who turned his back on our family the moment he discovered I was a mage and not his son, and from a mother who blamed me for the ruins she set ablaze with her own treachery and lies.

Judgment is a poor substitute for a parent's love, but still. He's offering him everything I never had.

No matter. My parents are dead now. Incinerated in the attack on my hometown conceived by Judgment and carried out by the Black Sun standing before me.

I may as well have lit the fuse myself.

The taste of blood and ash fills my mouth, and in this moment, I feel more connected to my own darkness than ever before. And for the span of a single deep breath, I'm almost ready to give up, to fade out of the flimsy existence I'm still clinging to and let the Dark Arcana take whatever they want.

But there on the cold, wet ground before us, Cass—my professor, my friend, my brother—finally coughs out a breath. It's labored and bloody, but the life hasn't left him yet. He's still fucking fighting. And as long as that's the case—for however long it lasts—I'm not going anywhere.

The Black Sun shoves the end of the Wand into Cass's bare chest, right over his heart. The mark of Judgment flares to life.

XX. Trump Twenty.

Cass's body spasms in pain, but he makes no sound. I run to him, dropping to my knees beside him and reaching for his hand, but he can't feel me any more than the others can see me. I'm no more substantial than the mist.

As far as the Dark Arcana are concerned, Ansel McCauley is dead and gone.

"Leave him," Judgment says, and the fiery mark fades into a charred black wound. "I have preparations to make with the others, and you must return to the Fool's Grave to await the professor's companions."

"Why are you so sure they'll be there?"

"The Light Arcana are not so foolish to believe they can

win this war without the sacred objects. They will most certainly attempt to retrieve them."

"But they're sealed in protective magick. They can't unlock it without my blood. Or his, for that matter." He kicks Cass's leg, unleashing another dreary moan from the wounded man's lips. Even in the dimness of the cave, the black blood shines wet on the back of his skull.

Goddess, what I wouldn't give for even a breath's worth of magick right now...

"Precisely," Judgment says. "Take what you need from the professor, then go to the Fool's Grave and wait. When the others arrive, you will play the part of their beloved Ansel."

He crouches beside me and retrieves a small vial from his pocket, then helps himself to the fresh blood still leaking from Cass's wounds.

"The Light Arcana are reckless and emotional," Judgment continues. "The moment they believe you've returned to them as their former friend and brother, logic and reason will flee. They'll trust you to help them unearth the objects, and then you'll valiantly offer to lead them back to Cassius Devane."

"You want me to bring them here? To the cave?"

"The Star would never resist a rescue mission. Especially when it comes to the men she claims to love." Judgment shows his teeth again, but his smile quickly turns into a sneer of mockery. "Her unabated feelings toward her precious Moon Arcana will be the final nail in her proverbial coffin."

His disdain and contempt toward the woman we love fills me with a fire so intense, I'm surprised I'm not glowing with it. Beneath my touch, Cass flinches as if the same fire burns inside his veins, but he doesn't open his eyes. Doesn't take another breath.

Judgment begins a tiresome speech about victories yet to be earned, magick yet to be harnessed, but I don't need to eavesdrop to understand his plans.

They're going to lead my brothers and our woman into a trap.

And then they're going to obliterate their souls, just like they did mine.

With the Keepers of the Grave turned dark and the sacred objects in the Magician's possession, their armies can easily tear the thin veil separating our realms. They will gather their undead soldiers and break upon the campus of Arcana Academy like a tidal wave unleashed on an anthill.

Once the Academy has been destroyed and all who live annihilated or enslaved, the armies will move on to the wider world.

The Magician will control magick for an eternity.

And everything around him—everything that doesn't serve him—will burn.

"So you mean to kill her then?" the Black Sun asks with a twisted grin of his own, and my heart—what's left of it—slams against my chest. "Gotta admit—didn't see that coming. I figured the Magician would have some other use for the Star."

"He has plenty of uses for her, none of which requires

her to be alive. At least not in the way that humans think of the word. Alas, as much as I'd love to be the one to redeem the fallen Star, *I'm* not going to kill her." Judgment glances down at the lump of human formerly known as Cass. "We're going to watch *him* do it. But not until he drives her to the absolute brink of madness."

"The professor? He's as lovesick as the rest of them. He'd die before he hurt that woman."

Judgment reaches for the man's shoulder again, his eyes full of an ancient wisdom so dark and deep—so *certain*—it fills this fading heart of mine with ice. "In the end, my Sun, every last one of them will atone. Only by seeking absolution for their sins will they come to know peace. But before such peace can be granted, first they *must* be broken."

The deadly, ominous warning echoes across the cave, and the vile assholes finally leave us. One to go kiss the boots of his master, the other to lead our brothers—and our bright, beautiful Star—to their deaths.

I close my eyes, and with everything I have, call on the very last shred of my magick, hoping to goddess I've got enough of *something* left inside me to reach across these forsaken realms and make him hear me.

"Cass? You need to wake up. Now."

TWO

STEVIE

Jareth is *not* having it.

His ear-piercing screech and the frantic beating of wings against the glass outside give me and the guys just enough warning. Without a second to spare, we dive behind the bed and take cover.

The fucking window explodes.

In a tempest of glass and fury, my owl swoops inside, circling the small room twice before finally coming to perch on my shoulder. He's trembling, tiny shards of glass raining from his wings like snow, but despite the epic break-in, he doesn't seem to be injured.

"Way to make an entrance, buddy." Gingerly, I rise from the rubble, careful not to jostle him too much. He hops down to my forearm, his weight familiar and comfortable, and for a single heartbeat I allow myself the luxury of closing my eyes and taking a deep breath.

All I smell is blood.

A tremor rolls down my spine, and Jareth's talons dig in deep. His energy fills me at once, his fear and rage mingling with my own, his protective magick pulsating through my body in warm, electric waves. It zips across my skin and makes the hairs on my arms stand on end.

Suddenly, I want to move.

To run.

To fucking *fly*. Out the window, across the desert sands, all the way to the ends of the known world until I've left every terrible nightmare behind.

Do it, Stevie... Just go...

A firm grip on the back of my neck brings me back to reality, and I open my eyes to find Baz standing before me, his eyes glowing with a strange light.

"Baz?" I reach up and touch his lips, my fingers trembling. His skin is hot, his breath ragged. "Are you... What's happening?"

"You tell me."

I draw back, my fingers still vibrating. It's not his light, I realize. It's mine. My skin, my hair, my entire body is bathed in a soft, golden fire, pulsing in time with my heartbeat.

"Rein it in, Little Bird," Baz whispers, sliding his hand up to cup my cheek. "I love a magick show as much as anyone, but right now we need you calm and focused."

"We need to get to Cass and Ani," I say, remembering the mission with sudden, shocking clarity. "Why are we still standing here? We need to go. We—"

"We *will*. But not like this." He brings his other hand up, cradling me, beseeching me with those deep, red-brown eyes. "Breathe it out, Stevie. Let it go."

I hold his gaze for a beat, then finally nod, blowing out a breath and stamping my feet to dissipate the energy. The glow fades away.

From his perch on my arm, Jareth lets out a soft hoot and tucks his head under my shoulder.

"Hello, Handsome." I pick a few shards of glass from his wings and stroke his feathers. "It's okay. We're all okay."

"Stevie? Kirin?" Muffled voices call out from the other side of the door, frantic and tight. The rest of our friends are still beating madly on the wood, but Ani's wards are holding strong.

With a quick spell, Kirin calls on his air magick, and Baz offers an assist with his earth magick, attacking the wood. The door begins to rattle in its frame, and with one last push from the outside, the whole thing finally gives.

Five witches rush into the room. Poor Jareth takes off, rocketing back out the window where he so dramatically entered only moments earlier.

He doesn't go far. I can feel his presence on the roof, my stately familiar keeping watch over us all.

"Goddess, what *happened*?" Professor Broome sweeps me into her arms, then pulls back to check me for injuries. "You're bleeding!"

"It's not my blood. I'm okay."

Nat, Isla, Carly, and Professor Maddox surround us, all eyes wide with shock as they take in the devastation.

Broken furniture.

Shattered glass and wood.

And blood. A river's worth, running in a wide black slick on the other side of the bed.

The smell of it curdles the air, threatening to make me retch.

Oh, Doc. I'm so, so sorry... Please, please be okay... You and Ani have to be okay...

"Stevie." The urgency in Professor Broome's voice yanks me out of my misery. Pushing the bloodied tangle of hair from my face, she says firmly, "What happened in here? Where are Dr. Devane and Ani?"

"Whose blood is that?" Nat asks, and Isla lets out a strangled gasp at the sight.

"Stevie?" Broome presses.

"Gone. They're just gone. Ani attacked us and..." My voice breaks, and I shake my head and turn away from her. I *have* to stay focused on the mission. There's no time for sorrow or regret. Only time to act.

I cross the bedroom, searching the dresser and night tables for any magickal supplies left unbroken—anything we might be able to use on our quest. Unfortunately, there doesn't seem to be an intact spell jar or candle in the place. Everything was decimated.

Professor Maddox runs her hand along the mattress, her eyes glazing with tears. "So much anger," she whispers. "So much violence. I can feel it in the very air."

"Ani," Baz says. "It was all Ani."

She nods, her shoulders slumping as if she already

knew Ani was the source. "What happened? How did he regain consciousness? That sedative should've kept him under for hours."

"The Nightmare's Lullaby potion was a bust," Baz explains. "Ani went completely ballistic. He's gone total dark side, just like Stevie feared. Cass was trying to do the spell and Ani just..." He shoves a hand into his hair, his eyes wide as if he's reliving the shock of it all over again. "Everything unraveled so fast. He flew into a rage and..."

The words die on his tongue, just like they died on mine. The others look to Kirin, but our Tower only shakes his head, eyes fixated on the pool of blood where—just *minutes* ago—Ani nearly bashed in Doc's skull.

Disgust and terror twine around my heart, making my chest hurt.

None of us can give voice to the horrors we've just witnessed. Horrors perpetuated by one of our own.

"He's got the Wand," Kirin finally admits.

Everyone sucks in a shocked breath at that.

"That would explain why he's so much more powerful than we imagined," Maddox says. "But the darkness in him... Goddess, I wouldn't believe it was possible if I couldn't feel it for myself. He's the Sun Arcana. Goodness and light, through and through."

"Ani's... not in his right mind," I say, "but we can get him back. Will *will* get him back. We just need a few supplies and... We'll bring them *both* back."

Carly narrows her eyes. "Back from where, exactly?"

When I don't respond, she grabs Baz's arm, her gaze

desperate—the complete opposite of the cool queen of snark I'm used to.

I swallow down another wave of terror. We're falling apart, one by one, and that's the *last* thing we can afford to do. We need to be strong and united. Unstoppable. Unbreakable.

"Tell me what's going on," she implores Baz. "Where are they?"

"You tell *me*, Carly." He turns away from her, his anger rising. It washes over me like lava, threatening to burn everything in its path. "Aren't you supposed to be the clairsentient one here?"

"Baz…" I shake my head in admonishment, but I know his anger isn't directed at Carly. We're all freaking out.

He finally meets my gaze again, and I nod for him to go on. As far as I'm concerned, everyone in this house is in the inner circle. Keeping secrets is *not* an option.

After a deep sigh, Baz turns back to Carly and says, "Stevie thinks Cass and Ani are being held captive in the spiral caves."

"Spiral caves?" she asks.

"Some ancient place beyond the Void where Dark Judgment calls the so-called sinners to atone." Absently, he rubs his chest, right on the spot where Judgment marked him. The mark itself is gone, but I'm sure the pain still lingers.

"The place from your visions?" Carly asks me, and I nod again.

"Stevie…" Professor Maddox presses her fingertips to her temples like she's trying to keep her head from exploding. "Your visions are powerful—I'm not questioning that. But so much of what you see is wrapped in metaphor and symbology. What you experience in your dreams and visions is unique to you and you alone. We're not even sure those caves exist in our realm—not in the way you've experienced them in your dreams."

"Well, they exist *somewhere*," I say. "I'm sure of it. As long as that's the case, then we've got a chance at finding Doc and Ani. And as long as *that's* the case, we have to take that chance."

"Okay," she says. "Let's assume you're right, and the caves exist somewhere we can actually get to them. Why are you so certain the mages are there?"

"The Magician. That's his prison of choice."

"You're certain?"

"He all but admitted it to me."

After my Solstice ritual earlier, there wasn't much time to get into the specifics of everything the Magician revealed to me—we were too focused on subduing Ani and trying to break him out of Judgment's hold. But I have to tell them now. They need to know what we're up against.

"All the witches and mages who've died recently— everyone they've framed, tortured, and executed—are fighting for the Dark Arcana now," I say. "Not willingly, but forcefully."

"But how can executed witches fight?" Isla asks.

It takes me a minute to find the courage to tell them the whole story, and when I do, the words threaten to choke me. I can barely speak above a whisper, but I force myself to continue, painting the same gruesome picture for my friends as the Magician painted for me.

"We're talking about *thousands* of people," I say. "So many more than what the media is reporting. Since this whole thing started in earnest, there have been *mass* executions, mass graves. With help from the dark mages in our realm, the Magician stripped out all those souls and replaced them with dark magick—some sort of spell that keeps them physically alive and bound to him."

"Alive isn't the word I'd use," Baz says.

"Undead," I say. "An entire army of them. They will keep fighting for him until their bodies literally disintegrate. As for the souls?" A deep, dark shudder wracks my body. "He's imprisoned them in the spiral caves beyond the Void."

"You've seen all of this?" Isla asks gently.

All I can do is nod.

"And if her other visions are any indication," Baz says, "the general of this fucked-up army is none other than Ansel McCauley."

"The Black Sun," I say. "That's what Dark Judgment called Ani in my nightmares. They said he'd be the one to lead the armies to victory."

"But… how?" Carly asks.

"Something to do with the Wand of Flame and Fury," I say. "We think it can literally raise the dead."

Maddox nods, her face as pale as the sheets. "Wands contain the very spark of life. If the Dark Arcana have found a way to harness that energy… Goddess, I can only imagine."

"There's more," I say. "Regular witches and mages aren't the only ones he's turning. With Judgment's help, the Magician is planning to turn all the Light Arcana dark, just like he did with Ani."

"But Ani isn't… he's not undead," Nat says.

"Right." I wrap my arms around myself to keep from shivering. "Apparently, Light Arcana don't need to be executed. He just… drives the light out of us. The physical body and consciousness remain, while everything else—the heart and soul, the light that makes us who we are—is imprisoned in those caves."

Nat sits on the edge of the bed, her toes mere inches from the pool of Doc's blood. "So you figure that's where Dr. Devane and Ani are too."

"Yes. Doc and the *real* Ani," I clarify. "Ani's soul. That's my best guess based on everything I've seen."

"It makes sense," Professor Maddox says. "But again, do the caves exist in our realm? From what you've described, it doesn't seem like the sort of place you just happen upon while hiking through Arcana Academy lands."

"No, a place like that *wouldn't* exist here," Professor Broome says. "If Judgment and the Magician are imprisoning souls, they wouldn't use a place from our realm. Doing so would require too much energy on their part—they can't fully manifest here. Not yet, anyway."

"Stevie, I'm with the professors on this one." Kirin plucks his glasses from a pile of broken glass on the floor

17

and pushes them back onto his face, his pale green eyes electrifying in the dimly lit room. "Any place the Dark Arcana are using to trap souls *has* to be in another realm. Even if it's touching our realm somehow, the only way we could access it is through the dream realm."

"If that's what it takes to get them back," I say, "then I'm in."

He glances over at Baz, then back to me, his face tight. "The three of us barely made it out alive last time. And Ani—"

Kirin cuts himself off with a quick shake of his head, dark hair falling into his eyes and hiding the pain I know he's feeling. I feel it too—his, mine, Baz's. It's all wrapped up together in a sharp, thorny bundle, piercing my heart with every breath.

Ani *didn't* make it out alive. That's the part Kirin can't bring himself to say out loud. Our Gingersnap overdosed on my dream potion and went into the realm alone, and now he's gone.

My eyes blur with tears, but I brush them away. I can cry later—a bucket full. A bathtub full. An *ocean* of tears for everything we've endured. But right now, I need to get everyone on board with this mission.

"That's just it," I say, picking up a cracked bottle of what used to contain Fairy's Breath. Like everything else in this room, it's useless now. "The boundaries between the realms are weakening. Otherwise the dark version of Ani wouldn't have materialized here like he did—we all saw it happen."

"Yes," Kirin says, "and then he and Doc vanished—likely to another realm."

"A realm we might be able to get to *if* we leave now. The longer we wait, the less chance we have at finding anything." I shove a hand through my hair, trying to ignore the matted blood drying in my curls. "Goddess! We're standing here debating the possible location of magickal realms while our brothers are trapped in one, held hostage by the same psychos plotting to enslave the magickal world and kill anyone who gets in their way. What is *wrong* with you guys?"

Kirin's eyes flash with pain, and I immediately regret my words. But before I can apologize, he crosses the room and takes my hands, squeezing tight. "I get that your instinct is to go after them. I want to bring them home too, Stevie. More than you know."

"Then help me," I whisper, the tears spilling despite my best efforts to contain them and Kirin's best efforts to comfort me. With every beat of my heart, pain floods my body, the thought of abandoning Doc and Ani turning me inside out with grief.

"There's nothing I won't do to fight for our brothers." He cups my face, stroking my cheek with his thumb. "Nothing *except* risking your and Baz's lives in the process. If we go into this thing half-cocked, we could get trapped out there."

"Wherever the hell 'out there' even is," Baz says.

"They're right." Professor Maddox sits on the bed next to Nat, putting an arm around her shoulder and slowly turning her away from the blood she's been staring at. "You could lose hours—days, even—wandering between realms, hoping for that one needle in the magickal haystack that's going to grant you entry to the right place."

"So what do we do, then? Just stay here and hope for the best?" Fresh frustration simmers in my blood, but I force myself to take a few deep breaths before speaking again. "Look. I know it's a long shot, and I know it's dangerous as hell. But I don't care *where* the caves are. All I know is the place I saw in my visions was out past the holly thicket. Out past the mists. Once we get there, we'll figure out next steps. But I can't just sit here and... and do nothing."

"No one's suggesting we do nothing," Professor Maddox says.

"So far, I'm not hearing any other ideas." I turn away from Kirin and head to the broken window, staring out across the night sky. The desert is calm and peaceful, the breeze as sweet as a freshly cut apple.

Jareth swoops down from the roof, his shadow cutting a dark path across the backyard, vanishing into a tree at the edge of the property. His white feathers are a beacon in the darkness, and once again the urge to flee rises up inside me.

I could go now. Just hop out the window and take off with Jareth...

A strong, warm touch lands on my shoulders, and Baz's love for me hits me all at once—a wave of emotion so strong, it nearly buckles my knees.

Behind us, I hear Kirin asking the others to give us a

minute alone. The witches shuffle out of the room, leaving me with my men.

Bringing his lips to my ear, Baz says, "Do you trust me?"

My answering nod comes without hesitation.

"Look at me," he breathes, and I turn around and gaze up into his eyes.

"Cernunnos…" I mouth his ancient name, my voice so soft and broken it's not even a whisper. "Goddess, I'm so sorry. For everything. I just wanted… We have to help them and I…"

"Shh. It's okay." His hands slide into my hair and hold me close, his lips hovering before mine, his gaze as fierce as I've ever seen it. "I need you to hear me on this, beautiful. Really hear me."

I close my eyes and nod.

"Ani's gone dark, and he's got the Wand. He's working for the enemy—one who's apparently far more powerful than any of us imagined. You say his soul is still out there somewhere? That he and Cass are being held captive? Fine. Yes. I believe it, Little Bird. And I swear to fucking *Goddess*, I will follow you anywhere—to the most terrible places in the most terrible realms in the universe. But *not* without a rock-solid plan and at least two backup plans behind it."

I open my eyes, and Kirin joins us at the window, once again taking my hands.

Somehow, everything else fades away. The broken glass, the blood, the awfulness of it all. Right now, it's just me and the men I love, their fierce protectiveness wrapping me in a bubble of warmth and loyalty nothing can shatter.

"You have to know we're with you on this," Kirin says. "We *will* find that cave. And when we do?" A new wave of emotion rolls through him, shooting straight into my heart. It's dark and terrifying, full of fire and vengeance—a rare glimpse at the unstoppable Tower magick he contains.

When he speaks again, his voice is trembling with power and conviction, bringing new tears to my eyes.

Tears of relief.

Tears of pride.

Tears of love.

"I promise you, Starla Milan," he growls, dark and dangerous. "We will find the monsters who took our brothers and put that look in your eyes, and we will fucking *obliterate* them. No bone will be left unbroken, no drop of blood unspilled, no soul unbanished. When this is over, the Dark Arcana will be nothing but a myth relegated to the darkest, dustiest corners of the library."

We watch each other in silence for a beat, Kirin's promises bolstering me.

Baz too, if the look of wonder on his face is any indication.

But then my Devil cracks a wry smile and says, "Wow. *Very* poetic, brother."

Kirin mirrors the grin. "I thought it had a nice ring to it."

"Me? I'm just gonna bash in their skulls and piss on their bones."

"Also a valid choice." Kirin gives him a playful shove as

the darkness begins to recede. "Nothing says 'fuck off for all eternity' like pissing on the bones."

A laugh bubbles up from deep inside my chest, finally shattering the last of the tension between us. "Okay, psychos. You've convinced me—we need a plan."

"Three at a minimum," Baz says.

"Right. Three. Got it." I blow out a long, hot breath, blinking away the remaining tears. "Guess I'd better go put on the kettle."

THREE

STEVIE

All good planning sessions require tea—especially the balls-out, last-chance, end-of-the-world-as-we-know it ones. So back out in the kitchen, I wash the blood from my hands, tie my hair back, and give myself one job. One fucking job—that's all I have to worry about for the next fifteen minutes.

Make the damn tea, girl. And make it count.

With excellent timing, agents Appleton and Quintana have just returned from an earlier recon mission on campus. So, while the guys catch them up on the latest and greatest Dark Arcana news and the witches bustle around the house taking stock—weapons, potions, magickal supplies, tactical gear—I pour my heart, soul, and not a small amount of magick into crafting the perfect brew.

Black tea for alertness, balanced by calming lavender. Rose petals for love—the love I feel for my mages as well as for the witches who've become my closest friends. A whisper of cinnamon for healing and luck—Goddess knows we'll need both. Crushed vanilla bean to remind us of home and hearth—a sweet memory to call us back safely. And finally, a few drops of essence of obsidian for protection from dark energies.

I'm calling it The Calm Before the Shitstorm—no further explanation required.

"I really hope we survive this thing, Stevie." Isla comes up behind me and wraps her arms around my waist, resting her chin on my shoulder as I pour the hot tea into mugs. "I want to live long enough to see you open your own shop. You're so amazing at this."

I smile and let out a soft sigh. "From your lips, Isla."

"I mean it, girl. I plan to be your first paying customer."

"I'll hold you to it, then."

"It's a date." Grinning, she helps me carry the mugs to the table, where everyone is already taking their seats.

"So here we are, witches." I raise my mug, skipping the preamble of small talk. "We thought we'd have more time to prepare for this battle, but we don't. Tonight is all we've got left. Tomorrow, we're going out swinging."

"And blazing, burning, fighting, kicking, spellcasting, and whatever the fuck else we need to do to beat those sonsofbitches." Baz winks at me across the table, the spark in his eyes giving me a bit more hope.

I salute everyone with my mug and take a long pull, and the rest follow suit, everyone doing their best to put on a brave face.

With the whole gang finally settled in around the table, I take the empty chair next to Kirin. He smiles and squeezes my knee beneath the table—a gesture that's even more soothing than my tea.

"So what do we know?" Casey asks.

"At this point," Kirin says, "we're running on the assumption that everything Stevie has seen in her visions is coming to fruition. Undead armies, unchecked magick, and the Dark Arcana themselves—the Magician, the Chariot, Judgment, and the Sun, as much as I hate admitting that last one. It's only a matter of time before they figure out how to break into our realm—Stevie's seen it. If they're not here by sunrise, I'll be shocked."

"Campus is the primary target we're worried about," I say. "That's what I kept seeing in the visions. Plus, it's the quickest way to take out a lot of witches and mages at once —to turn them into soldiers, who in turn can take out more witches and mages... You see where this is going."

Professor Broome reaches over and takes Nat's hand, giving her a quick squeeze. The poor girl has been completely silent since she saw Doc's blood.

Not that I blame her.

"We're facing a war on two fronts right now," Kirin continues. "The Dark Arcana are probably the bigger threat, but I worry Eastman is weakening our position from within the Academy. We need to shore up somehow—get the Academy's magickal and physical defenses in place—but we can't risk Eastman finding out about our plans."

Casey nods, the skin around her eyes tight with worry. "It was hard to get the full assessment in the short time Agent Quintana and I were on campus tonight, but I agree

—the Academy itself is our weakest link right now. Intel is limited, but one thing is certain—Eastman and his dark mages have the place on lockdown."

"How are the students holding up?" Baz asks. "People must be completely freaked."

"Yes and no." She sips her tea, then sets down the mug. "We went over there expecting a lot of panic and confusion. We'd hoped to slip into the chaos unnoticed, maybe extract some of the students and faculty back here via the portals. But there wasn't any chaos to speak of. The place was eerily quiet."

"It's like Trello said," Quintana adds. "Eastman has taken over management. He seems to be employing a two-pronged strategy of scaring the shit out of everyone, then sweeping in like a white knight, promising to keep them safe."

"Fucking fraud," Baz mutters.

"Yeah. Unfortunately, with Trello gone and no one else challenging the man, most of the students and faculty are buying his act. And we can't alert *them* without alerting *him*."

"They have no idea what they're up against," Casey says. "Eastman talks a good game, but he's not keeping anyone safe. He's buying time, readying for the attack."

"So you think he's coordinating with the Dark Arcana?" Carly asks. "I thought he was Mr. Magick-is-Evil, All-Mages-Must-Burn-in-Hell. Why would he get in bed with the most magickal of all magick users?"

Casey grips her mug so tightly her fingertips turn white.

"Despite his claims against it, Eastman has no problems accessing dark magick to further his own cause. I'm assuming he's got enough followers on the inside to make a stand, not to mention backers on the outside further supporting the hate campaign."

"It's only a matter of time before he finds a way to break the rest of the wards and bring those outsiders in," Quintana says. "Whether their faction ultimately wants to put down the Dark Arcana is irrelevant. At the moment, both factions have the same enemy: the students and faculty of Arcana Academy and…" He takes a deep inhale and shakes his head, as though he still can't believe the epic level of fuckery we're dealing with. "And everyone sitting around this table. Especially…"

His gaze lands on mine, and my stomach bottoms out, Trello's earlier words floating through my memory.

"Everything the Magician wants, everything he's chased, across the boundaries of time and space, for millennia—you already have the power to command. You can unite the Arcana objects and reclaim magick for the witches and mages who seek to honor it. You have the power to unite the Light Arcana in the battle against the coming darkness. And when the rest of the world wants to give up, to lay down their arms and walk away from this fight, you have the power to inspire hope. To give us all a reason to keep living. To keep loving. To keep fighting, no matter what the cost."

She was talking about the Magician, but she could have been talking about any one of our enemies. If I'm the one with all this so-called power—a woman literally brought into this world by magick itself—it's no wonder they all want to see my head on a pike.

Goddess, this all feels so impossible. I was created by magick—a wish made by my mother and granted by the Dark Magician himself—with my blood now being demanded as payment for Mom's debts. Enemies lurk in every shadow, and now we have to worry about them teaming up against us in some crazy magickal showdown no one on Team Good Guy is prepared for. And two of our best men—*my* men—are being held captive.

Injured and captive.

A shiver grips me tight, shaking me to the core. Every time I close my eyes for even a *second*, I see only Doc's blood, the storm in his eyes as I held him. I smell his fear, feel his love for me, feel his life force fading away with every labored breath...

"Where are the students being held?" Professor Maddox asks, and I blink away the terrible memories, forcing my attention back to the agents.

Information. That's what I need. Information is good. All part of the planning process. All part of keeping my mind focused on what has to be done.

"We don't know exactly," Casey says. "We didn't have time to do a complete assessment before Eastman's guards starting getting close."

"How many on-campus mages and witches are officially on Team Asshole?" I ask.

"That's another unknown," Quintana says.

"Best to assume the worst," Professor Broome says.

"The last thing any of us can afford is to underestimate our enemies. Especially now."

"What do you think we should do, Stevie?" Nat asks. It's the first she's spoken in an hour, and when I look at her now, all I see—all I *feel*—is hope. Hope that I can help. Hope that we can figure this out. Hope that we'll survive another day.

All of them are awaiting my answer—all of them holding the same spark of hope I see in Nat's eyes. Again, I hear Trello's voice in my head.

I close my eyes and take another sip of tea.

Goddess, I wish it wasn't me. But it is me. I may feel woefully unprepared, unqualified, un-*every* important quality necessary for leading the witches and mages into this fight. But that's just too fucking bad, isn't it? I've been blessed with magick and power that so many others would and *have* died for. I may not have wanted it, I may not fully understand it, I may not feel capable or worthy of it, but that doesn't matter now. It's mine. And right now, I want nothing more than to figure out how to use that power to help all the people I care about. All the witches and mages who are counting on me—as well as the ones who don't even know I exist. All the witches who died for what they believed in. For what they tried to honor in their everyday lives.

Magick. Love. Peace.

I don't know if what Trello said is true—if I'm really the one who can unite everyone and inspire hope and all that epic shit—but I guess it's like I said about finding Doc and

31

Ani. If there's even a *chance* I can do something here, I have to take it.

"We need to get word to campus," I finally say. "The students and faculty need to be prepared to fight." Everyone around the table shifts uncomfortably, arguments doubtlessly stacking up in their minds, but I press on anyway. "Look, I get it. I hate it too. I hate that it's come to this, especially since they've had no real warning, no guidance since this whole thing began, and even less training than most of us have had. But I can't see a way around it. We're outnumbered and out-magicked. *Everyone* needs to fight, or everyone is going to die."

I take another gulp of tea and brace myself for the pushback, but it doesn't come. I can feel their energy—the movements through all the stages: denial, anger, grief, and finally acceptance, followed by a grim resignation.

And then, right when I'm afraid I've made the wrong call after all and the weight of my heart is almost too much to bear…

A surge of renewed hope.

"You're right," Professor Maddox says. "Everyone has a stake in this war, and everyone must make a stand. Sitting on the sidelines is no longer an option—that was made clear when the so-called authorities tasked with keeping society safe suddenly decided witches and mages weren't part of that society."

"Okay," Casey says with a firm nod. "I'm with you on that. Here's the thing, though—and our tech guy confirmed it—Eastman's cut off the student internet and phone messaging. Outside of holding up signs in the windows, they can't communicate with anyone outside their dorm halls, and I'm betting most of them are too scared to leave. He's got them believing their lives are at stake and he's the only one who can keep them safe."

"Well, he's half right, anyway," Baz says. "Their lives *are* at stake. But Stevie's right—if they don't fight, they're totally screwed. All of us are."

"We need to get a message through," I say. "We need to figure something out, or they're just a sitting target waiting for the nuke."

Kirin drums his fingers on the table, his brow crinkling. "If I can figure out how to override the security protocols Eastman put in place, we might be able to get a message out campus-wide."

"That sounds promising," Professor Maddox says.

Kirin nods. "Yeah, but there's no foolproof way to do it without Eastman and his minions finding out. We'd immediately lose the element of surprise, and right now, that's one of the only things we've got going for us."

"We need more intel," Baz says. "We need a better idea of what we're up against—then we could *maybe* figure out how to sneak a message through without those fucks finding out."

"We could split up," Kirin says. "Some of us could slip back through the portal and—"

"No," Casey says emphatically. "Agent Quintana and I barely made it out without being spotted. None of us can risk going back to campus—not until we're ready to rock.

Because the second they see us, all hell's gonna break loose —with or *without* the Dark armies crashing the gates."

A heavy silence settles over the table as we stare into our teacups and ponder the total suckage that is our present situation.

"What the hell are we supposed to do?" I whisper, more to myself than to anyone else. The tea in my cup ripples, and for a second, I wonder if another one of Mom's Tarot cards is going to pop up out of the brew.

Instead, I get a different sort of message.

A flicker of white outside the glass deck door catches my eye, and I turn to see Jareth perched on the railing, posing and preening as if he's waiting for someone to state the obvious.

"Real subtle, J." I let out a soft laugh. Then, turning to the others with the first genuine smile I've managed since we all sat down tonight, I say, "No, none of us can risk going back there. But I know someone who can."

FOUR

CASS

For days, I've been clinging to the right side of morality and sanity, kept there by *one* thing: the pure, untarnished love of the woman who owns my heart.

But right now? That woman isn't here. She's back in Red Sands Canyon, likely plotting a rescue mission with Kirin, Baz, and the others. One that could very well lead to the demise of everyone I've ever cared about.

Especially her.

In her absence—forced upon me by the very monsters tormenting me in this cave now—the rage inside rises unchecked. Someone I manage to keep it locked up tight while the Dark assholes discuss their plans, but my silence is as temporary as my apparent inaction.

Like mental manipulation, violence too has its place, its time.

When that particular clock strikes twelve for me, I'll be ready.

Dark Judgment and his pet Sun are so blinded by their presumed victory they truly believe they'll get to Stevie. That they'll so much as fucking *breathe* on her, let alone bring her to harm or worse—force me to do it.

Hell, if I thought I could get to my feet right now without passing out from blood loss, Judgment would already be a pile of smoldering ash.

But again, I must wait for the right moment. One mistake, and we'll lose everything.

"In the end, my Sun," Judgment says now, "every last one of them will atone. Only by seeking absolution for their sins will they come to know peace. But before such peace can be granted, first they *must* be broken."

Not fucking likely, you twisted fuck...

I force myself to continue playing the wounded warrior, waiting in silence until the echo of their footsteps vanishes into the misty dark beyond.

Certain they're gone, I finally open my eyes and exhale a pained breath, waiting for my vision to adjust to the near-pitch blackness. Without the light of the Wand, there's nothing but shapes and shadows as far as I can see. Yet even in darkness, everything spins. A wave of nausea rolls through my gut, and I place both palms on the cold cave floor in a vain attempt to steady myself.

My head and mouth are still bleeding. The coppery taste of it fills my senses. Pinpricks of starlight dance across my vision, reminding me of Stevie. My Star.

Right now, that's what keeps me going.

After a few more deep breaths, I pull myself up into a

sitting position, bare back pressed against the damp rock. My head slumps forward, and my stubbled chin scrapes against the charred flesh over my heart, courtesy of my hosts.

I welcome the pain. The memory of that burn. As far as I'm concerned, it's just another torture to return in kind.

An eternity passes before the shadows around me stop spinning, and finally—Goddess, *finally*—my head clears enough to allow a few coherent thoughts.

One, I'm in a cave so dank and dark, the only light comes from a few moonlit cracks overhead. It's not enough to even orient myself, let alone find my way out of this forsaken prison.

Two, I'm in rough shape. I've lost a lot of blood, and every part of my body that can still feel anything throbs.

No wonder they didn't bind me. Only a fucking miracle could get me out of here now.

"Cass... Can you hear me?"

I startle at the whisper—so close I can feel its ghost on my cheek. But when I reach out, I grasp only cold air.

"Hearing things," I mutter. "Perfect. This head injury is more serious than I feared." I reach up to touch the back of my skull, wincing at the sharp pain. My fingers come away sticky, and another wave of dizziness barrels into me. "Fuck. *Fuck!*"

I'd bash my own head into the wall out of sheer frustration if I wasn't so certain the act would kill me.

"Cass," the call comes again, slightly louder than a whisper now. "You need to hear me. Please try."

That voice…

It's so faint, yet familiar. I could swear it's…

"Ani?" My own voice cracks at the effort of speaking.

A warmth I can't explain spreads across my shoulder, and a scent I recognize as my brother's—not his cruel doppelgänger, but my *true* brother—drifts past.

"Goddess, Ani. Where the hell are you? I can't see anything in this hole."

"Cass? You can hear me? Tell me you can hear me." The relief in his voice is palpable, and his touch solidifies on my shoulder. Before my eyes, an image of the mage I know and love flickers into view. He's crouching beside me, a faint golden light humming around him.

"Ani? Goddess, I wasn't sure I'd ever lay eyes on you again. I thought…" My voice trails off as I struggle to make sense of the image before me. "Why do you look so… thin?"

I reach for him, but my hand goes right through his body, leaving nothing but a warm buzz tingling across my skin.

"Insubstantial," he says. "That's the word you're looking for." Ani glances down at his chest and presses a hand to his heart. His body wavers like a warped film reel.

In all my years as a mage and professor of mental magicks, as the Moon Arcana, as a master of illusion and manipulation, I've never seen anything quite like it.

If this were a movie, I'd call Ani a ghost.

But this *isn't* a movie. And unless we figure this out—

and fast—none of us will live long enough for a happy ending.

"How are you existing like this?" I ask. "And what about your..." I gesture vaguely into the dark space the two Arcana monsters recently vacated, unsure what to call the Dark Sun. "The other one?"

Ani sighs. "He's not really an 'other,' Cass. He's me. Well, me with the soul stripped out. I'm the soul, essentially —something like it, anyway. They call him the Black Sun."

"I don't understand. How did this happen?"

"In the dream realm." The red-hot shame in his cheeks is clear even in the darkness. "I was completely taken in by the Wand. Judgment and Chariot did a spell. Somehow they... I'm not sure how to describe it. It was as if they split me in two. He has a consciousness—some dim, base-level instinct that keeps it alive. But the rest of him... I don't know. I feel like he's all the worst parts of me, left behind in my physical body while the rest of me got forced out and banished here."

"And where is *here*?" I glance around and try to get a sense of things again, but all I can see is mist and shadow. "Are we near the Void? Or in the dream realm?"

"Not exactly." Ani gets to his feet, his light dimming as he paces the small chamber. By that light alone, I get a better sense for the space—a smallish section that branches into the darker passageways of what's probably a vast cave system. The walls are slick and smooth, the mist making everything colder than it otherwise would be.

"From what I've managed to pick up from their conversations," he says, "this place—the cave, the mists, even the Void itself—is like a portal that exists in and connects multiple realms. The Dark Arcana can take form here, but they aren't yet strong enough to fully manifest on the material plane."

"But your... the Black Sun. He *has* manifested. He—" I cut myself before saying it out loud. Ani doesn't need to know what atrocities that monster committed in his name. Not now.

"I know, Cass. I know everything he's done. Every flame he's lit. Every life he's taken. Every wound he's inflicted. I may as well have torched that town myself."

"Ani, none of that is your—"

"Don't," he says, and no matter how badly I want to talk him out of his guilt, I know I can't. In this moment, all I can offer him is the respect of changing the subject.

"Stevie said something about the Magician planning to turn all the Light Arcana dark." I tell him about her Winter Solstice ritual—everything the bastard revealed about his plans, including the part about her being a magickal creation not entirely of this world.

Of course, Ani already knew that part—the Black Sun was lurking around the house at Red Sands when Trello told us the story of Stevie's conception, so Ani heard the whole story.

Still, at the mention of Stevie's name, the light around him brightens just a fraction. "She confronted the Magician?"

"She sure as hell did. Tried to make a trade with the

Arcana objects, but he wouldn't bite. He wants them, sure. But more than anything, he needs her blood for some ritual."

"Goddess, I can't believe she went up against him like that." His lips quirk into a momentary smile. "She's crazy."

"That she is," I say, but in the face of our current predicament, my answering grin is short-lived. "Is that how they turn the Light Arcana, then? The spell you mentioned?"

"I think so. But I'm guessing they probably need the Arcana objects too. For me, it was the Wand. For you it'll be the Chalice."

An icy chill rolls through me as I recall the feel of the Chalice of Blood and Sorrow the night Stevie and I recovered from the dream realm—the skull of the First Fool. "Guess that explains why I'm still intact. The Chalice is buried under rock and magick, just like the Pentacle and Sword."

"For now." Ani sighs. "Cass, it's not safe here for you. They'll be back. You need to be gone by the time that happens."

"I don't suppose we can just walk out the door?"

"There is no door. Not that I've seen. You need to find another way."

I take a deep breath and haul myself to a standing position. The pain comes swiftly, nearly driving me to my knees, but I force myself to remain upright. I *must* find a way out of here—for both of us.

"So the other Light Arcana," I say, still trying to piece

together a more complete picture. "Judgment, Chariot—before they went dark. Are their souls trapped here as well?"

"If they are, they haven't made contact." He appears to lean back against the cave wall, shivering when his shoulder blades make contact. "Likely they were cast out years ago. Decades, even. Honestly... the fact that I'm here at all feels like an anomaly. Judgment and Sun haven't acknowledged my presence once—not even to taunt me, which tells me they don't know I'm... lingering." He holds his hand before his face, and again his image flickers. "I don't know how much time I have left, especially now that the Dark Arcana are gathering so much strength. I—"

"We'll figure this out, Ani. We always figure it out."

He nods, but I can tell that his heart—wherever it now lies—isn't in it.

"Listen to me, Ani." I pull away from the wall and take a few steps toward him, feeling a bit stronger each time a foot connects with the rock beneath it. "We're going to get out of here. Both of us. And I swear to you just as I'd swear it to Stevie and Kirin and Baz if they were here... I'm going to kill the druid. It won't be quick or kind. You have my word on that."

Ani blinks up at me, his eyes suddenly luminescent in the darkness. I'm no empath, but you'd have to be a block of stone not to feel the weight of his deep sadness and regret.

His shame.

For a beat, neither of us speaks or moves. Then, on a

long sigh, he says, "Cass, what happened back at Red Sands tonight... I... I'm so sorry."

"You've nothing to apologize for. I won't even hear it."

"But—"

"It wasn't you at Red Sands any more than it was you in..." I trail off, again not wanting to remind him of the massacre in California, but of course it's already on his mind. It will likely be a constant companion every day for the rest of his life—yet another Dark Arcana cruelty I'm looking forward to repaying with interest.

"But it *is* me. That's what I'm telling you. The Black Sun *is* me, with certain aspects removed. He's me without morals, without shame, without fear. He's the darkness that's always lurking behind the smile—all the things I thought I'd dealt with years ago, but clearly didn't."

My memory jumps back to the night Stevie and the others were forced into the dream realm. It was thanks to Ani's witchfire that we finally got the upper hand with Janelle and Casey, both possessed by Phaines. But to conjure so much magick—to unleash so much devastation —Ani had to dig into the most terrifying parts of himself and bring them all to the surface. All of his pains and agonies, his disappointments, the abuses he suffered—all of it became fuel.

That single act of heroism—Ani raining hell on our enemies—was the crashing of the gate that eventually gave Judgment the entrance he needed.

And I should've been able to protect him from it. Then *and* now.

Instead, I've only subjected to him to further torment.

"That *thing* is no more you than a bag of flour is a chocolate chip cookie," I snap. "You are so much more than the sum of your parts, Ani. All of us have darkness inside us. What happened to you... That was Judgment's doing. Not yours."

Anger roils inside me, but I force it down, knowing I'll need to harness it later. Besides, Ani doesn't deserve my ire. Even if it's not directed at him, I don't want my brother exposed to it for even a second.

That particular bullet—rather, that *bomb*—has someone else's name on it.

Ani flickers again and turns his back on me, his head hanging low.

Fuck.

I'm losing him. I can feel our bond weakening as he retreats further into his own guilt.

I need to get us out of here, but I have neither the directional sense nor the stamina to search for an exit that may not even exist. Gingerly, I move along the wall, my hands seeking a sharp rock as my mind begins formulating a spell.

"You feel everything the Black Sun experiences?" I ask.

"Everything."

"So you understand I gave you Nightmare's Lullaby, yes?"

"The potion." Ani turns to face me again, but immediately drops his gaze, as if he's afraid to admit how badly I've hurt him. "It didn't work on him because he doesn't have the capacity for true fear. He has no conscience, no sense of morality or remorse, no sense of consequence."

My gut twists at the implication. The potion didn't work on his dark counterpart... but it worked on Ani.

Biting back the taste of bile in my throat, I force myself to continue. "I wanted to find another way. But Stevie knew there wasn't one. She also knew what it would do to you, whether it worked or not, but she was willing to take that risk, even on the good chance it would all backfire—which it did, quite spectacularly."

"Cass, we don't have to talk about it. I understand. You were trying to drive him out. I get it. I—"

"Do you know why she did it?" I move quickly along the wall, still searching the smooth, water-worn rocks for something sharp. "Why *I* ultimately agreed to it, even knowing the high chance of failure? Knowing the damage it would inflict?"

He stares at me again, his eyes so pained I can barely stand to look at him.

I know he heard the words Stevie spoke over his bedside—the Black Sun was there, feigning unconsciousness, so Ani heard everything. Still, I feel the need to repeat them now. To remind him how much he means to all of us —to Stevie most of all.

"Ani is *ours* to love and protect," I say, her sweet voice in my head. "Ours. The family he chose. The family that chose him. The family that wants and loves him. The family that needs his light in our lives—not because of some stupid prophecy or magickal war, not because we share DNA, but simply because he—"

"Please," he whispers. "Don't. I can't—"

"Because he *belongs* to us," I press on, my own voice thick with emotion. "Now and always."

Ani is my brother in every sense of the word—a brother like the one I never got the chance to have growing up. I screwed up with Xavier, and I screwed up with Ani too. The difference is—there's still a chance I can actually help Ani.

"I know you've looked to me for guidance over the years," I say now, "and I've done my best to honor that—to deserve it. But the truth is, I've utterly failed you, Ani. Tonight with the potion, that night you saved us from Janelle and Casey. Hell, I've been failing you ever since we came together as Keepers of the Grave. I should've better prepared you for..." I sigh, stopping my fevered pacing for just a moment.

Ani stands before me, blinking up at me with wide eyes.

I reach out for his shoulder, feeling just the slightest hint of him beneath my touch. "If anyone here has something to apologize for, it's me."

"You're not the one who allowed himself to be seduced by the magick of the Arcana. I should've been able to resist it."

"You were only trying to protect your brothers. I know what it cost you, Ani. Believe me. And for that, I'm truly sorry."

"I would do it again in a heartbeat."

"I know. I know you would." I squeeze his shoulder, and this time, he actually feels it too. He's not solid by any stretch, but he's a good deal more substantial than when we started. Fresh hope surges inside me. "But right now? Right now, I just need you to help me get us the fuck out of here. I can't do it without you."

He glances down at my hand resting on his shoulder, my skin still caked with blood.

Ani takes a deep breath and blows it out slowly. I feel the ghost of it on my cheeks.

"You and me, Ani. We're getting out. Okay?"

He meets my gaze again, a spark of hope shining in his. But then it's snuffed out like a spent candle, his shoulders drooping. "I can't help you anymore, Cass. I can't help anyone."

"That's unfortunate. Because the thing is... You don't have a choice."

FIVE

STEVIE

I light the candles and fan out my Tarot cards across the table on the back deck. With no more than my intuition as my guide and my friends by my side, I select the ones I feel most drawn to. The ones I know will aid me in strengthening my connection with Jareth.

My owl watches me from the eves, curious, but in no obvious hurry.

I've never intentionally called him like this—a spell to connect our magick so we can fly together. Whenever our energies merged before, it was more spontaneous—like when I was gazing out across the Iron and Bone lands from my window in the dorms, wondering what the guys were up to. Or when I was completely desperate—like that day on El Búho Grande back home, when he burst out of my very being to save me from the dark mage who'd possessed my friend Luke.

Well, we're certainly desperate tonight, right?

Glancing down at the four cards I chose, I take a deep breath and speak the words as they come to me.

I call on the Hermit for my wise owl friend
And the Star that shines bright within me
The Six of Swords keeps us safe to the end
As the Prince of Swords travels swiftly

With these as our guides, let our magick entwine
Beyond death and shadow we fly
My light flows through you as yours becomes mine
As one we shall soar through the sky

Repeating the spell, I close my eyes and let all other thoughts and worries fade away. All of my focus is on Jareth—the feel of his soft feathers, the weight of him perched on my arm, the scent of the breeze in his wings, the piercing glow of his bright, golden eyes. I recall the first time I felt his energy that day on El Búho Grande, and every time we've connected since—including tonight.

We've been through a lot together, my owl and I. There's no one I trust more to see this through.

A smile of pure gratitude graces my lips, and overhead, Jareth lets out a soft hoot. That and the gentle whoosh of his takeoff are all the warnings he offers before soaring away. I open my eyes and run out into the backyard, gazing up to track his path across the starry sky.

I watch until he turns into a tiny white dot.

The moment he's completely out of sight, my vision

shifts—the change so abrupt, I fall to my knees and squeeze my eyes shut to stop the sudden spin.

But soon enough it settles, and suddenly I'm no longer kneeling in the backyard. I'm sailing across the desert, across the magickal boundaries that separate Red Sands Canyon from the Academy and the lands beyond it—the Petrified Forest of Iron and Bone, where Baz and I shared our first kiss beneath the rocks I was failing at climbing that day. The Towers of Breath and Blade, where Kirin took me flying on a magick bike and taught me how to harness my air magick. The Cauldron of Flame and Fury, where Ani gave me the sunrise. The River of Blood and Sorrow, where Doc and I traveled in the dream realm after finally giving in to the wild passions that nearly consumed us both. That night, he helped me feel more worthy than I'd ever felt before—worthy of my magick, of the love of my Arcana brothers, of the friendship I've found at the Academy.

Every one of those sacred places holds important memories for me, and I hold on to those memories as we dip and glide across the currents, the wind rustling through Jareth's feathers as if they're my own.

It's not long before we're circling campus, and I force myself to focus on every detail, every shadow. We perch on top of dorms and classroom buildings, swoop over the fountain, dart between trees and follow the crisscrossing red stone paths.

I have no idea how much time passes. We cover the entire campus, then travel beyond once again, always watching. Always learning.

Our flight feels at once endless and momentary.

But at some point, I open my eyes again and get to my feet, and I find myself surrounded by my mages and the others, all of them eagerly awaiting our news.

Jareth lands on my shoulder and nuzzles my neck.

Stroking his head, I take a deep breath and get my bearings.

Then, I drop the fucking bomb.

"Guys? It's worse than we thought."

SIX

STEVIE

"He's got patrols across the entire campus," I say. "Guarding every dorm, building, portal, and pathway. Dozens more are arriving every hour—like freaking cockroaches."

"What? We didn't see anyone coming in," Casey says, exchanging a horrified glance with Quintana. "Are they using the portals?"

"Not the public ones." I bring a mug of piping hot peppermint tea to my lips, welcoming the burn. We're all in the living room, a roaring fire crackling, but I can't seem to chase off the chill. Even with Baz and Kirin on either side of me, and a fleece blanket wrapped around me like a burrito, I'm still shivering. "Jareth overheard some of the mages talking about secret access through the admin building."

"I've never heard of such a thing," Professor Broome says. "And I've been at the Academy for ages."

"I'm not sure if Trello herself even knows about it," I

say. "The men were talking as if they just created it. Or someone created it for them."

"Did you recognize any of them?" Quintana asks. He and Casey are wearing tracks in the carpet with all their incessant pacing. "Any faculty among them, any prominent political figures, anyone like that?"

I shake my head. "The mages were all pretty covered up, though. Dark robes, hoods. No symbols or insignias that we could see, but..." My skin erupts in goosebumps, the chill digging in for the long haul. "We heard more than a few references to the Soldiers of Light."

Agent Quintana lets loose a string of curses.

I don't blame him. The Soldiers of Light are the crackheads that claimed responsibility for the attack on Ani's hometown—a brutal act of terrorism that gave the human authorities carte blanche to detain all witches and mages, indefinitely and without cause. When Trello first told us about Eastman's mages taking control of campus, she'd said the group was dark and secretive, and Doc had wondered about a possible connection to the Soldiers, but we didn't have proof.

Now we do.

Not that it does us much good.

"What kind of numbers are we looking at?" Quintana asks.

"Best guess? He's got at *least* a hundred experienced magick-users firmly entrenched at the Academy, but that's just for starters." I down the rest of my tea in a few big, hot gulps, then set my mug on the side table. "According to the chatter, there are at least two hundred more so-called Soldiers of Light scheduled to arrive on campus before sunrise. And that's not counting anyone else he scares into submission before we're ready to make our move. For all we know, they could turn half the campus against us before we even step foot on Academy grounds."

Casey finally stops pacing and drops into a chair near the fireplace. "Goddess, by this time tomorrow, Eastman's ranks could triple. Quadruple. We just don't know."

"What about the students?" Professor Maddox asks.

"Most of the students seem to be lying low in the dorms," I say, "too terrified to defy lockdown orders. I saw a couple of graduate researchers trying to leave campus with two professors, but they were all detained by Eastman's mages and brought back to the admin building—that seems to be their HQ."

"What happened to them?" Isla asks, her eyes wide.

"The guards brought them to a room with a few other students. It didn't look like they were being harmed—just held against their will." I let out a breath, but the relief is short-lived. "Whether he's physically hurting them or not, he's keeping everyone in constant fear that he *could* hurt them."

"It's an old tactic." Kirin wraps an arm around my shoulders, and Baz shifts closer. "Effective too."

"If he terrifies them enough," I say, "they won't need much convincing to take his side when the fighting starts. Especially if he brainwashes them into believing he's their savior."

"Aside from Kirin's earlier idea about hacking the security protocols," Quintana says, "did you see any holes? Anything we might be able to leverage to get a message to the good guys and boots on the ground in there?"

"No. They're patrolling every nook and cranny on campus. They've emptied out all the classroom buildings and shops, closed up the restaurants and bars, and blocked access to the nature paths beyond the dorms. The whole place is a heavily guarded ghost town, with all the most vulnerable targets sequestered in the dorms. The faculty is there too, trying to keep everyone calm. It looked to me like the mages ordered it—the faculty housing was all empty, just like everywhere else."

"Any large-scale weapons?" Professor Maddox asks. "Military, police, anyone from outside services?"

"Not that I could tell. Just the mages working for Eastman. No witches either, now that I think of it—just men and their magick tricks."

The room falls silent, each of us marinating in our own gruesome thoughts about the days and nights to come. I wish I could just leave it at that, but there's more.

"In addition to our tour of campus," I say, "we did a few flyovers of the House lands."

"No patrols?" Quintana asks.

"Not beyond the initial access points behind the dorms. They seem pretty confident they've got everyone corralled inside their perimeter."

"So maybe that's our in," Quintana says. "Back door."

Casey shakes her head. "Even if we can get onto the

SPELLS OF MIST AND SPIRIT

lands without being noticed, there's no way we'll get past those patrols and onto the main campus without raising the alarm. We'd have to go for a distraction of some sort, but that's *extremely* risky."

"Not to mention," I remind them, "we wanted to get word to campus that the students and faculty need to be ready to fight. But Eastman's guys are already ready. They've got a full-on army in there, and that's *without* the Dark Arcana. It's too late to prepare anyone on campus for the attack. When the fighting starts, they're just going to have to pick a side."

"Let's hope it's ours," Kirin says.

"What else did you see?" Carly asks.

"We tried to find the caves from my vision, but no luck. Everything beyond Breath and Blade is completely enshrouded in—well, I'd call it mist, but this stuff is different."

"Different how?" Professor Broome leans forward in the chair across from me, her brow knitted with curiosity and concern.

"This stuff was like... like a magickal fog. Thick and roiling, but dark—almost like an indigo color. But shot through with flickering light. Like a lightning storm on the ground."

She exchanges a worried glance with Professor Maddox. "Sounds like a cloaking spell."

"That was my first thought too," Maddox replies. "Which means it's likely the Dark Arcana are already materializing in our realm—or readying for it."

57

"Regardless, the guys and I still need to get to the caves beyond the Void," I say. "That's where Doc and Ani are being held. I... I'm sure of it."

Kirin squeezes my shoulder, a deep sigh escaping his lips. "Why do I sense a but coming?"

"They took Doc because they *know* we'll come for our friends. And you can bet your magick wands they're planning one hell of a welcome party for us. Even if everyone in this room stormed the caves together, we aren't strong enough to face the Dark Arcana."

"Agreed. So where's that but?" Kirin asks.

"We can't leave Doc and Ani to the wolves. We need to get to those caves." I lean my head on his shoulder, hating the words before they're even out of my mouth. "*But...* we can't do it without the Arcana objects."

On my other side, Baz is already shaking his head. "Stevie, even if we wanted the objects, we can't get to them. The Fool's Grave was completely demolished. There wasn't a single rock wall left standing."

"I know," I say. "Jareth took us through the whole area. It's all rubble, just like we left it. But I could sense the objects there—especially the Sword. Everything is still safe and sound, locked up behind the magickal barrier we made."

"I suppose that's a bit of good news too, then," Nat says. "The Magician hasn't gotten his hands on the goods."

"Not yet," I say. "Rubble or not, no one can get to those things without the blood of all five members of the brotherhood. We need to get there first."

A wave of Baz's red-hot anger smashes straight into my chest. "Those fuckers already have Cass and Ani. Now you want the three of us to show up like some kind of offering, completing the magick circle? Why the fuck did we bury the objects in the first place, then? Why not just hand them over right from the start, save us all the fucking trouble?"

"Baz, I'm just—"

"Oh, and let's not even *talk* about the Magician's hard-on for *your* blood," he snaps. "No. No way. End of discussion, game over, pick another plan because that ain't it."

I squeeze his hand, trying to calm him. "Baz, we need those objects. Rail against it all you want, but you know damn well it's the only way we'll have enough power to make a stand."

"She's right, Baz," Kirin says.

"Yeah, no shit." He clenches his teeth so tightly, the muscle on his jaw ticks. "I hate it. I hate that you're right. I fucking hate everything about this, but… but I also don't see how we get our brothers back without those damn objects." The last of his anger dissipates into resignation, and he squeezes my hand back.

"What about the blood, though?" Casey asks. "Don't you need Cass and Ani's blood to unlock the protection magick?"

"Doc's blood is not the problem." I nod toward the back bedroom, where the blood is still pooling on the floor—more than enough to salvage for our purposes. "As for Ani… the Black Sun will be waiting for us at the Fool's

Grave. I know it in my bones, guys. You have to trust me on this."

"Why are you so sure he'll be there?" Kirin asks.

"He knows we'll be after the objects—either to use them to gain an advantage or to prevent the Dark Arcana from doing the same thing. We've seen what they did with the Wand—they know we won't make a move without securing the other three objects. And they want the objects too, obviously. The Fool's Grave is *everyone's* next play. No way around it."

"If only we had more time," Professor Broome says, her voice thin and full of regret. "I thought we could prepare. Train. Figure something else out. Reinforcements or... I thought... Well, no matter. We all must work with the cards we were dealt." She offers a tired smile, but her eyes still hold a spark of hope. "Tomorrow, Kelly and I will make our way back to campus through the portal. We'll turn ourselves in to Eastman—convince him we believe Trello's become completely unhinged. We'll go under the guise of seeking his protection. If we can get in his good graces—make him believe we're truly worried about our own safety and that of our students—well, that's two more experienced witches we'll have on the inside."

Professor Maddox doesn't even hesitate. "From there, we'll do what we can to spread the word about what's coming, and see who we can count on to fight on the right side of all this."

I return their kind smiles, my eyes misting. "A better witch would try to talk you out of this, but—"

"Wasn't it a better witch who said 'Everyone needs to fight, or everyone is going to die?'" Professor Broome winks at me and reaches forward to pat my knee. "We're all in this together, Starla Milan. Kelly and I will get onto campus and raise the proverbial alarm—leave that to us. You, Kirin, and Baz need to focus on Cass and Ani."

I nod, the knot of emotion in my throat making it difficult to speak. Thankfully, Baz seems to sense this and takes over.

"Once we've got the guys and the Arcana objects, we'll make our way to campus. I have no idea what we'll face along the way—if we'll need to cross realms or what—but we will find a way to get back to you. With any luck, we'll rendezvous before an attack from the Soldiers of Light or the Arcana assholes, strategize our own attack, and hit them before they know what's coming."

"The dark army's going to strike tomorrow," I finally manage. "There's no doubt in my mind. I'm not sure whether they'll hit us at the Fool's Grave, the Void, or hold back and launch their full attack on campus, but either way, we need to be ready for that fight. Even if we manage to recoup on campus before a strike, I doubt we'll have much time to plan our attack."

"Then I guess I'd better start planning it now." Casey rises from her chair and glances at her phone, paging through her contacts. "I'll see what help I can get from London. They may not be willing to spare any men, but they can at least spare a few minutes to talk. We need more intel on Eastman's black-mirror mages and any other tricks he might have up his sleeve. If we can get a better handle on some of the shit Eastman's been digging into, that could give us an advantage."

"So what's our next move, Case?" Quintana asks.

"After I get this intel, we'll see about sneaking in through the back door, like you said. That was actually a good call, given the options."

"Iron and Bone lands? Or maybe Breath and Blade—see if we can use that mist as a cover?"

Casey shakes her head. "Too close to Dark Arcana territory. If they're materializing already, we don't want to be anywhere near that." She taps her lips, then says, "River of Blood and Sorrow. That's our route."

Quintana sighs, but eventually nods his acceptance. "Good thing I know how to swim, because something tells me this mission is gonna get cold and wet."

"I'm not worried about our comfort level," she says. "I'm worried about getting spotted. We still need to figure out a way to distract the mages guarding the campus perimeter long enough for us to sneak past their lines."

"Distraction?" Carly beams, lighting up the room with her mischievous grin. Linking her arms with Nat and Isla's, she shakes out her lustrous raven hair and says, "You leave *that* to the hot-girl squad."

SEVEN

STEVIE

After a scalding hot shower and the fastest blow-drying job in history, I'm finally settling into the one place that could possibly bring me comfort tonight.

My bed.

With Baz.

Naked beside me, he traces his thumb back and forth across my forehead, his smile as soft and sad as his voice. "What's going on in there, Little Bird?"

"You mean, other than the fact that we're balls-deep in a magickal apocalypse that's probably going to destroy witch- and mage-kind as we know it?"

"Yeah, other than that. You can't fool me, Milan." A smile tugs at the corners of his mouth, and he presses a kiss to my eyebrow, still stroking my face. "This isn't your pondering-the-apocalypse face. You've got something else on your mind." He nudges my nose with his, a tiny spark of good-natured jealousy flaring in his energy. "You miss your Tower? The Devil's company isn't enough for you tonight?"

I smile back at him and offer a quick kiss. "Hmm. Sounds like *you're* the one missing him."

"Keep dreaming."

"Don't worry, Baz. Kirin will be here as soon as he's done reviewing those security protocols with Agent Quintana." At his mock frown, I rush to add, "Don't take my desires personally. You know your girl is insatiable when it comes to her mages."

"Sounds like a challenge to me. You know that, right?"

"Counting on it." I laugh, but it drifts away, quickly vanishing in the candlelit space.

"Seriously, Stevie. Where are you?"

With a deep sigh, I close my eyes and focus on his touch, each stroke as gentle as a breeze. Despite his delicious proximity, even the now-familiar warmth of his body isn't enough to blunt the chill that's held me hostage all night.

"I was just thinking about home," I finally admit. "I mean—home before. There's a place in the Santa Clarita called the Canyon of Ghosts. During the day, it gets so hot it's nearly impossible to hike there. I tried it once—it was like breathing straight fire. But at night?" A wistful *hmm* escapes. "At night, it always feels like winter. Bitter, freeze-your-eyeballs kind of cold. But you deal with it, because when you're out there under the stars, just you and the big world around you... Goddess, it's like nothing you've ever seen, Baz."

I tell him about the fairy lights in the sky, the way their ghostly glow illuminates the heavens. When the wind whispers in the canyons, it shifts through the sands and makes the dunes literally hum—a song as miraculous as it is haunting.

I never thought I'd miss the place so much.

"It sounds beautiful," he says, and I open my eyes, meeting his gaze.

"Do you think I'll ever see it again?"

"Stevie, I..." He cups my cheek and shakes his head, lips pressed together as if he just can't bring himself to speak what's on his mind. After another silent beat, he finally says, "I don't know if we'll even survive this thing."

"Right. Not one for sugar coating, are you?"

"Figured that out all on your own, huh?" His sexy, cocky grin finally breaks through, but it doesn't last. "Don't see much point in it. Whether we've got another fifty years or fifty minutes, I'm here with you now. *That's* what matters. You and me, Kirin, the guys, all the—wait. Are you seriously *laughing* at me right now? The world is teetering on the edge of annihilation, and you're laughing?"

Without waiting for a reply, he rolls on top of me, pinning me beneath his lean, muscular form. His grin widens again, matching mine.

"I was just remembering the day we met," I say. "Outside the Iron and Bone dorms. Goddess, you were so damn full of yourself. If someone would've told me I'd end up falling in love with you—"

"End up *what*?" He slides his hands into my hair and lowers his mouth to mine, just shy of kissing me. His warm breath holds a hint of whiskey and mint—a combination that makes me shiver.

"You heard me, Redgrave."

"Say it again anyway."

"Seriously?"

Nipping at my neck until I'm squealing beneath him, he says, "You wouldn't deny the last wish of a dying mage, would you?"

"*That's* your last wish? Wow. You could've asked me for just about anything, and you go with the love declaration?"

"I said what I said, and I stand by it."

"Fine. I fell in love with you, Baz Redgrave."

"I see." His lips buzz along my jaw, peppering me with hot, teasing kisses. "And when, exactly, did this alleged falling occur?"

I drag my nails lightly down his back, fingers memorizing every ridge, every plane. "Hmm. Well, it was a process. A long, slow one. Like, first I had to excuse away all your bad behavior and ridiculousness, and then—"

"You loved *every* second of it." His eyes blaze with fresh heat, and between my bare thighs, his cock grows hard. "Admit it."

"Yeah, I did. I still do." I press on his chest, forcing some space between us, but that only makes his hips grind against me, his cock all the more eager. "Goddess, I'm so in love with you, you big dumb ape. Are you happy now?"

"I am." He shrugs, as if he needs a bit more convincing.

"I mean, I *could* be happier." With a gentle roll of his hips, his cock teases my entrance, sending a jolt of pleasure through my core. He repeats the motion, slower this time, and then he's sliding inside me, filling me with his hot, hard length.

I grip his forearms and let out a soft hiss. The warmth, the gentle stroke, the way he moves inside me... all of it is conspiring to take me away from this place. The worries. The what-ifs.

"Any other questions, Little Bird," he teases, shifting so the base of his cock brushes against my clit with his next thrust. "Or did you lose your train of thought?"

"You..." I pant, quickly unraveling. "You always did have a knack for... making me... forget."

"Oh, but I don't want you to forget. Not this time." He grips my face with surprising urgency, then brands me with a kiss so deep and devastating I really *could* die right now and be a happy woman. When he finally pulls back, all the humor is gone from his gaze, replaced with a depravity that sets my insides on fire.

"Tonight," he warns, his voice dark and low, "I'm going to give you something to remember. Something to make you *ache*." Another searing hot kiss, another perfect thrust. "Tonight, I'm going to fuck you like there's no tomorrow."

Because there might not be.

He doesn't need to say that last part out loud. Love and passion ignite in his eyes, and then he's on me again, suffocating me with kisses, the weight of his body a warm, solid reminder that we're still here. That whatever's on tomorrow's horizon doesn't matter—we've still got tonight.

And *nothing* is over yet.

He drags his mouth down to my throat, then continues lower, capturing my nipple between his lips and sucking hard. The pain is exquisite, and my core clenches around him, throbbing with a need so desperate I'm not sure I'll survive the next five *minutes*, let alone the impending war.

Threading my fingers into his hair, I try to hold him to my breast, more than happy to lose myself to his hot, velvet kisses.

But my Devil in disguise has other plans.

Before I realize what's happening, he's pulling out of me and pulling away. I'm about to scream in protest, but then he flips around on the bed, repositioning himself with his cock near my mouth and his face between my thighs.

He goes down. Hard and deep and bruising and...

Holy

Fucking.

Hell.

With strong hands, he grips my thighs and pushes them open even wider, pinning them down as mouth descends on my superheated flesh again and again. Fisting him, I part my lips and guide his smooth, rock-hard cock into my mouth, relaxing my throat as I take him in deeper, the feel of his hot skin making me moan. His tongue flicks over my clit, that skilled mouth knowing exactly how much pressure to give me, exactly how much teasing I can take before I shatter.

Swirling my tongue around the head of his cock, I suck hard and bring him in deeper, suddenly desperate to taste every inch of him. My hips arch off the bed to get closer to his punishing mouth, a move that only makes him more frenzied.

He growls and sucks my clit between his lips, teasing and nipping as I gasp in pleasure, both of us driving each other wild. He fucks me everywhere at once, his tongue devouring me, his hips thrusting against my face, the weight of him hot and perfect on my body as we race to that delicious, white-hot edge…

I close my eyes and moan once more around the swell of his cock, and his tongue spears my core, a relentless lashing that has my vision swimming with images of our forbidden meadow, my legs trembling, my body close to bursting.

Goddess, he feels so good. Every touch, every kiss unravels me a little more.

He closes his lips over my clit and sucks, and then I'm gone, the meadow swirling into nothing but black skies and starlight as the pleasure explodes inside me. Baz tightens his grip on my thighs, his body going rigid as he chases his own orgasm, his tongue still swirling over my clit. With one last growl, he finally comes, his body going as boneless as mine.

I swallow him down, gently easing him out of my mouth.

Everything inside me is hot and buzzing.

We take a few seconds to catch our breaths, then he's shifting positions again, kissing his way back up my thighs, my stomach, my throat. He nuzzles against my neck, one hand spanning across my hips, the silence between us so comfortable and safe it nearly brings me to tears.

We lie together like that for a few long minutes, the candlelight throwing long, flickering shadows on the ceiling. Downstairs, I can hear the murmurs of whoever's still awake, the soft clink of spoons stirring sugar into coffee, the click of keys on a computer keyboard as someone undoubtedly searches for more intel. More answers. More anything.

I let out a deep sigh—content, mostly, but a little sad as well. It's such a simple thing, this feeling. Such a pure, everyday kind of magick—lying in the arms of someone you trust with your heart. The idea that anything could take this from me, that it won't be here tomorrow… Goddess, just imagining it is enough to nearly wreck me.

"Whatever you're thinking about," Baz whispers against my skin, "let it go. Just for tonight. Can you do that for me?"

I nod silently, relaxing into his soft kisses, the gentle trail of his fingers back and forth across my abdomen. "I guess I shouldn't get myself all stressed before going to sleep."

Baz lets out a soft chuckle, kissing my neck and shoulder as he rolls me forward onto my hip, my back to his chest.

"What the hell is so funny?" I tease.

"Sleep."

"And that's funny because…?"

"It's funny," he says, lifting the hair off the back of my

neck and running his nose up to my ear, "because it implies I'm letting you off the hook that easily."

I swallow hard, a rush of new anticipation flooding my insides, making my stomach dip. "You're... not?"

A possessive grip tightens on my hip, and a deep, feral rumble vibrates through Baz's chest.

"Oh, Little Bird," he warns. "I'm not even *close* to done with you tonight."

EIGHT

STEVIE

A soft moan slips from my mouth, and Baz slides his hand around my hip and down between my thighs. With a featherlight touch, he draws slow, gentle circles over my clit, heating me up all over again.

"I guess you were right," he teases. "You *are* insatiable for your mages."

"Your fault. You touch me with your... your magick Devil-hands and I just... oh, *fuck*..." I shudder as he dips a finger inside me, then eases out again, slowly drawing up to circle my clit.

"You just *what*, Little Bird?"

"I... I just..."

I'm spared the torture of formulating a coherent response by the sudden creak of the bedroom door. A sliver of light slices through the darkness as Kirin steps inside, but Baz doesn't stop touching me.

He dips inside me again.

And again.

Without a word, Kirin shuts the door, strips out of his clothes, and climbs into bed beside me, Baz's perfect torture setting my nerves ablaze. Kirin meets my gaze, his lips just inches from mine. I nod once, letting him know it's okay, and then he's closing the distance, capturing my mouth in a long, soft kiss.

Once again, I'm safe and protected in the arms of two of my Arcana brothers. Their presence calms and strengthens me, but it also deepens the ache in my heart.

Kirin finally breaks our kiss, pulling back to look into my eyes. I see my own fears reflected in his pale green gaze.

"They should be here too," I whisper, a lonely tear escaping, and of course the guys know who I'm talking about.

Kirin cups my face, his eyes searching mine in the soft amber light. The force of his love for me hits me hard, and it makes me believe—for just a moment—that anything is possible.

"They will be," he says. "The next time we set foot in this house, they'll be with us. I promise you."

"I believe you," I whisper, because it's the truth. Because I have to believe him. Because it feels like my Arcana brothers and I have only just found one another, and I refuse to let the darkness steal away what we haven't even fully *begun* to explore. To build. To nurture.

Baz pulls back, sliding his hand up my arm to caress my shoulder while Kirin presses his palm to my chest, right over my heart. Right now, they're holding me together.

"I love you both so much," I say, and Kirin grants me a sweet smile that reminds me of the first time I saw him in Kettle Black—my secret Mr. Cinnamon Buns crush. "And when I'm with you, somehow it feels like maybe we really *will* survive this thing. And even if we don't, at least—"

Kirin cuts me off with another kiss, this one so intense and possessive it sends a jolt of electric heat zipping down to my toes. When he finally breaks for air, his eyes are glassy, his lips red and puffy.

"Stevie, listen to me," he breathes. "I don't know what's going to happen tomorrow. But I *do* know you're going to survive it. You're our light. You *have* to survive it."

Behind me, Baz runs his fingers through my hair, tightening his grip in a hold as fierce and possessive as Kirin's kiss. "He's right, Little Bird. If anyone's going to make it to see another sunset, it's you."

"Screw you guys," I tease. "If I'm surviving, so are you. Package deal, non-negotiable."

"I'll take that deal," Baz says.

Kirin smiles and shrugs a shoulder. "Sure, why not? I'm in."

"Well, not yet, you're not. But the night is young, so…" I hook my leg over his hip, drawing him closer and cracking up at my own stupid innuendo. Kirin's hard length presses against me, already eager to grant my every wish. Behind me, Baz's equally rigid form presses against my curves. "Two hot men vying for my affections," I tease. "How will I ever choose?"

"I could challenge Genius Boy to a duel," Baz says, "but I feel like we should conserve our strength tonight."

I reach behind me and slide my fingers into his hair, pulling him closer. "Not all of it, I hope."

"I suppose I could spare some for you." His answering laugh trails into a soft sigh as he brings his lips to my ear and whispers, "I love you, Little Bird. More than you probably realize. You're truly my light."

"And my heart," Kirin says softly, his gaze fiery and serious as he slides into me. Behind me, Baz reaches forward and cups my breast, gently tugging my nipple as he teases the sensitive skin behind my ear with his tongue.

It's our last night before our last night.

Sounds funny to say it like that, but that's how it feels.

And there's nowhere else I'd rather be.

"I want you," I breathe, arching back against Baz again as Kirin draws out slowly, then slides back in, inch by torturous inch. "Both of you. Together."

Baz grabs my hand and guides it back to his cock, more than happy for my touch, but I pull away.

"Not like before," I insist. "Inside me. At the same time."

Low growls of pleasure rumble through them both, but I sense Baz's hesitance at once. He's worried he'll hurt me.

"In the nightstand," I say. "There's a pouch."

He rolls over and fumbles in the drawer, coming back with the gossamer pouch Professor Broome gave me the day I picked up my birth control potion—the one that made Kirin blush so adorably the first time he saw it. I grin, sending a silent thank-you to Carly and the girls. When they packed up the things from my suite before we all moved in here, they didn't skimp on the important stuff.

"There should be a small bottle inside," I said. "That's what you want."

"Right. The, uh…" He pauses as he reads the label. "Warming personal lubricant?"

Kirin and I exchange a wicked glance, both of us holding back a laugh.

"Do I even want to *know* why you have this?" Baz asks. "Not that I'm complaining, of course."

"No one wants to be caught without the essentials at the end of the world, Baz," Kirin says, mimicking the exact phrase I shot at him the night he discovered Professor Broome's bag of tricks.

Little did we know it would come in handy so soon.

The laughter passes, and Baz settles in behind me, bottle in hand. Still buried inside me, Kirin starts moving again, soft and slow, whipping me into a crazy-hot frenzy.

I hear the *snap* of the bottle cap, and a nervous excitement buzzes down my spine.

"Are you sure?" Baz asks, pressing another kiss to the shell of my ear.

"Yes. I want this. Right now." I turn my head to watch over my shoulder as Baz coats himself in lube, a shiver rolling across my shoulders. I've never done anything like this before. Never had two guys inside me at the same time, and never invited *anyone* in through the back door.

I've never trusted anyone enough to even consider it.

But all that changed the moment I fell for my Arcana mages.

With my leg still draped over Kirin and his cock growing even harder inside me, I shift to give Baz access. He teases me with a slick finger, then adds another, slowly gliding in and out, letting me get used to the sensation. There's a light pressure as I adjust to the strangeness of it, but between his masterful touch and the warming lube, it's…

"Oh, Goddess," I breathe. "That feels… It's… amazing."

He strokes me deeper, and Kirin matches his rhythm, in and out as the heat coils inside me.

"More," I whisper. "No teasing. I want more of you."

Baz slides his fingers out and positions himself at the back entrance, and Kirin goes completely still just long enough for Baz to slide in. It's slow and perfect and weird and hotter than anything I've ever imagined. Kirin starts rocking his hips again, and Baz follows suit, moving in a little deeper with each thrust.

When he finally pushes all the way in, my body clenches hard around him, and I suck in a sharp breath, unprepared for the sudden shock of pain. But then Kirin trails a hand down between us, fingers gliding over my clit in slow, perfect circles, and everything inside me relaxes, my body adjusting to accommodate my massive, impossibly hard mages.

"Okay?" Kirin asks, and I bite my lower lip and nod, my cheeks heating. He shifts again, making me gasp.

"Oh, *fuck*." They're both in so deep, hitting me in places

I've never felt before, unleashing intense, red-hot sensations I've never experienced.

Behind me, Baz lets out a deep groan of pure pleasure, and all at once, euphoria hits me. Tingles race across my scalp and down my spine, settling in my belly with a warm buzz that quickly ignites a fire. Flames of ecstasy lick across my skin, making me writhe and gasp, desperate for more of their hot, fevered strokes.

"Do you want us to stop?" Baz asks, blazing a trail of kisses down the back of my neck. A moan escapes my lips, and I arch back and bring him in deeper, deeper, deeper still, filling my body with a pulsing need that seems to demand more of him with every thrust. More of *both* of them.

Kirin increases the pressure on my clit and plunges in harder, he and Baz settling into an alternating rhythm, in and out and in and out, faster and deeper and hotter and suddenly my muscles are trembling with the need to fall, to implode, to fucking shatter.

Reaching up behind me, I fist Baz's hair and pull hard, rocking my hips forward and back, taking in one, then the other, my heart racing, my body a raging inferno that wants only to devour and consume and burn.

In a breathy, desperate voice I barely recognize, I give them my final command.

"Don't. You. *Dare*."

NINE

CASS

I reach past his head to a rock jutting from the wall behind him. The edge is sharp—just enough to do the trick.

"My father was a malicious sonofabitch," I say. "Probably had a lot in common with yours. But you know what? Fuck him. Fuck him, and fuck your father too. And your mother, for not knowing what a gift she had for a son. I don't presume to know what cruelties they heaped upon you, Ani, but I do know this: You're not alone. And you *do* have a family. Maybe the people who brought you into this world abandoned you, but your *real* family—me, your Arcana brothers, the woman who's doubtlessly fighting her way here as we speak—will *not* abandon you."

"Your valor is admirable, Cass, but—"

"Valor?" The idea is so ridiculous, a bitter laugh bubbles out. "That ship sailed long ago, my friend. This? This is love."

"For Stevie," he says. It's not a question.

"Yes, for Stevie. And for Kirin, Baz, and you. My *brothers*."

The tiniest bit of light flashes in his eyes again. "And what about our brotherhood? You're not doing this just to honor the vows?"

"I'd break them in a heartbeat if I had to choose between the two. Alas, I don't. And neither do you." I glance up toward the ceiling, a vast black dome marred only by a few pale slivers of moonlight. It isn't much, but like the rock, it's enough to get the job done.

"Okay, Ani. No more slacking off," I say with a grin that's only half forced. "You may be an imprisoned Arcana soul, but I'm still your professor, and I've got an assignment for you. One you *must* pass if you've got any hope of graduating."

At this, a warm smile finally breaks across his face, his body further solidifying. Maybe not enough to take on the dark armies, but hopefully enough to do the one thing I need him to do right now.

"Pop quiz," I say. "Which Arcana am I?"

"Damn, Cass. How hard did you hit your head?"

"Answer the question, Mr. McCauley."

Ani rolls his eyes. "Despite the fact that you're acting like a fool, *Dr. Devane*, you're the Moon."

"Correct. And you are…?"

Ani holds up his hands like a stage magician revealing his last trick. "Tada! The Sun."

"Excellent. Keep it up and you'll get that A in no time. Next question… What is moonlight?"

He rolls his eyes, but still plays along.

"It's... sunlight," he says, glancing up at the cracks in the ceiling and quickly catching my drift. "Reflected by the moon."

"Ah, there he is, the fiery Arcana genius we know and love. So, you see my dilemma, yes? I simply can *not* do this without you. You bail on me now, Mr. McCauley, and you're signing my death warrant as well as everyone else's."

"Laying it on a little thick, Doctor," he says with another eye roll, but a bit more of his old spirit shines through. "Where are you going with all this melodrama?"

"You and I have a strong bond," I continue. "Right now, we need to call on that bond to juice my mental magick. I don't need much—just enough to be able to reach out to the others. Stevie, primarily—she has the ability to dreamcast, which means she should be the most receptive to my communications."

"So we're sending a mental message?"

"Less of a message and more of a warning. A dire one."

Barring an escape route, we need to let the others know about Judgment's plans before they walk into an ambush at the Fool's Grave. That sick druid was right about one thing —our Star won't resist a rescue mission. And as soon as she and the others start plotting, they'll realize they need the Arcana objects. They probably already have.

It's precisely what Judgment's counting on.

"Okay, professor," Ani finally says, and I damn near fall to my knees in relief at the steely determination rising in his voice. Gone are the doubts, the insecurities, the guilt. Even the sarcasm takes a back seat, his love for Stevie and his brothers shining through. "What do you need me to do?"

"I need you to focus your energy on reconnecting with your human form."

"How?"

"Your gift is fire, but for this, you'll need to tap into the earth. Think about all of your physical senses—every part of your body you use to experience the world around you. Recall the scent and taste of your favorite foods, the feel of sun-warmed rocks as you climb in the Cauldron, the sounds of the river rushing through Blood and Sorrow's lands. Think of all those songs you and Stevie sing, and the tea she made for you, the music of her laughter, the taste of her sweet, soft lips as she—"

"Yes, thank you, I can take it from here." With a grin and a shake of his head, Ani is finally on board. The seeds have taken root, and he's slowly coming back into view.

"You may not be able to fully reclaim your body yet, but I'm fairly confident you can bring enough of yourself back to the physical plane to do what needs to be done."

"And what, exactly, is that?"

I offer a sly grin, then slice my palm open on the sharp rock. "*Bleed.*"

"Oh, is that all? Of course. Sure. No problem, professor psycho," he says, pushing up his sleeves. But there's no anger or concern in his gaze now. Only the same determination I hear in his voice. "Just so you know, I'm getting an A in your classes. All of them. For the rest of my academic career. Non-negotiable."

"Assuming we succeed, we will discuss grades later. Now, get to work. We don't have much time."

Ani nods, all the jokes finally fading as he closes his eyes and focuses his attention on the task. While he tries to reach out to his physical form, I kneel on the cave floor and squeeze my hand into a fist, dripping blood onto a spot illuminated by a thin shaft of moonlight.

Seconds later, Ani's crouching across from me and doing the same thing.

I smile at him with a raised eyebrow, surprised at how quickly he was able to do it. He's not a hundred percent solidified—his edges are still a bit blurry, and his image is still flickering, but he's bleeding. Real, actual, Sun Arcana blood.

Magick blood.

"You did good, Ani. Really good. Great, actually."

Ani returns my smile, his own warming me from the inside out. "Nothing says 'you did good-really-good-great-actually' like an A, Cass."

"Noted. Now, I need you to focus your attention on Stevie, Kirin, and Baz. She's the one I need to reach, but they're likely together, and the strength of their bond will amplify their power just as it does ours. Kirin and Baz can act as receivers, helping her to tune into our message even if they don't yet know we're sending it."

"And if we can't reach her after all this?"

"We're the Sun and Moon of the Major Arcana, Ansel

McCauley. Keepers of the Grave. Sworn protectors of magick. And most importantly—two of the four mages on whom Starla Milan's life depends. We *will* find a way."

He nods and closes his eyes again, doubtlessly calling up images and memories of Stevie and our brothers. I do the same, and after a few moments, when I've got them clear in my mind, I hold my palms over the moonlit pool of blood and chant my spell.

> *Magick of Moon, magick of Sun*
> *Bonded by light, let two become one*
> *From this realm to hers, the channel is clear*
> *Our message is sent, allow her to hear*

On the second recitation, Ani picks up the spell, and together we chant, over and over until we're both entranced. I open my eyes, and the cave around us begins to fade away.

"It's working," I say, unable to keep the excitement from my voice. "Keep going."

We repeat the verse faster and louder, our words echoing across the cave. With a final flicker, the cave vanishes, replaced with a vision that brings tears to my eyes and joy to my heart.

Ani seems to sense it too, and opens his eyes, gasping as he takes in what's undoubtedly the same sight.

"It's hers," he says, and I nod. Overhead, the night sky glitters with an endless field of stars, the air clear and crisp. A deep, calm pool of water shines below, the reflection of the sky so clear it looks like a bowl of stars. Behind it, the familiar standing stones keep watch, huddled in their eternal circle.

It's the Star card, save for only one missing element.

The Star herself.

Ani and I are still kneeling in place, and though our stone floor now looks like a grassy clearing, the blood we spilled remains.

I begin the chant again, nodding for him to do the same.

> *Magick of Moon, magick of Sun*
> *Bonded by light, let two become one*
> *From this realm to hers, the channel is clear*
> *Our message is sent, allow her to hear*

On our seventh recitation, the dark blood sizzles between us, spinning into a tight circle of red, then swirling outward into ribbons of glowing silver and gold, finally exploding in a supernova of light. Mist rises from the center, and as the light recedes, a new vision emerges.

Stevie, lying in her bed.

Wrapped up in the arms of our brothers.

And... gasping with pleasure.

Her cheeks are flush, her lips parted in ecstasy, her body glistening with sweat as her two lovers shower her with all manner of shared affections.

Jealousy flares in my chest, but Ani only laughs.

"Oh, and what a vision we've conjured." His eyes light up, utterly entertained. "Get it, girl!" Then, sparing me a momentary glance and a quick wink, "Suffice it to say, I'm *definitely* getting those A's now, professor."

If I wasn't so happy to see Ani's sense of humor rekindled, I might be forced to turn him back into a ghost.

Tamping down the green-eyed monster with a reminder that I'll have her in my arms again soon enough, no sharing required, I fix Ani with a pointed glare. "Less ogling, Mr. McCauley, and more concentrating. As much as we all love a good show, we actually have a message to convey."

"Yes, and let's just hope she can hear it over the sounds of all those—"

"Concentrating, Mr. McCauley," I command, but I can't help the smile quirking my lips as I see my woman taking charge in the bedroom. I may be a jealous bastard when it comes to her, but damn. She's *ferocious*.

Oh, my beautiful Star. The things I'm going to do to you when I get home...

TEN

BAZ

She's so fucking tight. So perfect. *Goddess*, the feel of her body and the sound of her soft, breathy moans fill me with as much desire as they do rage.

The thought that *any* pain or harm could ever touch her —let alone the end of the fucking world at the hands of an insane Arcana mage—unleashes a blinding fury not even the monsters of my past could inspire.

"Don't. You. *Dare*," she says now, ordering us not to stop, her searing desire making me even more painfully hard than I already am. I'm buried so deep inside her I can no longer tell our bodies apart, her every movement and moan conspiring to send me over the fucking edge.

Nothing outside this room exists. Nothing outside this bed. It's me, Kirin, and the woman we've all fallen in love with, the press and release of our bodies, the sound of wild heartbeats and ragged breath and low moans, the sound-track of our own finale.

SARAH PIPER

Without breaking contact, I shift her upright while Kirin rolls onto his back. Now I'm on my knees behind her, fucking her perfect ass while she rides his cock.

"Tell me how it feels," I grind out, desperate to hear her describe it.

"It's... oh, Goddess. What you're doing to me... I can feel you both inside me and it's so deep and hot and I... I want more. Just... more."

With one hand clamped hard over her hip, I shove the other into her wild mass of hair, tugging *just* hard enough— just how she likes it. The scent of her shampoo washes over me, and I bury my face beneath the dark curtain of curls, kissing the nape of her neck, tonguing her shoulder, my mouth seeking out every inch of silky-smooth skin within reach.

My balls tighten, and I know I won't be able to last much longer. The heat from the lube and the feel of Stevie's body and the sounds she's making... Goddess, it's a wonder I can even remember my own name.

Still fisting her hair, I push her forward until she's on her hands and knees straddling Kirin. She cries out in pleasure and arches her back, and I slide in deeper as Kirin brings his mouth to her nipple.

All of us are teetering on that same razor-thin edge. And fuck, it's the hottest thing I've ever seen.

"Baz," she moans softly, the sounds of my name on her breath sending a white-hot jolt to my balls. "Kirin, don't stop. Holy shit, I'm so close. I'm..."

Kirin sucks her deeper into his mouth, rubbing her clit

with a fevered intensity, and I groan, rocking harder against her backside, T-minus five seconds from losing it.

"Yes!" she cries out. "Right there. I'm… oh, fuck… *yes!*"

Her body grips me like a fist as she comes hard, and that's all it takes. I'm gone, exploding inside her in a hot rush, my whole body on fucking fire for this woman.

Kirin shudders beneath her, reaching around to cup her ass in both hands. He lets out a deep growl as he unleashes inside her, setting her off again. Stevie tosses her dark head back and rolls her hips, riding us both through her second orgasm, and everything around me fucking spins.

I suck in a ragged breath just as the room slides out of view, and Kirin's Tower energy reverberates through her body and barrels right into me, pulling us all into a crazy vision. Lightning arcs through a black sky, illuminating the jagged tower jutting up from the sea. Waves crash onto the shore, a storm gathering overhead. Raw power courses through the air itself, making every hair on my body stand on end.

Another bolt of lightning crashes overhead, and the tower collapses.

It's beautiful and terrifying and fills me with a sense of dark dread.

I open my mouth as a scream tears its way up my throat, but then the image shifts again, and the cry vanishes on my lips.

New images spin and flicker past my eyes—flashes of a dark cavern. Rock and mist and moonlight. Slowly, they come into a focus, finally going still.

A pool of blood swirling into ribbons of light.

Cass.

Ani.

I see them both as clearly as if they were in the room with us, their heads bent together over the blood, examining it closely.

"Doc!" Stevie cries out. I can't see her, but I feel her presence, hear her voice, and I swear Cass does too. His head jolts upright, his eyes scanning the space.

"Cass!" I reach for him even though logically I know he's not physically near. But seeing him there, knowing he's alive *somewhere*—and with Ani, besides—it gives me hope. "Ani!"

Again, Cass looks around, head swiveling as if he's trying to place the sound but can't quite make it out.

And then, just as soon as they appeared, our brothers vanish.

There's another flash of lightning, and then the vision fades out completely, leaving me back in bed with Stevie and Kirin. We're lying side by side now, arms and legs tangled together, all of us hot and sticky and spent.

The shock is plain on Kirin's face.

"You were there," Kirin says. "Both of you."

Stevie and I nod.

"But… how?" he asks. "I thought it was just me—my Tower energy going into overdrive after we… But it was a vision."

I nod again and tighten my hold on Stevie, brushing her shoulder with another kiss. "It's her. It's always her."

In all the time I've known Kirin and the guys, nothing like this ever happened to us. Yeah, we've always been close—always had this unbreakable Arcana bond, not to mention a damn tight friendship. There were times I thought I could read their minds, or they could read mine.

But this kind of connection goes beyond all of that.

And we owe it all to our Star. She brought us together, strengthening our bond even as she changed it.

"They're with us," she whispers, her eyes shining with wonder. "I could feel them. Both of them. I saw the caves, and they're together, just like I thought."

"I think they're trying to reach out," I say. "It looked like they were doing a spell."

"Cass *is* the mental magicks expert," Kirin says. "It's a smart move."

Stevie sits up between us, clutching the sheet against her breasts. "I think he's trying to… to get inside my head. I can still sense him."

"What do you mean?" I ask.

"It's hard to explain. It's not a manipulation or anything like that. More like… like someone testing the locks, looking for a way in."

I sit up next to her, running my hand up and down her bare back. "Makes sense. You're the one who can dream-cast. You've always had an ability to sense our Arcana energy. The visions—everything started when you got here."

"But that was…" Her brow furrows as she tries to piece it all together. "I mean, first it was Kirin's energy—I recognized it right away and figured it was just from the intensity of what we just did. But suddenly we were there with Doc and Ani... That wasn't just a vision or wishful thinking. It was a connection. We saw them—in real time. I just... I'm not sure how all this works."

"It's possible we opened the channel," Kirin says, the nerd-boy wheels already turning behind his eyes. "Or strengthened the signal."

"Yes, but how?" she asks.

"We got..." His cheeks darken, and he gestures awkwardly between us. "Close."

"*Real* close," I tease.

A slow, satisfied grin spreads across her lush mouth, her blue eyes dancing with new mischief. "In that case, we should probably try again. For Doc and Ani. You know—anything to bring them home safe and sound. Doc would want us to do it, don't you think?"

"Oh, definitely." Kirin nods like a bobble-head. "For research purposes, of course. As a professor, he can appreciate the need to recreate the conditions of the experiment in an attempt to replicate the results."

The two co-conspirators look at me expectantly.

I crack up, already climbing out of bed and heading for the shower. "Oh, like I'm gonna say no to *this* little science project?"

Fucking hell, I just came harder than I've ever come in my life, and I'm already hard again.

They follow me to the bathroom and the three of us hop

into a steaming shower, where Kirin and I fight the good fight over who gets to thoroughly soap up our girl.

In the end, we decide—once again—to share.

"For research purposes," he repeats, nodding like he's still trying to convince himself of his pure motives.

Sliding my hand up to cup her slick, sudsy breast, I grin, knowing Ani—and even Cass, though he'd never admit it —would approve. "For research purposes."

ELEVEN

KIRIN

"You look... bewildered." Casey smirks as I enter the kitchen, then hands over the mug of coffee she just poured for herself. "You need this more than I do."

"Yeah, I just... couldn't sleep." Gladly taking the offered brew, I duck her gaze, my cheeks burning at the insinuation.

No matter. I suppose it's obvious what I've been up to tonight—I couldn't keep this grin in check if my life depended on it.

"Can't imagine why." Casey rolls her eyes, but she's still smiling at me, warm and playful despite how exhausted she must be.

She's been hard at work all night, her tablet, phone, and notes spread all over the kitchen table. Her partner is passed out on the living room couch. Everyone else seems to have gone to bed, which is probably for the best. We've all got a big day ahead. Or *days*, maybe. I have no idea how long this battle will take—how many days and nights we'll be away from home, away from one another, away from any sense of normalcy.

If we'll ever get that back.

Don't think like that…

I take a seat at the table and sip the coffee, wincing at its knockout strength. "Damn, Case. I see you're still drinking the high-octane stuff."

"You know me," she says, pouring herself a fresh cup from the pot. "I like my coffee how I like my soul."

"Dark and damned," we say in unison, then crack up.

The memories come back easily, always swimming just below the surface—Mom in the kitchen, playfully scolding Casey and me over the pre-teen coffee habit we'd picked up. She used to tell us the caffeine would destroy our youthful souls and turn us into heathens. She was joking, but—as it turns out—not entirely wrong.

One memory unlocks another, and soon images of my old life flood my mind—my siblings, our childhood home, the love and the laughter that came before the destruction…

No. I can't go there.

Not tonight.

I force out the last memory with another sip of bitter coffee, patching up the dam before it crumbles completely.

Nostalgia is a dangerous drug.

"On second thought…" Casey sits across from me, her green eyes softening in the glow of her laptop screen. "You look bewildered *and* happy."

I shift uncomfortably under her scrutiny, but she doesn't seem to be instigating a fight tonight.

Still, a ribbon of guilt unfurls in my gut. "Seems wrong, doesn't it?"

"Being happy?"

"Considering what we're up against—and everything that's happened already..." I glance at the notes spread between us—frantic scribbles about the Soldiers of Light and Eastman's diabolical plans, circles and arrows and underlines on words like *black magick* and *cult*. "I don't know, Case. The whole world's going to hell, and my heart is shattered over everything we've already lost, yet somehow when I'm with Stevie... *Goddess*, even when I'm just thinking about her or someone says her name or I find one of her hair clips on the bathroom sink... I can't help it. Suddenly I'm a smiling, grinning, happy-ass idiot."

"You're *alive*. Stevie reminds you of that." She sips her coffee, gaze darting quickly to Agent Quintana, then back to me. Lowering her voice, she says, "Finding joy in the midst of pain isn't a bad thing, Kirin. If more of us could do that, humanity would be in a much better place."

"I told her," I blurt out suddenly, the words escaping before I've even thought them through. "I mean, Stevie's the only person I've ever talked to about... The only one I've told... everything."

I don't need to spell it out. Casey knows I'm referring to her APOA induction ceremony in London—the night I lost control of my Tower energy and demolished a hotel, paralyzed my grandfather, and injured scores more.

That night, I destroyed my career and sidelined Casey's dreams, causing a rift in my family that's never been repaired.

I don't have the strength to look up from my coffee, but I feel my sister's eyes on me, quietly assessing, likely wondering what—if anything—she should say to my admission.

I blow out a breath, sending a soft ripple across the coffee.

As badly as I want to, I still can't find the words to address this head-on.

To well and truly apologize for what I did—that night and after, when I walked out on my family, too broken and ashamed to face them. To let them continue to love me.

Shame burns through my chest, but I deserve that much. Casey hasn't bolted yet—she's remained by my side through all of this Academy and Dark Arcana craziness. The least I can do is sit here with my discomfort and let her judge me.

She's certainly earned the right.

Casey sighs, and I brace for the attack, expecting her to go right for the jugular like she always does.

You never even said goodbye...

"How did she take it?" she asks instead, surprising me.

At the unexpected kindness in her voice, I chance a quick glance across the table. The same kindness shines in her eyes.

"She basically told me I needed to get my head out of my ass," I reply.

Casey lets out a quiet laugh. "Knowing what I know of her, yeah, I can totally picture that."

"Well, she didn't use those *exact* words. She just *very* firmly reminded me the Tower isn't just about what crumbles, but what's left standing in the aftermath. What's worth fighting for. Then she told me to stop sifting through the old rubble and build something new instead."

"Wise words." Casey sips her coffee, watching me over the rim of her mug. "So, is that what you're doing now? Building something new?"

"I… yeah. I guess. I'm trying. Still getting the hang of it, though. It's a complicated procedure, removing one's head from one's ass."

"Especially *your* head. That thing is huge."

Another laugh bubbles up from inside her, and this time I return it.

When it fades away, we sit in silence for a few moments, sipping our coffee and listening to the sounds of Agent Quintana's light snoring.

Eventually, Casey gets up to grab the coffeepot.

"It's pretty easy to see why you fell so hard for her," she says, returning to top off our mugs. "She's amazing, Kirin. Fierce as hell too."

"Yeah, *that* part reminds me of someone else I know." I hold her gaze, still trying to find the right words.

There's just so much to say, and so much ground to cover, so much lost time to make up for.

Everything is a jumble inside my head, so in the end, I

blurt out the first coherent words I can string together. "Thank you."

"Thank Quintana. He made the coffee. Then the poor guy fell asleep before it was even ready."

"I mean… Thank you for… for not giving up on me. For not walking away when I've given you every reason to do just that."

She turns away from me and crosses the kitchen, returning the pot to the coffeemaker. Keeping her back to me, she says softly, "Does that mean you want me to stick around?"

"It means… it means I've got a lot of shit pent up inside —shit I've been wrestling with for years. It's not just going to disappear overnight. I fucked up, I was hurt, I hurt you and Derrick and Mom and Dad and everyone else I love, and I…"

The admissions burn their way through me, dark memories threatening to pull me under. But after a long pause, I take a deep breath and the pain finally eases, allowing me to say what I should've said years ago.

"I don't know, Case. I guess what I'm trying to say is… Yeah, I want you to stick around. If not here physically, here in my life. I know I have a lot to make up for. I'm willing to work to earn your forgiveness. I'd really like it if you'd give me that chance."

I look up from my mug, and Casey finally turns around, tears painting her cheeks.

"Forgiveness isn't something you need to work for," she says. "Believe it or not, my forgiving you doesn't even *involve* you. That choice is all on me—and it's one I made a long time ago. I've already forgiven you." She wipes away her tears with the heels of her hands, then takes the seat across from me again. "But forgiveness doesn't mean forgetting. It doesn't mean things automatically go back to normal."

I nod, lowering my gaze again. "No, I suppose not."

Casey blows out a breath. "Then again, what the fuck is normal, anyway?"

This time, I'm the one laughing. "You're asking a guy who can demo a building with little more than a bad mood? A guy who's the emanation of the Tower card, in love with the Star, in some kind of relationship with the Moon, the Sun, and the Devil?"

"When you put it *that* way..." Casey shrugs, her smile returning. She takes a few steadying gulps of coffee, then looks up at me again, her eyes bright. "Friends," she says firmly. "Maybe we can start with being friends."

"I'm in." I toss back another gulp of radioactive coffee. "So, as your *friend*... Am I allowed to ask how long you've had a thing for Quintana?"

"No," she snaps, but she can't hide the blush in her cheeks.

"Fine. Since we're new at this whole friends thing, I guess I'll let you off the hook... for now." Picking up one of her notebooks, I ask, "Any luck with the London office?"

"A bit. One of the tech witches—a new hire named Darla—was able to send over some promising leads. She dug through Eastman's online records and found some more of his—and this is a direct quote—'magickal spank-bank stash.'"

"That sounds… disgusting."

"Yeah, I could've done without the visual myself, but the intel is solid. Unsurprisingly, black-mirror magick is one of his favorite obsessions—we've already gotten a taste of that. But his interests span the black magick spectrum." She grabs her tablet, pulling up a few images. "Let's see, we've got blood sorcery and human vampirism, animal sacrifice, oh—and I bet this will make him a fan favorite at future office holiday parties —necromancy!"

"Guess that's why he's so interested in the Dark Magician's work," I say.

"We don't know for sure that they're plotting the attack together, but the evidence highly suggests some level of cooperation. And since we've agreed to assume the worst, I'm warning everyone Eastman and the Dark Arcana are on Team Asshole, just as we feared."

"So basically, we're dealing with a psychopath who hates all magick-users—including himself—knows just enough about the dark arts to be dangerous, and is either partnering with or just seriously fan-boying our main magickal enemy."

"He's obsessed with self-flagellation, Kirin." She trades the tablet for one of her notebooks, skimming over her research. "This whole thing feels like some kind of sick fantasy he designed to punish and publicly humiliate himself. Taking everyone else down in the process is all part of the grand plan, but my theory is he's going to take himself out too."

"Like a suicide bomb?"

"Could be. For these kinds of whackjobs, the more violent and terrible a show they can put on, the better. Something like that would certainly inspire his followers—and we've got no idea how many we're dealing with." She drops her notebook and sighs. "Whatever happens tomorrow, we need to take him out without getting too close."

I reach across the table and grab her hand. Her eyes widen in surprise, but she doesn't pull away.

"We'll nail the sonofabitch, Case," I say. "And when we do, APOA owes you a medal *and* a promotion. Two of them, actually."

"Hmm. Two medals or two promotions?"

"Both." I laugh—a thing that's suddenly a little easier with my sister. "You deserve both."

I finally release her hand and rise from the table, wanting to spend a little more time with Stevie before we have to be up in an hour.

But before I can wish my sister goodnight, my Queen of Leaves tumbles into the kitchen in a rush of frantic energy and crazy hair, Baz stumbling along behind her.

"He got through!" she says breathlessly, grabbing my hands. "Baz and I were asleep, and then Doc pulled me back into that same vision. And this time I stayed with them and Ani was there and Doc actually spoke to me!"

Quintana is up and instantly alert, rushing to join us in the kitchen. "What's going on?"

"I have no idea," Casey says, glancing from Stevie and Baz, then back to me.

"Earlier tonight," I say, "when we were... getting into bed..." I clear my throat, then start again. "The three of us kind of got sucked into a vision."

"The same one?" she asks.

"Yes. I think my Tower energy triggered it. Anyway, we saw Cass and Ani together in the caves and thought they might be trying to get a message out, but we couldn't hear anything."

"Until now," Stevie says. "He said—"

"Code red, people." Carly breezes into the kitchen next, her wide, frantic eyes belying her casual saunter. "I just got one of my intuitive hits, and it's *not* good."

"Describe not good," Casey says. "Like, you felt something bad happen? Saw something?"

Carly nods. "We're talking disaster-movie level hell here, guys. But then I crashed and went offline, so now I'm not sure what to think."

"Crashed and went... What does that even mean?" Casey rises from her chair, then shakes her head, muscles already bunching with new tension. "Wait. Before you answer that, I need you to go upstairs and rally the troops —tell them we're rolling out in an hour and we need to strategize. Then come straight back here and tell me about this disaster movie business."

"Fine," she says, forcing a bored yawn. I'm not sure who she thinks she's fooling—the woman is clearly freaked out. "But someone needs to get on coffee and breakfast duty,

SPELLS OF MIST AND SPIRIT

pronto. I am *not* trying to save the world without a good caffeine buzz."

Quintana salutes her and beelines for the coffeemaker.

"Better make it to-go," Casey orders, then turns back to me, Baz, and Stevie. "Okay, my little Tarot badasses. Start talking, and tell me *everything*."

TWELVE

STEVIE

"Try to describe it as best you can," Casey tells Carly. "What, exactly, did you feel?"

We're all crammed into the kitchen again, desperately shoving in food before heading out. I don't know why I thought our last big breakfast together would be more of an event, but clearly, that was wishful thinking.

I glance around at my friends and fellow witches, hating that we have to split up like this. We're all so much stronger together. But with enemies encroaching on multiple fronts, we need to be everywhere at once, and the only way to do that is to divide and conquer.

"You know when you're driving up at elevation, and your ears pop?" Carly says between bites of granola. "Imagine that same sensation on a much bigger scale. I just got out of bed to pee, and suddenly there was this strange pressure all around me—it literally drove me to my knees.

For a second, I thought I was having a heart attack, but then the feeling just hit me. Not a vision, really, just a knowing."

"A knowing?" Casey prods.

"Yep. In that moment, I knew without a doubt the sky was going to rip open and unleash a storm of immeasurable power strong enough to take out everyone on earth like fleas in a tornado." She forces a laugh, but it's awkward and nervous. "I know that sounds completely stupid, but I don't know how else to explain it. The feeling was there, clear as if it had already happened, then gone. When I tried to dive back into it, I couldn't pick it up again."

"Maybe it was… something else?" Casey raises her eyebrows, as if her prompting could make this whole thing any less horrifying. "A nightmare? Hallucination?"

"I wish." Carly sets her cereal bowl in the sink and shakes her head, her shoulders slumping. "After that, there was another pop, then my signal dropped. Completely. Permanently."

"Is that unusual after one of your insights?" Casey asks. "The dropped signal thing?"

"More than unusual. As far as I know, it's impossible." She turns around to face us again, crossing her arms over her chest and leaning back against the edge of the sink. "Basically, the feelings I get—that knowingness—it's like a constant hum in the background. Sometimes it comes at me in a strong wave, like that night when we saw Trello sneaking into the library with Phaines and I just *knew* something was wrong. Other times, I have to make an effort to tune into it and decipher the messages from the noise. But the noise itself is always there, whether I tune in or not. It's like a buzzing fridge—something you don't even notice until it stops. Well, it stopped."

No one says a word to that.

"Told you it sounded completely stupid." Carly shrugs and inspects her fingernails as if she doesn't care whether we believe her or not, but her fear is palpable.

"It's not stupid at all," Professor Maddox finally says, topping off her travel mug with a good dose of Quintana's jet fuel coffee. "What you've just described? That's a rift between realms, Carly."

Professor Broome gasps, realization dawning in her eyes. "Oh, no. You don't think…?"

"I do. She's a skilled clairsentient, Kate. What she felt was a premonition. That rift and the so-called storm that follows? That's the Dark Magician tearing the very fabric of our reality so he and his armies can slip in through the hole. *They* are the storm. And *we*—unless we can stop them—are the fleas." She snaps the lid of her travel mug into place, the sound making me flinch.

Then, turning to Carly with a kind smile, she says, "I don't want you to worry about your gifts, Carly. I know you haven't experienced a loss like this before, but I assure you—it's not impossible, and it *is* temporary."

Carly's fear evaporates, her relief a palpable surge. "Are you sure?"

Maddox nods. "It's not unusual for a gifted psychic to experience sensory overload from a particularly powerful hit. Your senses just need a little time to recover."

"Awesome," Carly deadpans. "I'll be back at a hundred percent just in time to greet the invading hoards."

With that, we spend the next fifteen minutes going over the plans, making sure everyone knows where they're supposed to be.

Casey, Quintana, and the self-named Hot-Girl Squad are driving out to the desert outpost, where they'll use the energy vortex there to portal onto Academy lands. The agents will follow the path along the River of Blood and Sorrow toward campus, swimming the final half-mile in.

As soon as they give the signal, the Hot Girls will portal in near the border checkpoint behind the Blood and Sorrow dorms, where they'll use a combination of—and I quote —"mysterious hot girl stuff and Dr. Devane's boring-ass mental magick lessons" to create a diversion, allowing Casey and Quintana need to cross into campus proper, where they'll attempt to locate and dismantle the secret portal Eastman is using to bring in his minions.

Assuming the girls can subdue the Blood and Sorrow guards, they'll sneak onto campus and link up with Professors Broome and Maddox, who'll be working from inside Eastman's inner circle to ferret out any allies and warn them of the impending attack.

Last night, Kirin and Quintana were able to hack into the student messaging network and schedule a message to go out campus-wide two hours after the professors portal in. Once that message hits, Team Asshole will know we're on to them, but so will everyone else. Hopefully, by the time those invading hoards hit prime time, we'll have more than a few witches and mages on our side, ready to fight.

This is it. We're down to our last few minutes of peace at the Red Sands House. Dressed to fight, geared up with a few small daggers from Casey and some attack and defense potions from Professor Broome, I take a step back and look around at my friends. My family.

Casey and Quintana are taking a final look at the Blood and Sorrow map spread out on the kitchen table. The professors are packing up the last of their potions, double-checking they haven't left anything behind. My guys are already waiting for me by the front closet where we'll portal out, each strapped with a backpack full of hiking gear, weapons, food, water, and a few vials of Doc's blood —everything we managed to collect from the bedroom floor.

Hopefully, it will be enough.

When my gaze lands on Carly, Isla, and Nat, a knot the size of a baseball lodges in my throat.

I take in the sight of my girls, trying to memorize every detail. Nat's huge smile and her wild, multi-colored hair. The light in Isla's expressive eyes and the teardrop pendant shining against her smooth brown skin. Carly's feistiness and flawlessly coordinated outfit. Even going to battle, she's a damn runway model.

Seeing them reminds me of Jessa, and a fresh pain lances my heart. I haven't seen her since her Harvest Eve visit, and I miss her so, so much. A hundred times this morning I thought to call her, to send a text, anything. But I was too scared it would be the last, so I stayed silent.

All I can think about now is hugging her again. Hearing her laugh. Smelling the scents of her chocolate and cinnamon scones.

I can only hope I'll have the chance again.

Tears sting my eyes, but I refuse to let them show.

"You okay?" Isla asks.

I force a smile and nod. "Just… worried about my witches. That's all."

"I'm worried too, girl," she says, tying her braids back beneath a dark headscarf. "But you know how it is. Sometimes you just have to go out there and do epic shit, right?"

A tear escapes. Brushing it away quickly before it unleashes a torrent, I say, "I just wish you all didn't have to be quite so epic today. The Dark Arcana are the responsibility of the Brotherhood. You shouldn't have to fight these—"

"I'm gonna have to stop you right there, Twink." Carly rolls her eyes as if I'm the most ridiculous person on the planet right now, then puts an arm around my shoulder. "I'll let you in a little secret. I *hate* winter holidays—especially New Year's Eve. It always leads to disappointment and loneliness and way too much self-medicating with my perpetual dates, Ben and Jerry. But this year is different. New Year's is less than two weeks away, I've got the best friends a girl could ask for, my psycho mother is locked away and out of my life, and for the first time ever, I'm actually looking forward to celebrating. So if you think I'm letting that shrivel-dicked asshole Magician and his variety pack of Tarot nutter butter psychopaths ruin it for me, forget about it. I already have the perfect outfit planned and everything, so fuck *that* guy."

I can't help but laugh. "So basically, you're doing this because you don't want to cancel your party plans?"

"Obviously! Do *you* want to cancel? Damn, girl. You've got four *seriously* hot dates. You're telling me you'd rather spend New Year's Eve dead instead of making out with them?"

I glance over at Kirin and Baz, utterly inspiring in their tight black T-shirts. "It's a trick question, right?"

"Obviously. Anyway, enough about you. How do I look?" She steps back and props a hand on her hip, showing off her ensemble—combat boots, camo pants with multiple secret pockets for multiple secret weapons, all topped off with a lace cami that somehow manages to conceal the sheathed dagger strapped to her back while still looking cute.

"Carly, only you could make camo and lace work so well together."

"Right?"

I take another look at each of them, relieved that Isla and Nat are wearing the protective hematite jewelry I got for them on one of our girls-night-out dates.

Carly and I weren't on the best of terms back then, so she missed out on the date night as well as the gifts. But in the short time since, she's become one of my closest friends. My sister-witch.

And she's not wearing a single protective stone.

Without a second thought, I unclasp my Eye of Horus necklace and fasten it around her neck.

"Whoa, girl." She touches her fingertips to the pendant and shakes her head. "If you like me *that* much, put a ring on it."

"Maybe for your birthday." I smile, then grab her hands, surprised when she squeezes back. "It's a protective amulet —it'll keep you grounded and safe. It was my mom's. Professor Broome made it for her."

Carly's eyes widen, her energy turning serious and heavy. "But... but what if I don't make it back, and—"

"Carly." I shoot her a pointed glare. "Tomorrow is Witch-'N-Bitch. Don't even *try* to get out of it." Looking up at the rest of the group, I say, "That goes for all of you ladies. Professors and Casey too. We've got a date tomorrow night, and I expect you all to be here with smiles, bubbles, and a champagne saber."

Casey laughs. "My first official Witch-'N-Bitch invite? I thought you'd never ask."

"So you'll be here?"

"Wouldn't miss it."

With a smile, I turn my attention back to Carly. "I really want you to wear the amulet. Please. You'll be doing me a *huge* favor."

"Oh *fine*, if you insist. But just so you know, I'm really putting myself out for you. This Egyptian style does *not* go with my ensemble." Carly rolls her eyes, but not before I catch the tears glittering in them. A surge of love and gratitude washes over me as she hauls me in for a hug. "Thank you," she whispers, softly enough that I'm sure no one else hears. "You have no idea what this means to me."

"Actually…"

Carly laughs. "Right. Empathic, spirit-blessed snowflake. How could I forget?"

With that settled, Professors Broome and Maddox quiz us once more on all the different potions we're packing, triple-check their own stash, and review their plan one more time.

"Please, *please* be careful," I tell them. "I meant what I said—I expect us all to be here tomorrow night. Conscious, walking, and ready to pop that bubbly."

Professor Broome winks. "Just because we're practically senior citizens compared to the Hot Girl Squad doesn't mean we've forgotten how to do epic shit."

I crack up at that, but Carly shakes her head.

"Are you serious right now?" she asks. "You two are hot-girl life goals. The rest of us can only *hope* to achieve your level of badassery one day."

"Did you hear that, Kelly?" Professor Broome asks, her eyes sparkling. "Hot-girl life goals! Maybe we should offer *that* class next semester."

"I'd sign up," Nat says, and Isla raises her hand. "Me too!"

Goddess, I love these witches.

"Okay people," Casey says. "Hate to break it up, but we really need to get moving."

She's right. All the levity and warmth from the last few

minutes evaporates, replaced with a cold dread so thick and heavy I can almost taste it.

"What about you?" Casey asks me. "All set?"

I look over at the guys, still waiting for me by the closet like silent sentries.

"All set," I assure her. "And don't worry—I'm in good hands."

"You're certain your intel is good? You know where you're going?"

She's talking about the message from Doc. Last night, we could only manage to hold the connection for a few minutes, but it was enough time for him to confirm my theories that Judgment is holding them in the caves by the Void, and that the whole area *is* accessible from the Breath and Blade lands. He said it's a portal and connecting point for several realms, including our own. Finding our way won't be the problem.

Dealing with whatever so-called welcome party awaits us? That's another story—one whose ending I can't even *pretend* to know.

"We're good," I reply anyway.

She watches me another beat, concern flashing through her eyes, then hugs me close. In a low, imploring voice, she says, "Take care of my brother, okay?"

"You know I will."

"And take care of *you*. We're just getting to know each other, Stevie. I'm expecting lots more Witch-'N-Bitch invites to come, okay?" She pulls back and smiles at me, looking so much like her brother, it almost takes my breath away.

"We're practically sisters-in-law at this point, so there's not much you can do to escape me, anyway."

Sisters-in-law…

I gasp as the realization suddenly hits me.

My mother… She saw this moment. She knew it would come.

> *By Queen of Earth you may be vexed*
> *But trust you must her diligence*
> *Sisterhood too, you'll find within*
> *But only when it's welcomed in*

"Casey, you're an earth witch, right?" I ask.

"Yep. My affinity is the Queen of Pentacles. Why do you ask?"

"No reason." I smile, feeling my mother's presence surround me like a hug.

When Casey turns to leave, a Tarot card flutters to the ground behind her.

I don't have to look at it to know it's the Queen of Pentacles.

With nothing left to say, nothing left to eat, and nothing left to pack, the house empties in a surprisingly quiet rush. Car engines start, then fade away. The sun rises a little higher above the horizon, already baking the red stones around us like a clay oven. Jareth swoops down to land on a tree in the front yard, letting me know he's ready to rock.

"One more time," Baz says, opening the closet door.

"Phase one," I say. "Blast our way back into the Fool's Grave, courtesy of our own personal wrecking ball."

Kirin gives a tiny bow.

"Phase two," I continue, "do the ritual to bust the Arcana objects out of magickal protection. Phase three, nab said objects, hightail it to the Void, and break our guys out of prison. Hopefully kill a few Dark Arcana dicks in the process. And if we survive *that* fun, then it's onto phase four—"

"Make our way to campus and roast the dark mage brigade," Baz says, "along with any other yellow-eyed, undead corpse bent on murdering the people we love and stealing away our magick."

"Sounds like a party," I say.

Kirin sighs. "I still wish we didn't need Ani's blood for this. It would be a hell of a lot easier if we didn't have to involve him at all."

"Not only do we need his blood," Baz says grimly, "but we need to steal it from him and take him down before he figures out we're onto him, and all without seriously hurting him. That body is still Ani's."

"The timing has to be just right," Kirin says, not for the first time this morning. "We can't let him know we're onto him too quickly."

"No, but the longer we play along," I say, "the more danger we're in and the greater the risk to Doc and *our* Ani.

What if he makes a move on us before we make ours? What if he brings backup? What if he leaves the Wand with Judgment and we can't get it back? What if we're not strong enough to break through the rocks at the Fool's Grave?"

Baz puts a hand on my shoulder, letting out a deep sigh. "There's a lot of what-ifs in this scenario, Little Bird."

His words hit me hard. There *are* a lot of what-ifs. So many, in fact, that if I keep trying to list them all, I'm going to scare us all into running upstairs and hiding under the blankets while the world burns down around us.

As witches and mages born in a time where our kind is feared at best, murdered at worst, we all grew up with targets on our back.

As Keepers of the Grave, we'll probably *always* be at risk, no matter what we achieve today.

But the coming war is the most dangerous, high-stakes, life-altering thing any of us have ever faced. So many things could go wrong, and despite Baz's insistence on multiple contingency plans, when it comes down to it, this time we don't have an inch of wiggle room.

But we *do* have one another.

A deep calm settles into my bones.

As long as my mages are with me, I'm ready to face those insane odds.

"You know what, though?" I say, finally finding my strength. My confidence. My inner doer of epic shit. "*We're* not a what-if."

I stretch up on my toes and kiss him breathless. Then,

turning to Kirin, I press my lips to his, inhaling his scent and kissing him until my head spins.

Out front, Jareth swoops down from his perch, letting me know he's with us before soaring up to the skies again.

"You ready?" Baz asks, his red-brown eyes searching mine in the morning light.

With one last glance around the house I've come to know as home, I strap on my pack, shake off the last of my jitters, and step into the closet.

"Let's go hocus-pocus those raging fuckwaffles to oblivion."

THIRTEEN

ANSEL

Pathetic.

As I watch the three Arcana imbeciles pick their way through the decimated, rock-strewn passageway, disgust and disappointment churn inside me.

Even after all the druid's assurances that they'd come, some part of me still believed they were smarter than that. Especially *her.*

No matter. Their ignorance and blind faith in their bond certainly make *my* life easier. Perched on a rise overlooking the passage, I've been waiting for them all night. And now, with the sun burning high over the infernal Petrified Forest of Iron and Bone, they're nearly here. In a matter of minutes, the Arcana objects will be freed from their magickal bonds, and the Devil, the Tower, and their precious Star will meet their doom.

A rush of power races down my spine, and the Wand glows red in my fist.

I was made for this…

As if reading my very thoughts, the Wand heats beneath my skin, eager to unleash more of its fury. It's glory. I hate to be parted from it for even a moment, but I can't risk letting them know I'm carrying it. Not until I've won their trust.

Shouldn't be too difficult, given how eager they are to save the day—how desperate they are to see their sweet little Sun Arcana returned to his former innocence.

My mouth fills with the taste of bitter rage. It almost feels like a waste to use my pure, untarnished magick on creatures so unworthy. But in the end, I'll do what I must do to appease my so-called masters.

Soon enough, the tables will be turned, and *I'll* decide how and when to use magick. Who deserves it.

Which subjects I'll claim, which I'll convert, and which I'll destroy.

The Arcana are nearing the cave mouth. I slip behind a petrified tree and tuck the Wand out of sight. They've brought her owl familiar, but I doubt even *that* wise creature can see me. Like his bonded witch, he's too focused on what may be following them rather than on what's awaiting in the darkness.

Too bad for him.

"This is it," the woman says when they've gone as far as they can go.

"Great." The Tower drops his backpack and folds his arms over his chest, clearly upset. Tension radiates among them like an electrical current.

Trouble in paradise? I can't help but grin.

"Drop the attitude, Kirin," she says. "You agreed to help. If you're not interested, you can go back home."

"Where we should've stayed," the Devil says, looking even more dark and brooding than usual.

"Do whatever you want," she snaps. "But I'm seeing this through."

The Tower doesn't like that answer one bit. "Stevie, even if we can get through this rock, we can't unlock the protection spell without Ani's blood."

"Told you we shouldn't have listened to her," the Devil says. "This is a fucking waste of time. Ani's dead. Cass is probably right there with him."

The Star glares at him, her eyes bright with anger and pain. "Don't talk like that. We're not giving up on them."

"Baz is right," the Tower says. "It's over. Time to turn ourselves in, throw ourselves on the Dark One's mercy, and hope to Goddess he lets us live."

Oh, you'll get your opportunity soon enough, mage...

"We have to at least try to get those objects out first. I know we don't have everyone's blood, but we could try a new spell, or more of our own blood to compensate, or stronger magick... I don't know, guys. I don't care. We have to find a way."

The Devil kicks a rock into the massive pile before them. "The only thing we're gonna find a way to today is our fucking graves."

Excitement flutters through me. Their bonds are breaking. Their love is failing. And it's turning them desperate, weak, and stupid.

The perfect storm.

This is going to be less troublesome than I thought.

Through a good deal of grumbling and bickering, the three inspect the massive pile of rock and rubble blocking their entrance into the cave, all of them sweaty and panting.

"We're fucked," the Devil says.

You have no idea…

Ignoring him, the woman turns to the Tower, her eyes filling with tears. "Please, Kirin," she begs, and it's just like I said. Desperate, weak, and stupid. "You said you'd help me."

"Yep. And then we're *done*," he snaps. "That was the deal. We help you, then we go our separate ways."

The coldness in his voice shocks me, simultaneously filling me with a surge of new power.

Me. They're breaking because of me. What I did to their little Gingersnap, to their professor… I don't know what happened in the moments after I left them in that house last night, but it's clear now that whatever went down, it was enough to shatter their trust in love and brotherhood.

It was enough to destroy their hope.

"I *will* honor the deal," she says, her voice turning just as cold. "Just get me in there."

The Tower nods and lifts his hands, his brow knitting in concentration. At first, I don't think his plan is going to work, but then it begins—a low rumble in the ground beneath me, a skittering of rocks and debris.

The man unleashes a primal roar, his body trembling as deeply as the earth itself. A bolt of white lightning sizzles down from the sky and smashes into the rocks, pulverizing them.

My wide eyes match the Star's and the Devil's both, all of us doubtlessly awed by the show of force.

It takes me a moment to recognize the new feeling coursing through my body.

Jealousy.

No matter. That little show will look like a mere party trick compared to the power I'll soon claim.

When the Tower has finally used up his reserves, the Devil takes over, calling on his earth magick to clear away the remaining debris.

After what feels like an age, a dark entrance and path appear before them, granting them access to the deeper caves where the Fool's Grave lies.

In silence, they make their way in. Grabbing a sharp, discarded rock, I make a few non-lethal cuts on my face and arms for effect, then trail them at a safe distance behind.

When they finally reach the ruined inner chamber, they wait for the Tower to clear away the large slabs of rock that crashed there the night Chariot decided to test her powers.

I swear the effort nearly kills him.

The Star seems completely unaffected by his weakened condition.

"Do you think we need to do the Keepers of the Grave ritual?" she asks when they finally have enough room to maneuver.

The Devil shakes his dark head. "Let's skip the damn ritual and get this over with. The sooner you realize we've got no power here, the sooner we can leave."

"You are *such* an asshole," she mutters.

The man doesn't even flinch.

It's nearly impossible for me to reconcile the sight of this broken trio of enemies with the once-loyal Brotherhood, but it doesn't surprise me. Love? Honor? Loyalty? In the face of *true* power, those things are as insubstantial as the dust beneath my feet.

Again, my palms burn with the need to hold the Wand, to feel its limitless magick connecting with my own.

But I must time this perfectly.

"It's right here," she says, crouching low and placing her hands on the ground. "I can sense the magick."

"Great. You found the spot." The Tower sighs, still exhausted from the whole ordeal. "Now what?"

"I don't know, Kirin," she bites back, getting to her feet and dusting off her hands. "Maybe we could put our heads together and figure this out."

"There's nothing to figure out!" he shouts. "We don't have Ani's blood. Game over."

"He's right," the Devil says. "We've indulged you this far, okay? But this is bullshit, Milan. It's over. We lost."

"So that's it?" She forces out a laugh, but tears track through the dirt on her cheeks. "Wow. I can't believe I ever felt something other than disgust for you guys. You're both spineless dickheads. I'm glad Doc and Ani aren't here to see this."

"The feeling is more than mutual, sweetheart," the Devil says. "Believe me."

The whole thing is beyond nauseating, but I'm glad for it. Their anger and bitterness will keep them distracted.

I give them another few minutes to trade their last barbs, take a deep breath before my performance, and finally make my move.

FOURTEEN

ANSEL

"St-Stevie?" I stammer, grunting as I drag myself into the chamber. "Baz? Kirin? Oh, thank Goddess! I thought I'd never see you guys again!"

Her blue eyes widen, then fill with fresh tears. "Ani?"

The Devil immediately steps in front of her, shooting an arm out and holding her back. The move almost seems protective, but then I realize he's just assessing the threat for himself.

Marginally more intelligent than I've given him credit for, but no genius by any stretch.

He approaches me cautiously and clamps his hands on my upper arms, and I let him, forcing myself to appear both relieved and terrified.

"Everything is so messed up," I whisper, forcing out a few tears. "It's my fault. I needed to get out of there, and... Goddess, I can't believe I actually found you guys. The Black Sun... he's... somehow I forced him out, and..." I close my eyes and shake my head as if the memories are just too traumatic to recall.

"Ani?" the Devil asks, and I open my eyes to meet his gaze again, offering the meekest of smiles. "Fucking hell, Gingersnap. We thought you were dead." He pulls me in for a hug, and the Star sneaks out around him, practically launching herself at me.

"It *is* you," she whispers through her sappy tears, nudging the Devil away so she can embrace me herself. "I knew you'd find us. I knew you'd come back."

The Tower joins the reunion, clapping me once on the shoulder, a thin smile breaking through his grim visage. "Welcome back, Ani. Unfortunately, we're all in hell at the moment."

The Devil drops his backpack and retrieves something from inside—a vial containing what can only be blood. Cass's blood, I'm guessing. He holds it up, tipping it back and forth, coating the glass in red. "And unfortunately, we've got a mission to accomplish, and not much time to get it done."

"Is that… blood?" I ask, my eyes wide.

The Star nods. "It's Doc's. It was everywhere, after you… The Black Sun, he…" The pain rises in her eyes, deep and endless, but she forces it away and gives me another pathetic smile. "It doesn't matter. You're here now, and we can do the ritual. Everything else can wait."

"Do you think the objects can actually help you win?" The words are out before I can stop them, harsher than I intended. "I mean... the Dark Arcana are beyond powerful. Trust me—I had a front-row seat."

"Not win, no," the Star says. If she thought my comment or tone odd, she doesn't show it. "But if we can reunite the four objects, we might be able to offer the Magician what he wants before he completely destroys the campus and roasts everyone on it. We're hoping for a deal."

"Not a deal," the Devil says, clearly unhappy about it. "A surrender. There's no other choice."

"Surrender?" I shake my head, and this time, I don't have to fake the disappointment and disgust. Does the Dark One even realize how weak the Light are? Why would he bother turning them at all? "But I thought... You mean you don't want to fight him?"

"We don't have the numbers, Ani," she says. "All of this is Dark Arcana territory now. We just want to get out of it alive."

"But then what?" I ask.

She sighs. "I don't know. Go our separate ways, I guess. Try to live a quiet life somewhere away from all this."

It's with great effort that I hide my shock.

My, my, how easily the righteous fall...

"You've missed a few things during your... possession," the Tower says. "Everything is completely fucked. We just want to end this thing and move on."

If the Light Arcana give up this easily, I can only imagine how quickly the rest of mage- and witch-kind will fall in line.

More and more, the Magician's war is looking like a

skirmish. He thought he needed the Light. Thought he needed to turn them, to enslave them, to own them.

The Star takes my hand, and it's all I can do not to jerk away at her vile touch.

"Do you have the Wand?" she asks. "*Please* tell me you have the Wand."

"I... I wish I could." I lower my eyes. "I tried to take it from them, but once I freed myself from the Black Sun's clutches, it was all I could do to escape that prison alive. I... Goddess, I'm so sorry. I had no idea you would want it for this."

"Oh, Ani." She smiles at me, her wide eyes annoyingly bright. "It's not your fault. I'm just glad you made it out."

Was she *always* this sweet and saccharine? It's a wonder the other two haven't died of it yet.

"The best I can do is take you to it," I tell her, coughing and clutching at my chest. The weaker I seem, the less likely they are to be on guard on our way out, and I'll need them docile when I retrieve my Wand. "They keep it in the druid's cave. It's... it's where they've got Cass."

"Wait. Cass is *alive*?" Her mouth rounds with shock and hope.

Aww, the poor little thing. Tormenting her is almost too easy.

"*Barely* alive," I croak out. "I told him if I made it out, I would try to get help. We were both hoping you'd be here. We sensed it. I just... I don't know how we can help him, Stevie. He's... in bad shape."

A low growl echoes behind me, but when I turn around,

I see only the Devil kicking at the ground, his eyes downcast.

The Star grabs my face, turning my attention back to her. "You did the right thing, Ani. You saved yourself. That's the most important thing—look out for number one, because no one else will."

I slip away from the sick burn of her touch and look again at the others, then back to the Star. Narrowing my eyes in confusion, I ask, "What's going on with you three? You're barely speaking. And earlier, I swore I heard arguing. Is everything—"

"It's *fine*." She shoots the men a harsh glare. "We'll catch you up later. Let's just do the ritual, get what we need, and get out of here before anything *else* falls apart."

I nod, ducking my head to hide my smile.

They really *are* broken. Ruined.

It's a beautiful thing, witnessing the disintegration of a love once thought unbreakable.

The Devil retrieves an athame from his backpack, and we form a circle around the cleared space where the Star claimed she felt the magick.

After pouring the professor's blood onto the ground, the Devil slices his palm, then passes the blade around. The Tower and the Star do the same, each of them spilling blood before finally handing the weapon to me. I make a quick slice across my palm and add my blood to the mix.

She recites the spell, and the rest of us join in, repeating it three times.

Blood that binds, blood that shields
At our command, the magick yields

Seconds later, I watch with abject fascination as the magickal dome rises up from solid ground. Our blood coats it, thick and shiny and mesmerizing. Again, the ground vibrates, but this time it's not the Tower's doing.

The bubble of protection vanishes.

And there, gleaming among the ruins, the sacred objects shine.

The Princes of the Tarot sit at each cardinal point, but those cards are useless now.

Wasting no time, the Star crouches down and claims the Sword of Breath and Blade, while the Tower claims both the Pentacle of Iron and Bone and the Chalice of Blood and Sorrow, carefully fitting them into his pack.

The Devil takes nothing.

Of all the Arcana, he is the most weak-minded. The most susceptible to temptation. It's no wonder they won't allow him to touch the objects.

In the Star's hand, the Sword glows like pale moonlight, and for the briefest instant, its power shines in her blue eyes.

I wonder if it's a mistake letting her hold it so long. I'm not sure I can take all three of them without the Wand, but—

"Happy now?" The Devil barks, breaking her fixation. "Can we get the fuck out of here, please?"

"Baz…" The Tower shakes his head in warning. Then,

turning to me, he says, "Sorry, Ani. The three of us have some shit to work out. We'll… we'll catch you up on the way."

"Is it because of me?" I ask, unable to resist. "Because of what the Black Sun did?"

He hesitates only a moment before shaking his head, but that fraction of time—that momentary pause—is all the confirmation I need.

I've driven them apart.

The rest will be easy.

Again, I'm forced to hide a smile.

"I don't want you to worry about it," he says. "We're just glad you're back. Now let's get Cass, get rid of these cursed objects, and get the *hell* off these forsaken lands."

The Tower and the Star lead us back out into the daylight, and I fall in behind them, acting as feeble and cowed as they'd expect from a broken mage who narrowly escaped death at the hands of the enemy.

With the Devil at my back, we clear the passageway and head into the Petrified Forest. Our route will soon take us past the petrified tree where I hid the Wand. Once it's back in my hands, I can take them down and claim the objects for myself.

Keeping my eyes on the ground before me, I bite back another smile. Judgment wanted me to lead them back to his cave, but what's the point? There's no strength left in any of them. They're used-up and empty. And now, I'm but minutes away from claiming the power of all *four* Arcana weapons. No longer must I rely on the Dark Arcana to set my path. I will forge my own with fire and fury. Magick will be *mine*. I'll—

"Baz, *now*!"

The woman's sudden command shatters my thoughts, and I snap my head up just in time to see the Wand—*my* Wand—glowing in the hands of the Tower. Perched on the petrified tree beside him, that damnable owl peers down at me with eerie, glowing eyes.

"No!" I shout, but before I take a single step forward, the Devil is on me, kicking my legs out from under me and shoving me face-down into the dirt.

With a knee jammed firmly in my back, he binds my wrists behind me, then hauls me to my feet, keeping a firm grip on my wrists. "Don't even *try* it, asshole."

I *can't* try it. I know it's futile. Without the Wand, I'm nothing. I'm as weak and broken as they are.

The Star stalks toward me, that Sword held high and mighty in her hand. It glows even brighter now, humming in the presence of the other three objects just as my Wand is glowing.

Rage and frustration churn inside me.

"You are an abomination." With a swift flick of her wrist, the Star brings the Sword to my throat, the tip piercing the skin and drawing blood.

"Giving up on your precious little gingersnap already?" I sneer at her, unable to hold in my disgust for another minute. "That's typical. Then again, you've already given up on each other, so why should the red-headed stepchild get special treatment? So go ahead then. Slit my throat."

She laughs. The woman actually laughs. "Oh, I don't think so. You see, Sunshine, unlike you and your Dark Arcana fuckstains, we will *never* give up on each other. The fact that you believed our little show today is just further proof you're not Ani."

"Oh, but I am him. *Your* Ani is dead and gone. I'm all that's left." My words hit the mark, making her wince. A flicker of doubt shines in her eyes.

"Don't listen to him, Little Bird," the Devil says, soft and gentle in ways the Devil shouldn't be. "We'll get Ani and Cass back, just like we said."

I wrench my head around and spit in his face, offering one last promise. "All of you will die. That is certain. But I'm going to enjoy watching the Star burn the *most*."

"And I'm going to enjoy *this*." He flashes a malicious smirk, then launches a fist into my face. "Lights out, Sunshine."

FIFTEEN

STEVIE

"You couldn't have knocked him out *after* we got here?"

Covered in sweat and grime, his glasses smudged beyond usefulness, my Genius Boy grunts under the weight of the unconscious Black Sun slung over his shoulder.

"He *really* had it coming," Baz says as we cross the last rise. "Anyway, I thought I'd be able to portal us out of Iron and Bone, but I'm still spent from shifting all that rock."

"I'm actually a little surprised about that," Kirin says thoughtfully. "Shoots my theory to hell."

"What theory?" I ask, stopping to double-check our route. We made it out past the edges of Breath and Blade on foot, but the dark mist Jareth and I spotted last night is starting to creep in, obscuring some of the paths.

I should probably be grateful to see mist.

On the one hand, it means we're getting close.

On the other hand, well. It means we're getting close.

Kirin sets Ani on the ground, careful not to jostle him.

Not only did Baz knock him unconscious, but we sealed the deal with one of Professor Broome's potions, ensuring he wouldn't wake up for several more hours at least. We can't risk it, especially given what he's already done with the Wand, but we didn't want to leave him behind, either.

He's still Ani. Still ours to protect.

The Wand is in Baz's hands now. Kirin's got the Pentacle and Chalice secured in his pack, and I've got the Sword strapped to the side of my own pack in a sheath I made from a spare T-shirt, just in case I need to grab it quickly.

When it comes to the ancient artifacts, we're locked, stocked, and loaded. But will it do us a damned bit of good?

Kirin stretches his arms and back, his joints popping. "I thought once all four objects were in close proximity, and in the possession of Arcana mages and a witch, they'd act as chargers."

"Like, to power us up?" Baz asks, and Kirin nods.

"I wondered about that too." I slide the pack off my shoulders and roll my neck, grateful for even a short break. "Other than the glowing and random buzzing, they don't seem to be doing anything special."

"Maybe we need Cass and Ani too?" Kirin asks. "*Our* Ani?"

I shrug. The truth is, none of us has any idea how these magickal objects work. The Magician sure seems to think they're the key to everything, but he's not exactly a reliable narrator here. So far, all we've really seen is the Black Sun carving a path of fiery destruction with that Wand.

Flame and Fury indeed.

I arch into a stretch, catching sight of Jareth soaring overhead, still with us. As tempting as it is to try to connect with him for another fly-over, I don't want to risk merging our energies now. We could be attacked at any moment by any number of enemies.

I need to remain in my own body, alert and ready for anything.

Besides, I trust Jared will turn up exactly when we need him to. He always does.

"So, who wants to carry sleeping beauty the rest of the way?" Kirin asks. "I nominate Baz, since he's the one who knocked him out."

"No can do, brother. Maybe if you'd been able to handle those rocks on your own, I wouldn't have had to jump in with the assist and burn up most of my magick."

Kirin laughs. "Assist? More like—"

"Hey." I roll my eyes. "If you two don't stop bickering, we're breaking up for real."

"Yeah, that's a no from me," Baz says, pulling me against his chest for a quick hug. He kisses the top of my head and sighs into my hair. "Faking it for Sunshine's sake was shitty enough."

"Agreed," Kirin says. "Let's never do *that* again, shall we?"

I give them each a quick kiss. "Deal. Now, see that rise over there, where the mist gets thicker?" I point across the expanse of land. "I'm pretty sure that's our destination."

"Because of the mist?" Kirin asks.

"That, and it feels familiar to me." I recall the nightmares that led me here—me in a makeshift wedding gown stained with holly berries, a bouquet of black dahlias in my hand as I stumbled out of the mist. "That darker patch at the base of the rise? I'm pretty sure that's the holly thicket, which means the rise itself is the top of the cave system. If what Doc told me last night still holds true, that's where they've got our guys."

"So that's where we're going, then," Baz says. "We'll find our way into the caves, find Doc, see what we can do about Ani's soul, and…"

He trails off, because all we've got is a vague plan and an even more vague hope that we can harness the magick in the Arcana objects to heal Doc and reunite Ani's soul with his body—preferably before this version regains consciousness or gets help from his Dark masters.

A chill rises along my arms, but I fight back the urge to shiver. "Okay, guys. Last chance to eat, drink, and take a bathroom break. No more jokes, complaints, or other random commentary after this, either. From here on out, we're in absolute stealth mode."

Kirin gazes out through the mist. In the distance, we can just make out the flickering of its magick. "We're walking into a trap, Stevie."

"No," I insist. "We're *creeping* into a trap. Creeping into a trap is… marginally safer."

Baz laughs. "I'll remember you said that when I have to save your ass from a Dark Arcana ambush."

"Such confidence!" I tease, whipping my Sword from its

bonds and holding it high. "Maybe *I'll* be saving you, mortal."

"Don't." His eyes flare with heat. "When you do those Viking warrior princess moves, all I can think about is seeing you in a little fur-trimmed leather bikini studded with—"

"Pro tip, asshole." Kirin smacks me on the back. "Stealth mode? Doesn't include sharing your depraved fantasies about our girl with the rest of the class."

Baz smirks, his gaze trailing down to the sudden bulge in Kirin's pants. "Yeah, I can see you *hate* my depraved fantasies."

"Tell you what, boys." I put away the Sword and flash them a wicked grin. "We make it through this alive? I'll wear whatever your barbarian little hearts, minds, dicks, and everything else desires. But seriously—no more talking."

With that, we finish up our break, reassemble the packs and Ani, and head off into the mist.

SIXTEEN

STEVIE

"Whatever happens," Kirin whispers darkly, doing his best to carry Ani through the holly thicket without hurting him, "do *not* go near the Void."

We've managed to get this far without alerting our enemies to our presence. But at the mere mention of the Void, the dark mist shrinks away from us, revealing a brief glimpse of the ground. The earth is stained red with crushed berries, and all around us, black dahlias bloom, choking out the once-vibrant ivy.

Goddess, even in the waking world, this place gives me the fucking *creeps*.

Somewhere in the distance, the Void exists. Awaits. Though I've never seen it up close, I can still hear its call.

Starla… it whispers. *Wish upon a falling star… Starla…*

Forcing the reminder of my mother's prophecy from my mind, I keep moving, one foot in front of the other, hoping that on the other side of this thicket, our destination still exists.

I look up and try to spot Jareth, but it's no use. The mist is so thick now, it may as well be midnight.

It's another hour or so of grueling, bone-chilling hiking through mud and tangled vines before the mist finally parts before us like a curtain opening on a new act.

And there, as clear as it was in my nightmares, is the ancient, spiral-carved stone wall. Like the holly, the mistletoe that once grew wild at its base is now choked with black dahlias.

"Is there an entrance?" Baz whispers. The wall before is solid and unbroken, stretching for what seems like miles in either direction.

Assuming things work like they did in my nightmares, I press my hands to the carved spirals and wait. The magick stirs to life behind the rock, pulsing through me like a heartbeat. This time, there's no great bellowing of the druid's horn, but the rock still rumbles and cracks, breaking away into a makeshift doorway.

On my first visit here, the Fool emerged in the form of a baby, whom Judgment promptly ate. Thankfully, there's no one to greet us today.

Of course it's a fucking trap, but I'll take whatever small blessings we can get right now.

On silent footsteps, we enter the cave, and I follow the tug of my intuition through dark and winding paths deeper into the earth. The mist follows us even here, rising waist-high in a deep cavern lit only by the flickering magick of the mist itself.

I have no idea where I'm leading us, but the guys follow me without question. I'm beginning to fear I've led us all to our doom when a faint but familiar voice echoes across the stone.

"My... beautiful... Star."

"Doc!" Forgetting my temporary vow of silence, I race toward the source, the mist parting before me as if it's somehow conspiring to help us.

And there, sitting half-slumped against the cave wall, is our Moon.

I fall to my knees, taking his pale face between my hands. He's cool to the touch, his breathing labored, but he's still alive.

"You... came," he says, a thin smile gracing his lips.

I nod, then press a soft kiss to his cheek. "We're going to get you out of here. But first I have to heal you."

He's still bleeding from the back of his head, and his bare chest is scored with burns and cuts. His knuckles are swollen and bruised, some of them split nearly to the bone.

His condition has definitely worsened since we spoke last night.

"Ani's... gone," he says, struggling to speak as the guys set their packs and Ani's body down beside us. "Said he'd be back... but... hours ago."

I don't know what that means, but right now, I don't have time to figure it out.

"We'll worry about Ani next," I say, hoping my soothing

voice detracts from the tears in my eyes. Goddess, seeing him like this... It's breaking my damn heart. I can only hope I've got the strength to heal him, or...

No. I have the strength. Failing at this particular mission is *not* an option.

Working quickly, I retrieve the Chalice of Blood and Sorrow from Kirin's pack and place it in Doc's hands.

"I need you to hold on to this, okay?" I give him a gentle smile as I take out an athame. "I'm not totally sure what I'm doing, but if it turns out I suck at this, you can take it out of my grade."

Doc's return smile is more than I could've hoped for.

As the guys explore what they can see of the chamber we're in, I slice my hand and squeeze my blood into the Chalice—as much as I'm willing to lose before I get lightheaded. Fortunately, my body heals quickly on its own. I'm hoping I can transfer some of that magick to Doc.

His eyes widen as my blood splashes into the bowl.

"I know it's gross," I say, "but it's the best I could do on short notice, and—"

He presses a fingertip to my lips. "You are magick, my... my Star. Don't... don't doubt."

Blinking back tears, I nod, making a silent vow to follow his command.

Don't doubt. Trust. Believe. *Know.*

With Doc holding the Chalice on his lap, I call the Star card into my mind, picturing myself at the center of it—naked, kneeling in the healing waters before the standing stones.

Then I dip my fingers into the blood and recite my spell.

> *I call upon my healing gift*
> *I call upon the sight*
> *I call upon my love for you*
> *Which burns forever bright*
>
> *I share my grace with you tonight*
> *And thus your body shall mend*
> *I offer my heart, my soul, my light*
> *Now your pain shall end*

Repeating the verses again and again, I paint Doc's wounds with my blood. I start with the cuts on his face, gently massaging them with my fingertips. The moment my blood touches his skin, it turns silver, glowing with healing magick.

Keeping his gaze locked on mine, Doc doesn't flinch or gasp.

Coating my fingers in more blood, I slide them behind his head, swallowing back my own pain at the wounds I find there. His hair is matted with blood and bits of bone, but I do my best to work past it, coating everything with my magick.

I paint in symbols of love over his chest, covering Judgment's cruel burns. I gently coat his split knuckles, the cuts on his hands and arms, the bruises beneath his eyes. I don't stop until my blood has been wiped clean from the Chalice and every last of his injuries is glowing silver.

"And now your pain shall end," I finish, pressing a kiss to his lips.

When I pull back, he's still watching me, unmoving but alert. Then, he sucks in a deep, sharp breath, and his eyes flash the same bright sliver as the blood.

By the time he exhales, the silver is gone from his eyes and body both.

I remove the Chalice from his hands and set it to the side, then inspect his arms and chest, his face. His skin is completely unmarred.

"How do you feel?" I ask, tentatively reaching for the back of his head.

He doesn't let me get that far. With a surge of renewed strength, he gets to his knees and hauls me into a crushing embrace. His hands tangle into my hair, his mouth pressing against mine with a kiss so demanding, he draws blood.

When he finally pulls back, we're both panting. His stormy gray eyes are wild and fierce. "You," he says firmly, "are a fucking *miracle*."

I can't help but laugh. "I take it the spell worked?"

"Yes, and the moment we get home, I'm going to show you just how *well* it worked."

"I'm holding you to it," I whisper.

We get to our feet and join the guys, our reunion happy but short-lived.

"What about Ani?" Kirin asks, glancing over the Black Sun's body, still unconscious. We give Doc a quick recap of what went down at the Fool's Grave, and our hope that we could somehow reunite Ani's soul and body with the Wand.

"Ani's soul is tied to this place," Doc says. "It took a lot for him to manifest long enough to do the spell last night. He faded pretty quickly after that. I don't think he's gone permanently, but it was getting more and more difficult for him to remain in tangible form here."

"What do we do?" I ask. "We can't just leave him."

"The presence of the Black Sun—of Ani's physical body —isn't enough to reunite them," he says. "The only way we can save Ani is to undo the dark magick that fragmented him in the first place, and that means going after the Magician and the Chariot."

I kneel down beside Ani's body and run my fingers through his hair, my chest filling with pain.

Doc's touch on the back of my neck is as warm and gentle as his voice. "I don't want to leave him either, Stevie, but we can't stay here. We need to get out and fight. Only then can we save him."

I blow out a breath and get back to my feet. Doc's right.

Survival rule number one: Deal with the most pressing problem first.

"Okay," I say, glancing around the dark space. The mist is back now, pulsing with magick light at our feet. "How the hell do we get out of here? The way we came in is just… gone."

"This place is an ever-shifting labyrinth," Doc says. "We can't walk out. We need magick."

"Another spell," I say, agreeing. "Something to clear the mist and show us the way forward."

Kirin nods. "Air magick. Swords. We'll call on it to clear the fog and guide us out."

"You want to do the honors?" I ask.

"Let's do it together. I'm stronger in air magick, but you've already bonded with the Sword of Breath and Blade. We can use both."

I unsheathe the Sword, holding it out like a divining rod. Kirin grabs my free hand, his magick heating up my skin, making my nerves tingle. At his nod, I draw his magick into me, and speak the first words that come to mind:

> *Paths obscured and paths unknown*
> *The road bends left and right*
> *Show us the way that leads us home*
> *From darkness into light*

All at once, the mist surrounding us condenses, settling into a thicker, whiter path at our feet that stretches ahead and curves around to the left. The Sword glows bright in my hand.

"That's our way." Releasing Kirin's hand and clasping Doc's instead, I lead us along the path of the white mist, winding deeper into the caves before taking a sharp curve through another chamber. It's a good thirty or forty minutes of walking through the darkness, my glowing Sword our only light. My eyes are so used to its silvery glow that I almost don't recognize what's right ahead.

"There's light," Doc says, pointing toward a wedge of sunlight illuminating the black rock ahead. It's the first natural light we've seen since we entered these deplorable caves.

The sight of it brings tears to my eyes.

"Our spell worked!" I gasp.

"Was there any doubt?" Doc teases, squeezing my hand.

"Only a little. You know how it is—first time escaping an ancient druid's evil lair and all."

"I told you, Miss Milan. You're magick." He leans in for another kiss, and together, my mages and I step out into the light.

Directly into an ambush.

SEVENTEEN

STEVIE

I have no idea where we are.

The mist is gone, and the sun-dappled meadow before us is a beautiful spring day come to life. Trees bloom in shades of white and pale pink. A brook runs along one side, murmuring softly over the rocks. Overhead, birds flutter and sing, chasing one another through the warm, floral-scented breeze.

It would almost be perfect.

Almost... if not for the several dozen dark mages standing in formation, hoods drawn low, hands crackling with magick as malicious as their false grins.

From the front of the line, one of the mages steps forward and lowers his hood.

William Eastman.

My heart drops right into my stomach.

If he's here, who's back on campus? Does his presence at

the caves mean Casey and the others were able to sneak into the Academy undetected? Or did he catch them and—

"Playtime is over, little Arcana slaves," he sneers. "Hand over the Star and the artifacts and we'll grant the rest of you a quick death."

All three of my mages step in front of me.

"Or," Baz says, "we'll keep her *and* the artifacts, torture you for sport, and leave you for the buzzards."

"You forgot the skull-bashing, pissing-on-the-bones part," Kirin mutters to Baz, just loud enough for Eastman to hear.

"Either way, they're going to suffer," Baz says.

"Suffer doesn't even come close to describing it," Doc says.

The ferocious heat of their energy crashes through me, so powerful it almost brings me to my knees. Pushing my way through it, I step out from behind their wall of over-protective man-muscle and raise my Sword, pointing it right at Agent Seen-Some-Shit.

"Sorry, dickhead," I say. "I really, really like this thing. So no, you can't have it. Or me, for that matter. Care to make a better offer?"

Eastman doesn't laugh maniacally or sling back a sharp retort. He merely shakes his head and sighs, as if he's greatly disappointed in our response.

Did he seriously think we'd just give up so easily? That the guys would just hand me over?

"It didn't have to be this way," he says matter-of-factly. Behind him, the hands of his mages still crackle with magick, sparks of black and indigo racing over their skin. I get the sense they're charging up for something, but other than our demise, I can't imagine what else they're planning.

"I was searching for a way to eradicate *magick*," Eastman says, "not its unfortunate practitioners."

"You say that as if you're not one of us," I say. "All of you. You're nothing but hypocrites."

"Oh, I'm very much one of you, Starla Milan. As are all the mages marching with me today. Our absolution will come through the purging of magick from this realm, if absolution comes at all. And if it doesn't? Well, that's the great sacrifice one must be prepared to make when undertaking such important work."

A dark, bitter laugh erupts from Kirin's mouth. "You think you can kill and torture witches and mages—living, breathing human beings—and bypass your one-way trip to hell?"

"That remains to be seen, doesn't it?"

"You won't survive to see your grand vision come to fruition, *traitor*," I hiss. "You won't survive the night—*that* is a promise."

Eastman offers a casual shrug. The mages behind him remain unmoving, their ominous presence at complete odds with the beautiful meadow beyond.

"Survival is not a necessary outcome," he says. "I'm but one man in an army of righteousness. Death is an honor for the Soldiers of Light."

Beside me, I sense my mages inching backward, probably looking for an escape. Their intent is clear—retreat into the caves, find another way out. But while we might be able to lose Eastman's mages in the darkness, there's an equally good chance we'll get trapped in there, making it even easier for them to hunt us down and roast us.

Still, Eastman seems to be fixated on me for the moment. Maybe I can buy the guys a bit of time to figure something out. I just need to keep the asshole talking.

"Soldiers of *Light*?" I call out. "You twisted fucks let the government—the entire *world*—believe witches and mages committed acts of terror, knowing all along it was the Dark Arcana. You got into bed with the Magician, helped him commit murder, then fed false information to the authorities just to fan the flames of rage against your own kind. Against people who worked for you. Who trusted you. Goddess, that's fucking *mental*, Eastman!"

"We no more got in bed with the Magician than we did with the government, Starla. The goals of all three of our organizations happen to dovetail nicely. The Soldiers of Light want magick gone from our realm, the Dark Arcana want to reclaim it for their own, and the government is happy to put down dangerous criminals. Furthermore, we claimed responsibility for the purging—or, as you call it, the act of terrorism. The fact that your government assumed the Academy was at the heart of it only proves my point—magick and all who wield it are a danger to civilized society and do not belong in this realm. If they did, the authorities would not be so eager to put them down. It's that simple."

My composure is chipping away. This man has utterly no capacity for remorse, for compassion, for even a shred of anything human. He's also woefully misinformed about the authorities—unsurprising, given the level of his ignorance.

I point the Sword at him again, still trying to keep his attention on me and not on the guys. "You're so deep in the Dark Magician's pockets, you may as well be eating out of his asshole."

"Your crudeness is only a sign of how badly magick has weakened your mind," he says, again with the disappointed sigh. Then, holding out a hand and gesturing me forward, "Come with us, Starla. Free the ones you claim to care about from the burden of your presence."

"Stevie!" Baz calls from behind. "Now!"

Without hesitation, I spin on my heel and charge back into the cave after my men.

We make it less than ten feet before a new threat emerges from the mist.

In a blur of fire and rage, the Black Sun barrels into Baz, punching him in the mouth and sending the Wand clattering to the ground. Kirin tries to dive for it, but he's too late.

Another assailant has already claimed it.

Baz scrambles to his feet, but he's as powerless against our attackers as the rest of us.

"Unworthy," comes the hiss from the shadows. "All who are deemed unworthy shall burn."

Judgment steps forth, the Wand glowing in his hands like a hot poker. He flicks his wrist, and a wall of invisible heat slams into us, forcing us back out into the light.

We're trapped. On one side, we've got Judgment and his

Black Sun. On the other, Eastman and his cult brigade. At this point, I don't know what's worse.

We are well and truly fucked. After all we came through, *this* is how it ends—we get fried by a creepy druid with a penchant for arson, or murdered by a bunch of self-righteous assholes drinking the anti-witch Kool-Aid.

We didn't even get a chance to fight for our friends. For each other.

We don't even know if our friends are still *alive*.

Anger boils up inside me.

No. We aren't going out like this. Not here, not now.

Fuck.

This.

Bullshit.

A scream burns its way out of my lungs. Sword raised, I spin around and slice open Judgment's throat.

"Holy shit!" Baz cries, then grabs my arm, recovering from the shock just as Judgment falls to his knees. "Fucking *move*, Stevie! Move!"

Judgment claws at his throat, eyes bulging as he gasps for air. Black blood surges from the wound and soaks his robe.

"Choke on it, fuckface," I snarl, but that's all I manage to get out before Baz hauls me away. We hightail it out of the caves, deciding to take our chances with the mages in the meadow.

My whole body is vibrating with rage and adrenaline, muscles burning as I push myself to my limits, running hard and holding onto that blade with everything I've got.

The Black Sun is close on our heels, his fury a palpable force, squeezing my lungs and making it hard to breathe, much less run. But still, I don't dare stop.

It's only when we've cleared the meadow that I realize what the fuck is wrong with this picture.

Eastman and his mages haven't moved.

But Judgment has.

Trailing his little pet Sun, the monster I just slice-and-diced is back on his feet and quickly gaining ground, the blood-drenched robe the only evidence of my attack.

"Unworthy!" he calls out, taunting. "You shall burn at his command! For *his* pleasure! Then you shall rise for mine!"

Baz whips around, calling on his earth magick to bring up a wall of rocks and debris, buying us a few seconds to catch our breaths.

Behind the makeshift protection, the Black Sun shouts at Eastman and his mages. "Do it now! Hurry, before they get away with the artifacts!"

"Why aren't they attacking?" I ask Baz.

"Don't care," Baz says, still holding up the wall. He turns his head and spits out a mouthful of blood. "We need to get out of here. Now."

"Can you portal us out?"

"No can do." Baz's arms begin to tremble, and the wall he erected falls away. "I'm tapped out."

We're about to run again when a string of curses slips from Doc's mouth, so low and dark I'm not even sure it was really him.

But the fear in his eyes is unmistakable.

I follow his line of sight—first to Eastman and his mages, their arms outstretched like they're about to receive a blessing. Then to Judgment, holding the Wand of Flame and Fury up toward the sky, the wood letting out a low hum. Beside him, the Black Sun bows his head.

The three objects still in our possession—my Sword, and the Chalice and Pentacle in Kirin's pack, let out the same hum as the Wand, as if answering its call.

A wave of dark, terrifying magick sweeps across the meadow. The once beautiful trees ignite in flames, a raging fire that spreads across the grassy earth, devouring everything in its path.

Still, the mages don't move. If anything, the fire seems to be feeding their own magick. Judgment lifts the Wand higher, and the mages raise their hands, dark indigo light shooting from their palms and up to the heavens.

The air shimmers overhead, and an arc of black lightning splits the sky. It's terrifying and awesome, as if the very fabric of space is being torn apart.

"Carly's premonition," I whisper, momentarily stunned by the sight. "The mages must've cast some sort of spell, or maybe it was Judgment, or… oh, *fuck*."

"What now?" Kirin asks.

"The Arcana objects. Lala told me that not only could they act as homing beacons for the Magician, but as anchors. She said the Dark Arcana could somehow harness the magick and use it to manifest in physical form here."

"But they've already manifested here," Doc says. "Judgment and the Black Sun, at least."

"*Here*, yes. But this area is all part of that magickal overlap where the realms connect. Technically, we're not a hundred percent in our realm right now. Ani—rather, the Black Sun—is the only one we know for *sure* manifested outside all this. And that's probably due to Ani's connection to us."

Kirin gestures toward the rift in the sky, the hole getting blacker and more ominous by the second. "So this is what, then?"

"This is the doorway for the rest of them," I say. "And we need to get as far away from it as possible."

"Yeah, I think we missed that train, Little Bird," Baz says, and I know in my gut he's right.

We're too late.

Overhead, the black hole in the sky opens wider, a storm raging inside of it. It touches down on the earth in a tempest of lightning and fire and wind and hail.

And then, through the chaos, an army emerges.

Scores of witches and mages—*dead* witches and mages—shamble forth, their eyes glowing yellow, their skin as pale as mist, their mouths full of blood.

It's just as I saw in my visions. The Dark Magician's undead army, forged from the bodies of the witches and mages his minions killed.

They spill onto the earth, the meadow still burning behind them. Some of them get caught up in the blaze, but for every body that burns, another forms from its ashes.

Behind them, the Chariot manifests, her eyes on fire with a single purpose: death to the Light.

I look at Kirin, his eyes shining with the same fear I feel in my heart. I know he's remembering Mom's prophecy—the one we found the day the Black Sun burned Ani's home town.

> *Cities kneel before the flames*
> *Thus begins the deadly game*
> *When hope is lost the Star shall fall*
> *As Death arrives to conquer all*
>
> *From the ashes, called to rise*
> *With blackened hearts and golden eyes*
> *Souls imprisoned in a tomb*
> *Soldiers marching for our doom*

Tears streak down my face. I can't move—none of us can. We're paralyzed by the sight. So many witches and mages. So many innocents, stolen and tortured and corrupted. The Dark Magician siphoned my mother's magick for this—all part of the deal to bring me into the world.

I might as well have forged the army myself.

And now, these brutal undead soldiers are charging straight for us, commanded by their Black Sun, driven forth by the Chariot and her war horses.

"We will end you, Little Star," she calls out, her voice clear and resonant above the chaos, just as it was the night she tried to manifest near the Fool's Grave, making the same threat. Her green cape flutters behind her as she drives the feral horses onward, plowing through the undead army. No matter—the fallen rise, again and again, ever eager to resume their brutal march.

Somewhere in the melee, the Magician waits. I can't see him, but I know he's here. I can feel his sickness. His desire. He wants my blood, and he'll take it—dead or alive.

We turn to run, but the dead are closing in behind us. In front of us. Everywhere.

The army marches on.

The ground rumbles with the sound of a thousand horses.

They're closing in fast.

Baz doesn't have the energy to portal us out.

With so many soldiers on the ground, neither he nor Kirin can bend the earth to our will.

There's truly no escape.

Swallowing hard, I raise my Sword and grab Kirin's hand. On his other side, Baz puts an arm around him. Doc stands next to me, one hand on my back.

Their love—for me, for one another—wraps me in warmth and peace. I feel the lightest touch of another mage, a brush of a kiss on my lips, and I know Ani's with us too. The *real* Ani.

There are no declarations, no last words. We all know we're going to die here—absent a miracle, that's certain now.

But when we finally go down, we'll be going down together. In light. In magick. In love.

Seconds before the Chariot barrels into us, a blinding white light flashes, and a burst of heat explodes in my chest. I suck in a breath and try to get my bearings, but the world is spinning away from me so fast, I can't tell up from down.

Jareth.

His energy surrounds and fills me at the same time, yanking me away from the chaos.

But we're not flying.

We're just... gone.

EIGHTEEN

STEVIE

I hit the ground hard and unbalanced, tottering on my feet with my mages at my side and Jareth spiraling away overhead.

"What the fuck was that?" Baz asks.

Kirin removes his glasses and squints up at the sky. "The owl can portal?"

"That… wasn't a portal." I suck in a deep breath and blink the stinging sweat from my eyes. "I think the realms are collapsing. The magick they used to open the rift must've…"

My words evaporate as the sight comes into full view.

We're no longer in the burning meadow.

We're on the burning campus. Not the Academy as we last saw it, with its pristine classroom buildings, lush Tarot fountain, and silver-and-black house flags snapping in the breeze.

No. *This* is the campus I saw in my nightmare visions.

Black smoke billows from the tops of the dorms. Fires burn out of control, devouring the landscape. The pungent scents of blood and metal and magick permeate the air. And everywhere we turn, Eastman's mages are attacking students and faculty. Our friends.

"Get down!" Doc shoves me hard, crashing down on top of me as we all drop to our bellies, narrowly ducking a volley of flaming arrows.

"Chariot!" I shout, catching sight of her green cape in the distance. "She must've followed us. Move!"

As fast as we can, we crawl behind one of the classroom buildings. At least, I think that's what it is. Only half of it still stands.

Above us, the same dark rift we saw near the caves continues to spew the Magician's armies into our realm.

"What the fuck is happening?" Baz pants, the three of us getting to our feet and leaning against the bricks, still trying to get our bearings. "I thought the owl was about to blow up those mages back there."

"Jareth *was* trying to protect us," I say. "It felt like that night at the Fool's Grave. But before he could fully unleash, we must've gotten sucked into... I don't know. We were there, and then we were here."

"But how is this place already so fucked up?" he asks. Another volley of flaming arrows sails past, hitting a nearby saguaro. It ignites in a brutal magickal fire. "The rift *just* opened."

"Not here, it didn't," Kirin says. He's lost his glasses, and his face is completely pale. "I think Stevie's right about the realms. Whatever the mages did back at the caves had a ripple effect. Time and space are bending to accommodate them."

"So how long has campus been under attack?" Doc asks. Behind our wall, the shouts of dozens of mages and witches fill the air.

This way!

Throw the stun potion!

Run!

In here—quick!

Help me! Help!

"Long enough to fuck up a whole lot of unprepared mages and witches," Baz says. He flinches with every new shout. "We can't stay here. We have to help them."

"We need to get to the admin building," Kirin says. "See if we can find Casey and Quintana and the others. We'll regroup, make a plan, and—"

"Look out!" I shove them out of the way just before a huge section of brick topples from the wall above us, smashing to bits on the ground. "We need to move. Now."

We slip out from behind the wall, heading in the opposite direction from where we entered, hoping to dodge Chariot's relentless hunt.

But it doesn't matter. The entire campus is swarming with undead soldiers. Every time one of our own takes down an enemy, the monster rises again, yellow eyes glowing, teeth gnashing.

"They can't be killed," Kirin breathes.

"They're already dead." Still gripping my Sword, I take

a quick scan of the campus—what I can see of it, anyway. There's no way to know how long they've been fighting. No way to know how many have already died.

The smell of blood makes my stomach churn.

And still, the undead armies keep marching.

"How is this possible?" Doc asks. "There are so many of them. And they're just… relentless."

"*He's* how they're possible," Baz says, his voice heavy with a mix of sadness, fear, and anger.

It matches his energy.

Following his gaze, I see the source. The general. The Black Sun.

He stands on top of the Chalice inside the fountain at the center of campus, one hand raised, the other brandishing the flaming Wand as if it were an Olympic torch. Despite the distance between us, his spell is a clarion call on the smoky air.

> *From the fury to the flame*
> *What once was dead shall rise again*
> *Reign of terror, reign of might*
> *Let darkness now consume the light*

With every word, more monsters spill from the rift. They snap and claw, chase and devour. Living witches and mages—students and professors alike—throw spells, weapons, and their own bodies at the attackers, desperate to beat back the encroaching waves.

But for every one they kill, more rise from the blackened ruins of battle.

"Stevie! Run!" a familiar voice shouts, and I spin on my heel to see Nat running straight for us. In a flash, I remember my vision. The arrows. Her death.

"Nat! Get down!" I charge at her, crashing in to her and bringing her down. Two arrows zip over our heads. I glance up to see three hooded mages nocking their arrows, preparing for another shot.

"Time to go." Kirin hauls me up, Doc dragging Nat, and we all bolt into another half-demolished classroom building.

"Isla and Carly are gone," Nat says, breathless. Her silver-and-teal hair is matted with dirt and blood. "We got separated, and—"

"Nat, listen to me." I grip her shoulder, my voice firm. "They're strong. They're fine. I can *feel* it."

She swallows hard and nods.

"Where are the agents and the professors?" I ask.

"I don't know. We never met up. I saw Agent Quinta running toward some of the mages a few minutes ago, but I was too busy trying not to die to stop and ask any questions."

"Understandable." I smile, then close my eyes, sucking in a deep breath. In my hand, the Sword of Breath and Blade tingles, its magick stirring to life.

When I open my eyes again, I see them. Four Tarot cards face up on the ground before me.

My Princesses.

"Did you see Casey?" Kirin asks.

Nat shakes her head.

"Fuck." Doc shoves a hand through his hair. "We are vastly outnumbered and completely out-magicked."

"Not *completely*." I look into his stormy-sea eyes, a smile touching my lips. The Sword glows faintly, and with it, the spell rushes into my mind.

I waste no time calling it into existence.

> *Swords and Pentacles, Cups and Wands*
> *I call on you now to honor our bonds*
> *By foes we're outnumbered, by magick outspelled*
> *So let's send these assholes straight back to hell*

"That's one way to do it," Baz says with a chuckle. "You sure they heard you?"

"Oh, they heard me all right." I grin into the darkness behind us. And one by one, my Arcana Princesses appear, looking as badass as ever—Swords, dressed in her tattered blue gown, her sword and black raven at the ready. Cups, with her flowing red hair and golden chalice. Pentacles, curious and open, wise beyond her years. And Wands, rocking a fierce, fiery energy and a powerful staff to rival that of the Black Sun.

Suddenly, I'm overcome with a wave of emotion—gratitude, mostly. Grief for those we've already lost. But also—rising above all that—honor.

Fighting with my mages, my friends, my Princesses... It

fills me with a sense of duty and hope and lightness that not even the darkest evil can dim.

"Whatever happens out there," I whisper, but Doc cuts me off with a kiss.

"Whatever happens out there, Miss Milan, we will discuss it later."

I nod once, borrowing a bit of his courage and certainty.

Later. The word is my new mantra.

Later. Later. Later.

There's *definitely* going to be a later, otherwise he wouldn't have said it.

With one last smile, I look at each of my mages in turn, my Princesses bookending them, two on each side. I look at my friend Nat. I think of our other friends out there somewhere—Carly, Isla, Professor Maddox, Professor Broome, Casey, Agent Quintana. I think of our fellow students and Academy staff.

And last, I think of Danika Lewis, the witch our enemies executed on live television. It feels like a lifetime ago.

It's her words I borrow now—the only ones that matter.

Raising my Sword, I unleash those words with a roar loud enough for everyone on campus to hear, friend and enemy like.

"Fucking *fight*!"

With my friends and mages at my side and my Princesses at my back, we charge out into the fray.

NINETEEN

KIRIN

The minute we're back out in the open, two cloaked mages come straight at me, magick crackling in their hands. Baz is covering my back, but Stevie, Cass, and Nat are already charging ahead into a mob of undead fighters.

I lose sight of them in a matter of seconds.

"You good, brother?" Baz calls over his shoulder.

"I got them—just watch your eyes." I chuck a blinding potion at the mages' feet and shield my eyes from the imminent flash. White light explodes between us, disorienting the mages and buying me about thirty seconds. Dagger in hand, I quickly dart behind them, shoving the blade into the closest one's back.

Mage number one goes down hard and fast. I yank out the blade and stab the other asshole, but the dagger slides right through him, and he vanishes.

"Black-mirror mages!" I shout. Baz whips around just as

two more appear before me, rising from the ground like black smoke.

It's the same dark projection magick we fought in the library basement the night Trello killed Phaines and we found the jars of siphoned magick. It means any one of them could be an attacker or an illusion. If we're not careful, they'll drain our energy and leave us wasted, all without lifting a finger.

I spin around and catch one from behind again, but he isn't real. Neither is the second.

"Fuck," Baz growls. "We need to see what we're dealing with, or we're toast. We need a spell to—"

A cacophony of screams and shouts cuts him off. We turn and see a group of a dozen students fleeing toward the library, where they huddle together in a broken alcove. I recognize Carly's friends Emory and Blue among them.

Not far in the distance, Chariot drives her war horses hard. Their hooves hit the ground with so much force bits of rock and earth fly up in their wake.

She's heading right for them, just like Stevie saw in her vision.

Damn it, those cracked walls are no match for her power.

Without a word, Baz and I take off at a run. My backpack slaps against my back—I can only hope the Pentacle and Chalice are safe.

"Watch your left!" Baz shouts, and I duck just before a mage lets a bolt of magick fly. It smashes into an undead soldier behind me, splitting his skull like an overripe melon. I chuck another blinding potion at the mage, stunning him.

More undead soldiers come at us from all sides, but they're not particularly skilled fighters. We take them down easily, stabbing and slashing our way through the mob. They drop around us like dead weight.

Seconds later, they're up again—smashed skulls be damned.

"This is fucking impossible!" Baz shouts, taking another one down with a quick jab of his dagger. With every kill, their rotten blood sprays our faces, but there's no time to think about it. We're too busy ducking and weaving through the knot of bodies, narrowly avoiding mage magick, hoping like hell we can get to those students in time.

The mob is closing in tight, cutting off our exit points.

"Fuck!" Baz shouts again. "Kirin, hold tight!" He raises his hands and mutters a quick spell, and the ground between us rumbles and shifts. It's a minor quake, but it's enough to knock a few bodies off-balance and give us a clear path. He grabs my arm, and together we bolt through the tight clearing.

"Baz! Kirin!" a voice calls out across the chaos. It's Professor Broome, frantically waving us on toward the huddled students. When we reach her, she says, "We need to do a spell. Set up a protective boundary. Hurry!"

Stopping a few yards in front of the alcove, Baz and I slice our palms and draw a line of blood on the ground.

"Listen up, everyone," Broome says. "I need you all to

take a deep breath, ground and center, and focus all your energy on envisioning a protective bubble rising up around us. It doesn't matter what your elemental affinity is, or how much practice you've had. Just trust yourselves and one another. Okay?"

Chariot is closing in fast. Close enough I can see the sheen of sweat on her brow, the froth of the horses' mouths, the hatred burning in her eyes.

"Now!" Broome shouts to the students. Then, clasping our hands, she shouts her spell.

> *Power of earth, power of air*
> *Power of many and all*
> *Make me a shield against the dark mares*
> *Make an unbreakable wall*

Baz and I take up the chant, driving all of our power into the words.

"Don't stop!" Broome shouts. "She's nearly on us!"

We repeat the chant again, so loud and forceful my throat burns.

Chariot's here. Ten seconds to impact. Five. Three.

The air shimmers before us like a gossamer curtain, and the horses stop short, rearing up hard as if the magick burns them. The chariot flips and rolls, dragging the horses back with the force, tangling them in the reins.

"Hold it!" Broome orders. "Don't let her in!"

Seconds later, the broken, bloodied woman emerges

from the wreckage, wounded but refusing to stay down. With a sword in one hand, she charges right for us.

She hits the magick boundary with a crash, her eyes wild and furious. The curtain warbles like a heat wave, but doesn't break. She throws herself at it again and again, tries from another angle, darts to the other side, charges at us with her sword drawn.

But we've truly created an unbreakable boundary.

She can't touch us. Can't touch the students behind us.

Choking on her own rage, the Chariot cuts her horses loose from the ruined apparatus, then mounts the larger horse. It rears up under her weight, screaming into the air like a beast of hell.

Then—finally—she and her war horses retreat, no doubt heading for some other target.

We hold the magickal barrier for a few more minutes, scanning the surroundings. It seems like it's only been minutes, yet half the campus already lies in ruins. Bodies litter the pathways—our own witches and mages, Eastman's mages, undead soldiers in various states of decomposition. Magick both good and evil sizzles through the air. At every turn, witches and mages are fighting. Screaming. Holding back death and mayhem as best they can. Smoke and ash choke out the sun.

"Professor Maddox?" I ask, and Broome nods.

"Kelly's in the admin building with Carly. Isla went with your sister and Agent Quintana to look for Nat. Last I knew, everyone was still…"

She trails off without saying the word.

Alive.

Nodding, I cling to it anyway. Of course they're alive. They have to be.

I peer through the smoke, trying to decide on our next move. I can't see Stevie or Cass. Can't see the Princesses, though Stevie assured us they were with her. I've lost sight of the Chariot too, but I can still hear the cries of her war horses.

The rift in the sky has finally closed, but the campus is crawling with the Dark Magician's undead forces.

From his perch on the Tarot fountain, the Black Sun still reigns supreme, bringing them back to life with his evil spells. With the corrupted Wand.

"The Magician?" Baz asks.

"No sign of him so far," Broome says.

"We can't hold this up forever," I say, my limbs burning with the effort of channeling so much magick.

The professor nods, then glances back at the students still huddled in the alcove. "I'll get them to safety. You two need to—"

"Guys!" Stevie's voice rings out across the quad. She's with Cass, a dozen mages on their tails. I have no idea if they're real or projections, but we can't take the risk.

"Go!" Broome says.

At once we drop the shield, Broome heading for the students, Baz and I beelining for Stevie and Cass. In a clash of magick and daggers, we slam into the mages, taking down the three real ones at the front of the line. Stevie and Cass spin around to take down two more. Just before another goes down, he shoots out a bolt of magick, sizzling across my shoulder.

Cass takes down the remaining live ones, and the others vanish—more projections.

"You good?" Baz asks me.

"Just a flesh wound. Let's move." I grab Stevie's hand and make for the admin building, hoping we can find Casey and the others. But once again, we're trapped by the mutant army.

Every time we take them down, they rise again—an unstoppable, undead wave of destruction bent on one thing.

Our complete annihilation.

With another burst of energy, we fight our way through the fray, finally taking shelter between two small office buildings. It's a brief respite from the screams of agony and battle cries. Even tucked away in here, the smell of blood and charred flesh is overwhelming.

From this vantage point, we've got a semi-clear view of the fountain. Of Ani.

"Status?" Cass asks. "Is anyone seriously injured? Kirin?"

I rotate my shoulder, relieved that it still works. The skin burns with pain, but the wound doesn't seem to go very deep. "Nothing a stiff drink won't fix later. You?"

"Still breathing," Cass says, and Baz nods as well.

All four of us are covered with scrapes and gashes and burns, but so far it seems we've managed to avoid the life-threatening injuries.

"What's next?" I ask. "This situation is—"

"Fucked, screwed, jacked, and fucked again," Baz says.

"I was going for *complicated*," I say, "but I think you covered it."

"The good news is the rift has closed," Cass says. "That seems to have stabilized the realms for now. Bad news is… it doesn't really matter. Whether we're dealing with a thousand or ten thousand, that army is basically immortal."

"There *has* to be a spell," Stevie says.

"What about the Princesses?" I ask.

"They're with me, but not in a physical way. It's more like… they lend me their gifts. So if there was a spell, they would probably be able to amplify it."

"I'm not sure what magick could take them down," Cass says. "Nothing we've tried so far has worked. And physical attacks are pointless."

Baz cracks his knuckles. "What about a brute force attack? Or beheading them? Would that work?"

We all fall silent for a few moments, trying not to flinch with every explosion and scream outside our temporary shelter.

It's hard not to feel the hopelessness creeping in. The dread.

"I'm afraid there's only one way out of this." Stevie leans back against the wall and closes her eyes, still panting for air. After gulping down a few more deep breaths, she looks at us again and says, "Ani."

"What about him?" Cass asks.

"We have to stop him. He's the one with the Wand—

he's their general. We stop him, we stop his minions. Then we just have the mages and the Dark Arcana to deal with."

"But how?" Baz asks. "If we kill the Black Sun, *our* Ani dies too. And then his soul is trapped who the fuck knows where."

"I'm not going to kill him," she says simply. "I'm going to heal him."

A spark of hope flames to life in my chest, but... no. How is that even possible? "Stevie—"

She turns to me with a ferociously determined glare that tells me there will be no talking her out of this, no matter how terrible the risk. "I just need to get to him, Kirin. If I can get to him, I can do this. I know I can."

"It's risky as hell," Baz says. "What if—"

"Look. Magick won't work against these monsters. Neither will weapons. Every second we waste talking about it is another second one of our friends dies. Another second the Dark Magician closes in on his ultimate goal. Those are the stakes here, and while I'm sure we could come up with a million and one better plans if we had more time, we don't."

"What *is* your plan, then?" I ask.

"There's no time to explain. Just... I need to get to Ani alone."

"No." Baz folds his arms over his chest. "Not happening."

"It is happening," she says. "It's the only way I can get him to drop his guard long enough to do what needs to be done. If we all show up together, he'll know we're trying to take him down."

He curses under his breath. We all know she's right.

"So," she says, "will you guys cover me?"

"Of course we will." I brush my bruised, cracked knuckles over her cheek. It feels like warm satin, and my heart nearly breaks at the softness of it. For a brief second, I'm back in Tres Búhos, ordering cinnamon buns at Kettle Black just for another excuse to be near her.

"Queen of Leaves," I whisper, "you know I trust you implicitly."

This gets the smile I was hoping for—a ray of sunlight in a face smudged with blood and ash.

"I told you you'd live to regret that one day," she teases.

"And I told you… Not a chance." With one last smile in return, I kiss her—all too briefly before the wall behind us gives way.

With no more time to discuss the nuances of her plan, we're off again, Cass and Baz at my back, Stevie disappearing into the smoky haze.

We don't watch her go. We turn all of our efforts toward keeping her safe.

With my brothers fighting at my side, we take down as many mages and yellow-eyed ghouls as we can. No matter that half the mages aren't real. No matter that the undead soldiers rise up moments after we break them. No matter that we're losing this war.

As long as our girl gets to the fountain, it's a win. That's the only thing I care about right now—keeping her safe.

Mages close ranks around us as more of them follow in Stevie's footsteps, but they won't even get close. As one, the three of us fight our way through them, stabbing and slashing, throwing potion after potion—spells to blind and stun, spells to choke, spells to kill. We're running on pure adrenaline now, covered in blood and rot, growling and snapping like animals as we take down our foes.

Stevie finally makes it to the fountain. To the Black Sun, commander of the dark armies. I see her wild hair whipping in the hot winds that surround him, and suddenly I'm filled with so much pride. So much warmth.

The hope she sparked inside me earlier rekindles with a vengeance, burning bright inside me.

Our Star is a fucking badass.

My eyes blur with tears.

I stop to take a deep breath, to get one last, long look at her. She's so fucking fierce I suddenly can't remember why I ever thought we'd lose this thing…

"Unworthy filth! You will *burn!*"

The vicious words cut through my momentary haze, and I whip around, following their terrible echo.

Judgment stands on the red stone path, blood covering his robes, his hands engulfed in magick fire. Slumped at his feet, a lone witch hunches over the broken body of a mage, his blood pooling out around them.

My heart hammers against my ribs, the hope in my chest exploding in a burst of fear and pain.

The mage is Agent Quintana.

The witch is my sister.

"Baz! Cass!" I shout for them even as I'm already running toward her, leaping over dead bodies, ducking more magick attacks. My brothers follow in my wake, all three of us charging toward the path.

"Don't you fucking touch her!" I bellow. "Don't you dare!"

Slow and unconcerned, Judgment turns his vicious glare on me. A smile twists his bloodied mouth.

"Such heroic little Arcana mages," he sneers. "So predictable."

Fisting my dagger so tightly my knuckles turn white beneath the bruises, I growl, "Let them go."

"Kirin," Casey chokes out. Her face is streaked with tears, but her eyes hold a quiet strength. "Don't—"

"That's enough." Judgment stomps on Quintana's hand, making the already battered mage cry out in pain.

He's alive, but barely.

"Let them *go!*" I demand, raising my dagger. Beside me, Cass and Baz hold up their own daggers.

Not that they'll do any good against Dark Judgment.

Judgment glares at us like we're no more than a nuisance. Flies to be shooed away.

"Fine," he says, and my blood turns cold as ice. There's no way he'd agree to it, unless—

"Hand over the Arcana objects, and I'll let your sister and her little pet go free."

"Kirin, don't even *think* about it," Casey snaps.

But her pleas fall on deaf ears. There's no way I'm letting him touch her.

I unhook my pack and slide it off my shoulders, dropping it at my feet. "The Chalice and Pentacle are inside. That's all we have."

"Take the bag and go," Cass says.

In a blur, Judgment scoops up the pack, unzipping to confirm its contents. "Excellent, excellent," he mutters. "All seems to be in order. The Dark One will be quite pleased with me."

"Satisfied?" Baz asks.

The vile beast offers a non-committal shrug. Then, with another twisted grin and a gleam in his dead eyes, he says, "Just one more thing to seal the deal."

Before any of us can say another word, he hits us with a wave of searing-hot magick that makes me feel like I'm being skinned alive and turned inside out. The world collapses, then spins away, taking my breath with it.

My sister's scream is the very last thing I hear—the soundtrack to my demise.

TWENTY

ANSEL

From the fury to the flame
What once was dead shall rise again
Reign of terror, reign of might
Let darkness now consume the light

I repeat the vicious spell, my voice so powerful and all-encompassing it's nearly unrecognizable. Magick sizzles through the air. A wall of fire rises before me, burning the bodies of the dead to ash. Seconds later, they reform, rising once again to take up arms—not at Judgment's command, or Chariot's, or even the Dark Magician's.

But at *my* command.

Everywhere I look, the earth runs red with the blood of the dead—the broken witches and mages of Arcana Academy.

They fall like dominoes because of me. *For* me.

The sight of it makes my cock hard with something far greater than lust.

This is power. This is what I was *made* for.

> *From the fury to the flame*
> *What once was dead shall rise again*
> *Reign of terror, reign of might*
> *Let darkness now consume the light*

I'm shouting the words now. A hot wind gathers around me, whipping my flames into a frenzy. With every recitation, the power inside me intensifies, rippling outward and transforming the landscape before my eyes. Where proud buildings once stood, suddenly there's only rubble and ash. Trees bend and melt, jagged obsidian spires rising in their place. The screams of the fallen ring out across the burning campus, a near-deafening cacophony of pain.

With smoke and fire and ash and terror, I've finally done it. I've turned the sun black.

It's devastating. It's destructive. And it's utterly intoxicating.

Yet through it all—through the snap of bones breaking and fire crackling, through the singe of magick in the air, through the haze of smoke and brimstone, through the stench of blood and death and rot—somehow, *she* remains.

And she's come for me.

I can sense her. Feel the ancient magick flowing through her Sword. Hear it singing in her very blood.

It calls to me as deeply as the fire in my Wand once did.

"Ansel McCauley!" she cries out across the blood-soaked ground. Her voice raises the hairs on the back of my neck. "I'm here to take you home!"

My lips curl into a sneer as I jump down from the fountain and turn to face her.

Her hair is wild and windblown, her face smeared with blood and grime. Her clothing is torn and tattered. A shoe is missing.

This war has stolen the shine from her eyes.

Yet the sword in her hands remains unblemished, a gleaming beacon.

The woman is as beautiful as she is formidable.

If only she'd chosen sides more wisely.

"So the Star Arcana lives," I say. "Another miracle for the precious spirit-blessed witch. I'd offer a slow clap, but as you can see, I've got my hands full." I shift the Wand from my right hand to my left, then back again.

If its raw power impresses her, she doesn't show it. Her eyes never leave mine.

"I'm here for my family," she announces. "It's time for the Dark Arcana to leave this realm."

"I see." I approach her slowly, my steps unhurried as my boots squelch through the blood-drenched patch of earth that separates us. "Is this little speech intended to move me? Because the way I see it, you're not really in a position to make demands."

"And yet, here I am. Demanding."

"Look around you, Star. Not even the fabled Arcana Princesses could help you win this battle. It's over."

Her face softens, her eyes alight with some new tenderness that crawls across my skin like scorpions.

"Oh, Ani." Tightening her grip on the Sword, she says, "We've tried everything we could think of to bring you back. Doc's magick couldn't help you. Taking the Wand couldn't help. Knocking you out, poisoning you… Nothing worked."

"Because I'm *not* Ani, and I don't need to be helped. So unless you're here to surrender yourself and that weapon, I suggest—"

"Excuse me, *asshole*." The softness in her face hardens into bitter hatred. She points the sword at my chest, the tip of it just a few inches from my heart. "I'm talking to Ani, not you."

Laughter and annoyance war for dominance inside me.

Petulant little bitch.

In the end, laughter wins out, and I let it loose.

"By all means, witch-girl." I give her an exaggerated bow. "Continue boring us all with your long and desperate goodbye. I assure you, it will be your last."

She looks at me as if I'm not here. As if she truly believes she's talking to *him*.

"Ani, I know you're still here with us. I may not be able to see you, but I can *feel* you." She presses a hand to her heart, the raw, unguarded emotion in her voice making my stomach churn in a way the mutilated corpses around us do not.

If the Light Arcana spent less time sharing their feelings

and more time tending to their magick, they might not find themselves on the losing end of this war.

"Honestly, witch." I take a step back and gesture to the carnage that surrounds us. "You're wasting your breath. Ani was broken and corruptible—just like the rest of you. He—"

"Ani was and *is* pure of heart and soul. He is an Arcana mage, a devoted friend, and one hell of a man."

Again, my humor battles with my irritation. Again, the laughter wins out.

"Then what, I wonder, am I?" I ask. "Serious question. I'm desperate to know."

"You are nothing but a cheap and soulless imitation. A husk who's so weak, he has to hijack another man's body just to do his master's bidding. As far as I'm concerned, you can fucking *burn*."

That's it. No more games. No more laughter. Now she's just pissing me off.

"I'm not the one who'll burn today, Starla Milan." I lift my hands, the Wand raised toward the heavens. The fires jump at my command, drawing closer, hemming us in.

Black smoke continues to rise, choking out the light.

And still, the bitch will not surrender.

"I'm sorry. Ani, I'm so sorry. I love you." She lowers her blade—fatal mistake. "Do you hear me? With everything I am—magickal, mundane, and everything in between—I *love* you."

"No. I can say with certainty Ani *can't* hear you. That

man is gone." I swing the Wand in a wide arc, smashing it into the side of her exposed ribcage. The force of it cracks bone, and she drops to her knees, all the breath rushing from her lungs. "Accept it or die in denial. I'm good either way."

Blood trickles from her mouth, pathetic tears drawing twin tracks down her filthy cheeks.

"I love you, Ani," she chokes out again. "I love you."

"You love a dead man." I jab the Wand into her chest, right above her heart. The fabric of her shirt burns away where the Wand touches it, her flesh blackening beneath it. "Stop babbling, and perhaps you'll die with a shred of dignity."

"Ani..." The woman barely has strength to draw breath, yet she refuses to listen to reason. She speaks to her Arcana brother as if he's with her. As if *I* don't even exist. "I will *never* give up on you. Never."

"No matter," I grind out, frustration simmering with the magick inside me. "He's given up on *you*."

"Who gathers here as bonded brothers?" she whispers.

"You and your bonded brothers will burn."

"We, the Keepers of the Grave," she breathes, her face pale.

I shove the Wand harder against her flesh, making it sizzle.

After a deep, painful cough, she sputters, "Who spills his blood as... as a symbol of our commitment to one another... and in the service and protection of the First?"

"No more, witch-girl. You've had enough."

"We, the Keepers of the Grave." She sucks in another

ragged breath, then continues. "Who vows, by his life or his death... by his silence or... or his words... in this and all incarnations henceforth, to... to protect the one true source?"

"Let me guess," I grumble.

"We, the Keepers of the Grave. We, the Keepers of the Grave. We, the Keepers of the Grave. We, the Keepers of—"

"*Enough!*" In a fit of rage, I toss the Wand aside and leap, knocking her onto her back and pinning her beneath my body.

She doesn't struggle.

With tears in her eyes, she whispers it again. Again, and again, and *again*, like some desperate mantra. "We, the Keepers of the Grave. We, the Keepers of the Grave. We, the Keepers of the Grave."

"Fitting, as now I'm sending you to yours." I wrap my hands around her delicate throat, fury rushing through my veins. "I will *break* you."

And this woman—this fragile eggshell of a woman, with blood in her mouth and stars in her eyes—looks upon my rage-twisted face and smiles.

Reaching up to touch my cheek, she whispers one last promise. "I *will* find you again, my friend. In this life or another."

And then, with a surge of strength and impeccable aim, she shoves the Sword of Breath and Blade right through my fucking chest.

I gasp. The pain is blinding. It's fire. It's ice. It's a thousand deaths on a thousand brutal battlefields in a thousand terrible lifetimes, all condensed to *this* moment. This battle. This death.

Through a mess of tears and grime and blood, she beams up at me at strokes my hair, a light in the brutal darkness. But that smile is not for me. It was never for me.

It was always for him.

Blood pools at the back of my throat. I can't breathe. My body is on fire.

"You... killed... him?" I sputter, my vision already dimming as I collapse against her chest, driving the blade in deeper.

"No." Tightening her fingers in my hair—*his* hair—she whispers the last words I'll ever hear. "I set him free."

TWENTY-ONE

ANSEL

By blood of the World, by light of the Star
Let body remember its soul and its heart
All is reborn, but first it must die
In shadow he fell, in light he shall rise

The Star's gentle chant floats up to through smoke-clotted sky in a sweet melody, wrapping me in warmth. I want so badly to follow the cadence of it, follow it back to her, follow it home…

Goddess, more than anything, I want to go home.

I don't know the Star, but I feel like I should. Like maybe she meant something to me. *Means* something.

But as hard as I strain to hear her now, to *feel* her, that beautiful magick is quickly drowned by another kind.

I can't see him, but Dark Judgment's voice is a deep and deadly threat on the wind, beating back the purity of her light with his foulest curse.

The one that broke me in the first place.

Flame and fury, will and might
Rend the shadow from the light
Dark desires now revealed
Heart and soul shall be concealed

At his words, my vilest memories flicker back to life. The pain and anguish, the agony, the festering wounds of a broken, discarded boy who grew up to become a shattered man. Wounds that fueled my rage and allowed me to welcome in the darkness. Wounds that led me to this—the battle raging below. The dead rising.

Flame and fury, will and might
Rend the shadow from the light
Dark desires now revealed
Heart and soul shall be concealed

But the dead, I realize, are no longer rising. The robed mages continue their relentless attack, aided by the Dark Magician and his companion, the Chariot, but their armies are being decimated by the witches and mages of Arcana Academy.

By attacks both magickal and mundane, my friends and fellow students are reclaiming our school. Our home. Our lives.

The dead are staying dead.

Desperate, Judgment recites his spell again, the words

churning inside me, twisting like a hot knife, digging into the deepest aches in search of his Black Sun.

He doesn't realize the darkness has already left me. I felt it go, vanquished by the magick of the Star's blade and the ferocity of her love.

The Black Sun's body—*my* body, hijacked by corrupt magick and ill intent—lies broken in her arms. She's on her knees, holding me close. Blood soaks through my shirt. The bright, coppery taste of it fills my mouth, my breath. I watch us from above. My head on her shoulder, eyes closed. Sword protruding from my chest. All that blood. All her tears.

She should be mourning me. Burying me.

Yet she refuses to give up.

> *Blood of the World, light of the Star*
> *Let body remember the soul and the heart*
> *All is reborn, but first it must die*
> *In shadow he fell, in light he shall rise*

Slowly, the Star withdraws her blade from my chest, her spell a healing balm. Silver light emanates from the wound.

But I don't feel them. Not the light, not the Sword, not the spell, not the mending of bone and skin that follows.

She presses her lips to the top of my head, still chanting.

I wish I could remember her. I wish I could feel the warmth of that kiss.

But I feel nothing.

I'm dying.

I'm dead.

I'm floating away.

I'm leaving my body. I'm leaving her.

I want to go home, but I'm leaving her, drifting endlessly upward into the smoke…

"Come back to me, Ani," she whispers, rocking me in her arms. "Come back to me."

Then, like a beacon of light and hope, the sun breaks through the haze. She tilts her face toward the light and closes her eyes, basking in its warmth. Her face fills my vision, beautiful and luminescent.

And suddenly, I remember what she is to me.

My Star.

Stevie…

"I love you, Ansel McCauley," she whispers.

Her kindness loosens some of the bitterness cemented inside me. It's slipping away, piece by piece.

Placing a hand on my chest, she repeats her spell, soothing and gentle, calling me home.

> *Blood of the World, light of the Star*
> *Let body remember the soul and the heart*
> *All is reborn, but first it must die*
> *In shadow he fell, in light he shall rise*

Dark Judgment tries again, but this time it's his spell that's drowned by the light. Stevie's magick echoes through my body and up toward my soul, soft tendrils of pure silver reaching for me. They wrap around my limbs, warm and inviting.

A gentle tugging sensation pulls me forward.

I'm no longer floating away, but toward.

Stevie utters her spell once more, then brings her mouth to my ear, her plea soft and sweet. I can finally feel it, warm breath tickling my skin, igniting every one of my senses until I'm aware of absolutely everything about her.

The touch of her wild curls whispering across my cheeks. The scent of her skin, still lingering beneath the sweat and grime. The clarity and purpose in her voice. The homey familiarity of her embrace.

The memory of everything we were to each other. The promise of everything still to come.

All because she didn't give up on me.

"Come on, Ani," she says. "Please come back. I know you're still with us. Please, please come home."

I'm coming, I try to tell her, but the words won't form.

"Do you know what Lala told me once?" She brushes her fingers through my hair, her touch as soothing as her voice. The silver tendrils thicken around my body, leading me closer to her. "Lala said true love is a formidable force—that when it sees itself reflected in the heart of another, it will lay bare and burn down anything that stands in the way of that union."

I see you, Stevie, I try to say. *Goddess, you're all I see right now. And I promise you, nothing will ever get in the way of us again. Just don't let me go...*

"I know it's scary, Ani," she says. "I know it. But you

have to try. Feel that love—remember it. Not just what you and I share, but the brotherhood. Friendship. Your family—we're all here, waiting for you."

I feel it! All of it!

"Lala says love has the power to dismantle our fears and set free the pure, limitless heart within," she continues. "And you know what? I believe her. So don't make me eat my words, okay? Follow it back. Feel it and come back to me."

I'm so close now, I'm practically on top of her.

She presses another kiss to my head.

And that's it.

The silver tendrils holding me finally snap, releasing me. In a whoosh of warm air and a blur of color, my soul slips into place, filling that broken body with light. With wonder. With joy.

With pure Arcana Sun energy.

It returns to me in earnest—a tiny bubble that expands and expands and expands inside me until it explodes, sending tiny bursts of warmth and laughter and wonder into every shadow, every cell, until there is no room for terror. No room for hatred. No room for shame. No room for rage.

Only love.

"You are *not* going to fucking die out here, Ansel McCauley," she demands, her voice clearer than I've ever heard it. "We haven't even finished working our way through the eighties karaoke songs, let along the nineties. We have *decades* to perfect. And you are not fucking leaving that to me. Got it?"

I got it! I want to shout, but I can't seem to draw breath. Can't open my eyes.

"Okay then," she says, her tone resigned. "Big guns. You've left me no choice."

Stevie clears her throat.

Takes a deep breath.

Then, with my blood-soaked body in her arms and the sun blazing down on us both, my girl breaks into an ear-splitting, glass-shattering rendition of Whitney Houston's *I Will Always Love You.*

And oh, Goddess, she's *terrible.*

But somehow, that's all it takes.

My breath returns. My heartbeat returns. My life and my soul and my magick... all of it returns.

And I suck in a deep breath and open my eyes, gazing up into the face of an angel.

"Ani! Holy shit, you're alive!"

"Stevie," I gasp, reaching for her face with a trembling hand. My throat is dry and cracked, my breathing labored. "I just have one... one request."

"Oh, Goddess, Ani." She can barely speak through her tears. "Anything. Name it. I can't believe you're here. Holy shitballs, you're here. Just name it."

Magick and energy zip through my limbs. I want to jump up and run. Dance. Shout.

But I keep my face somber, my eyes partially lidded.

"Don't... don't ever..." I cough, clutching at my chest

for effect. And then my face splits into a grin. "Don't sing that song again. No, seriously."

"I... what?"

"When you tried for the high note on that last 'love you-oo?' I was *this* close to bailing on this whole resurrection thing." I sit up on my own. "You should've opened this fight with that one, girl. You could've wiped out the whole Dark army without even lifting a finger."

"You little *fucker*!" She laughs until she's sobbing, then laughing again. She hugs me close, then shoves me away again, tears leaking from her eyes unbidden, her smile huge. "You are such a *dick*! A glorious, amazing, miraculous, beautiful dick!"

She launches herself at me again, tackling me down into the dusty dirt, rolling us over twice until she ends up on top of me, grinning down at me.

"You impaled me with a Sword, and *I'm* the dick?" I fist her wild hair in both hands, desperate to feel it again. To touch her. To see her face. To breathe her in. "Goddess, you're a sight, Stevie Boo Boo."

She touches her nose to mine. "You're not so bad yourself, Gingersnap."

"How did you... I mean, how did you know that would work? The Sword and the spell... I can't believe I'm not dead. Like, *dead* dead."

"You have Judgment to thank for that," she says. "The only thing he was good for."

"How so?"

"I slit his throat. It should've killed him—he went down

—but after a few minutes, he returned to his body like it never happened. *Returned* being the key word. I realized the Sword must've driven his essence out. It was temporary, but it gave me the idea."

"I'm not following. You stabbed me, but you didn't drive my essence out. The opposite, actually."

"I drove the *dark* essence out. My hope was that in the time it would take him to return, I could reunite your *real* soul with your body."

I can't help the laugh that escapes. "Your *hope*? You mean, you weren't totally sure this would work?"

"Well, it's imprecise magick, bringing the guy you love back from the nearly dead." Returning my smile, she shrugs. It's adorable. I'm a goner.

"I'm glad it worked. I still don't totally understand it, but I'm grateful."

"Basically, in those few minutes where you were just a body without a soul, I healed your wounds and undid the magick Judgment and Chariot used to fuck you up in the first place. So when I called you back, you were free to return and be... you know. *You* again."

"I felt it. Your magick. Your love. They pulled me back."

She places her hand on my chest, palm flat against the spot where she stabbed me. "Does anything hurt?"

I grimace. "Only where your knee is pressing against my—"

"Oh, shit! I'm sorry!"

"Don't be. I missed you. Everything about you. Especially your terrible singing voice."

"Such a romantic." Stevie laughs and rolls her beautiful blue eyes. Then, in a whisper as soft as the breeze, "You're back."

"I'm back." I tighten my hands in her hair, drawing her close. "I love you. And I swear to you, Starla Milan, I will never leave your side again. I—"

"Another *unworthy* promise made, another unworthy promise broken." The words come sharp and sudden, a dark shadow sweeping over us both.

We sit up in a flash as the monster comes into view.

Blood-stained robes.

A cruel grin full of sharp teeth.

Dark Judgment looms over us, the Wand clutched in his hand.

Before we can even scramble to our feet, he raises the Wand and hits us with a shock wave of dark magick. The world bends around us, sucking us into the vortex, tearing us apart once more.

TWENTY-TWO

STEVIE

It feels like an eternity before I can breathe or see again, and when I finally suck in that first deep breath and open my eyes, I'm kneeling in the holly thicket, gazing up into the black mouth of the druid's spiral cave.

Mist surrounds me like a death shroud.

Gone is the burning meadow. Gone are the armies of Eastman's mages.

My Princesses gave me strength and magick to fight my way through campus, but like all magick, even they eventually faded.

Here, there is only me, the sound of my ragged heartbeat like a drum in my ears.

Even my Sword is gone, lost in the rush of relief that overtook me when Ani finally came back to me.

Ani...

Slowly, I climb to my feet. My hair, hopelessly tangled

before, is now wrapped in elegant braids that twist around my crown and fall in a cascade down my back. My ruined clothing is gone, replaced with a strapless black gown. The bodice is studded with tiny silk rosebuds that trail down to the full skirt in spiral patterns that shift and swirl when I move. Beneath the blood-red roses, black satin shimmers in the mist.

Stunning, if not for the fact that it's one of the Dark Magician's sacrificial gowns.

"If you think you're going to kill me now, fuckface," I mutter, "you're going to be dead *and* disappointed when I send your ass to oblivion."

Gathering up the heavy skirts, I pick my way through the holly thicket and head for the cave, hoping my mages will be there. With every step I take, the mist grows thicker, until I can't see more than a few inches in front of me.

I don't want to call out to my mages and risk alerting anyone else who might be lurking, but I can't just stand here and do nothing. I have to find them. We have to get back to campus and finish this thing once and for all.

I've just opened my mouth to call Ani's name when a shadow moves before me.

"Who's there?" I whisper. "Ani?"

"You fought well today," a dark voice answers from the mist, casting my skin in goosebumps. "But this is where it ends."

The figure steps forward. The mist parts around him, retreating to give me a clear view of the cave entrance.

Of him.

The goosebumps turn into a full-bodied shiver.

"Hello, my Star," the Dark Magician says. His blue eyes are wild and bright, his skin pink and healthy. His beard is trimmed, his hair combed back, his normally ratty clothes freshly laundered. He looks more alive and vibrant than I've ever seen him.

That... can't be a good sign.

I swallow the knot of fear stuck in my throat.

"I've been waiting for you," he says.

"For me?" I force out a laugh I certainly don't feel. "Didn't I tell you to wait for your death?"

"Indeed, you did. Alas, I won't be the man saying his last words today." He turns his back on me, gesturing with a jerk of his head for me to follow him. "You look breathtaking, by the way."

"Breathtaking... Is that a pun? Because that's exactly what I'm going to take from you if you don't tell me where my men are."

"Relax, child. I'm taking you to them now." He stops before the cave entrance and clasps his hands behind him, rocking back on his heels. He seems imminently pleased with himself.

The knot of fear in my throat returns, bigger and tighter than ever.

What the fuck game is this asshole playing now?

He gives me a head-to-toe once over, then turns toward the cave.

"She's arrived," he says into the darkness. "You may begin the ceremony."

The last of the mist fades away, leaving us in a pale, colorless light. From the yawning mouth of the spiral cave, another man steps forward. His pristine white tunic and bright green cape are a sharp contrast to the gloom that surrounds us. Without the blood and filth, it takes me a moment to recognize him.

Dark Judgment.

Beneath my dress, my knees wobble, but I force myself to keep my voice steady. "You boys got a date tonight? Don't tell me you cleaned up on *my* account."

Ignoring me, he steps to the side, and another person emerges—a woman this time.

Just like her Dark Arcana counterparts, the Chariot is shiny and new, wearing a bright blue tunic and green velvet cape, her auburn hair braided and glossy.

Before I can unleash another smartass remark about all the ridiculous pomp and circumstance, Judgment lifts the ancient horn to his lips and blows.

The sound rings out across the landscape, echoing all the way to the Void and back.

Through a dark smile, Judgment says, "I warned you this day would come, Starla Milan. I warned you all the unworthy would stand before the Dark One, sentenced to eternal torment. I warned you the men you claimed to love would burn."

"The only ones burning today are..." The words die on my tongue as the next figures emerge from the cave. Naked and scrubbed clean, with shaved heads and lifeless eyes devoid of recognition or light, four men answer the call of Judgment's horn.

One by one, my Arcana mages—my heart, my soul, my love, my *everything*—step out into the pale gray gloom.

TWENTY-THREE

STEVIE

Shock and terror hold me in a tight grip, squeezing the air from my lungs and paralyzing my limbs.

At the Magician's order, the Chariot places the Chalice of Blood and Sorrow at Doc's feet, the Pentacle of Iron and Bone at Baz's. Neither of them so much as blink.

The Wand appears in Judgment's hands, glowing red at his touch. He raises it ever so slightly, and his horrible mark burns into the flesh of each of my men, right over their hearts.

"Stop it!" I scream, finally finding my voice. "Stop!" I try to run toward them, but some invisible force holds me in place. Not shock or terror, but magick. Dark magick, eddying around me like a polluted river.

My mages do nothing. Say nothing. Their flesh blisters and cracks, blood leaking from the XX-shaped wounds, but they don't even flinch.

"What have you done to them?" I whisper. Tears spill

into my mouth, heart pounding as images from my terrible visions come back to me unbidden.

This is it. This is where my men will die. He's going to fucking incinerate them.

"You have two choices, Starla Milan." Dark Judgment flashes another cruel smile, his mental fangs glinting. "You hand over the Sword of Breath and Blade and surrender yourself completely and absolutely to the Dark One, or…" He lifts the Wand again, and a fresh wound burns into each of my men, just below the first.

Again, they don't flinch. I can smell the burning flesh, yet none of them make a sound.

"Anything," I choke out. Because in this moment, there's absolutely nothing I won't do to end this torture. To stop this terrible nightmare from coming true.

I reach behind my back for the sheath, only to remember the Sword is gone.

Panic chews through my gut.

"I… I don't have the Sword. I must've dropped it on campus—probably by the fountain. If you take me back, I'll—"

"That isn't necessary." Judgment's gaze slides upward, and I follow it. My owl soars overhead, the blade glinting in his strong talons.

Jareth…

"Call to him," Judgment orders. "Order him to release the Sword. No tricks, no magick, no sneak attacks. He releases the Sword, then he leaves."

"And then you'll release my mages?"

"Your mages will be released."

I have no doubt he's telling the truth, but something tells me our definitions of "released" are wildly different.

I close my eyes and take a deep breath, desperate to come up with some solution—any solution that involves me and the guys getting the fuck out of here, with or without the damn Arcana objects. Silently I call on my Princesses. I call on my mother. I call on my magick. I call on Lala. I call on Anna Trello—the Justice Arcana—whom no one has heard from since she told me about how my mother conspired to bring me into this world. I call on the goddesses and witches of old. I call on the very elemental beings who gifted the First Fool with magick.

I don't know who responds, but eventually, my answer comes.

I feel the Tarot cards in my hands, their edges digging into my palm.

Pretending to adjust my skirts, I glance down at them. In one, I see the Moon. The message whispers through my mind at once—the same message I got the very first time I met Doc. It was in that awful prison when he placed the Moon card on the table between us.

A great deception is upon us.

Death is only the beginning.

The moon casts not its own light; in its glow, nothing is what it seems…

In the other card, a youthful man in a tunic and forest-green wrap gazes up at me, a stick and bundle slung over his shoulder, a bouquet of mistletoe in his hand. He and his black dog skip happily—obliviously—toward the edge of a cliff.

The Fool.

I stifle a gasp as another message rushes through me.

A new journey awaits you. Leap, and the net will appear.

There is no question about what I must do now. No debate. Not even a pause for breath.

I close my eyes and call on Jareth, ordering him to hand over the Sword at once.

Seconds later, he swoops down and releases it. It arrows straight into the earth, vibrating with the force of the impact. Chariot jerks it free at once, then lays it at Kirin's feet.

Reunited once again, all four objects emanate a faint magickal glow.

"Release them!" I shout, some part of me still holding out hope that maybe—just maybe—the cards were wrong. That I don't have to make that leap of faith after all, and these Dark Arcana assholes will simply take their toys, fuck off into the sunset, and forget all about us.

But those are the hopes and dreams of a naïve school-girl, not the reality of a spirit-blessed Arcana witch. One whose blood is the last ingredient in some arcane spell the Magician wants more than anything in this world—the spell that will allow him to reclaim his supposed birthright.

To control magick for eternity, forever dominating all who wield it.

He's planning to do the ceremony right here. All the objects are in place.

All he needs now is me.

And he's keeping me here, exactly where he wants me, paralyzed by fear. My greatest fear, as a matter of fact— losing the men I love, knowing there isn't a damn thing I can do to save them.

In a flash, Judgment raises his Wand one last time, and I know what comes next. The horror of it crashes over me hard, driving me to my knees.

He opens his mouth, condemning my men to death.

> Ashes to ashes, dust to dust
> With flame and with fury, the ends are just
> Cleansed by fire, Arcana must die
> From Death we return, in Darkness we rise

He touches the Wand to the ground before them. The fire ignites at once.

My instincts tell me to close my eyes, to hold my breath, but I can't. I force myself to watch. To take in every moment.

It's the least I can do for the men I so desperately love.

My heart shatters.

Still imprisoned by the magick, I watch in stunned horror as white-hot flames devour the men I love. Kirin's sunset-behind-the-saguaros eyes. The sound of Doc's laugh breaking through his no-nonsense demeanor. The devilish grin that can only belong to Baz. And Ani, my sweet Gingersnap, singing 80s duets with me until the very end...

Skin and blood and bone turn to ash.

And in a matter of seconds, they're gone. Just… gone.

But… no. They're *not* gone. I can still feel their energy. Their love. Their protectiveness. Every one of them is reaching out to me, even now.

How is this possible?

I close my eyes and steady my breath, trying to get a grip. Judgment plays on fear. On guilt. The Magician needs me weak and distracted. Both of them know what losing my men would do to me.

Another of Doc's early lessons comes rushing back at me.

Fear is our most primal, most powerful emotion. It leaves an imprint—almost like a ghost in the room. When I pulled the trigger, it didn't matter that the gun wasn't loaded. Your fear of death by gunshot was completely sincere, and left an intense imprint that my spell was able to amplify. That imprint, combined with the power of suggestion planted in the rich soil of a soft mind, was enough to make the guard truly believe that I killed us…

Holy shit. Of course.

A great deception is upon us.

Death is only the beginning.

The moon casts not its own light; in its glow, nothing is what it seems…

At the Magician's behest, Judgment is manipulating my mind, making me believe my greatest fear has come to life. He planted the seed long ago—the vision I saw on one of my earliest trips to the dream realm.

And now, he's using that against me.

But my fear *hasn't* manifested. No fucking way. They're

still alive. I can feel it—a wave so strong it lifts me to my feet, filling me with hope.

The magick holding me in place vanishes. The Dark Magician smiles, his eyes sparkling with pride. He thinks this is a done deal. That I'm broken, that he can take whatever he wants from me with no resistance.

I lift up my skirts and take a step back into the holly thicket—back into the mist.

"Where are you going, little Star?" the Dark Magician laughs, but makes no move to stop me. He can't even *begin* to imagine my plan. It amuses him, my pain. He'd probably get off on letting me wander around through the mist all day, crying my eyes out until he's bored and ready for his final ritual.

But despite what he believes, he *hasn't* destroyed me.

I still have my men. And I still have a choice.

Trello once told me something about choice: *You either choose to act through your own free will, or you choose to let the river of fate carry you where it may. In choosing to act, you don't always have the luxury of acting justly for all of the people all of the time. You simply make the best decision you can with the information available to you. Again and again and again. After that, all that's left is hope.*

Right now, I'm choosing that hope. I'm choosing to believe this isn't the end. I'm choosing to believe that no matter how desperate things might seem, there is *always* a light to be found in the darkness.

And if there isn't?

Then you find a way to be your *own* fucking light.

With one last call to Jareth—a final plea I know he won't ignore—I turn my back on the Magician and his monstrous entourage, turn my back on the vision of the ashes of the men I love, turn my back on all the darkness. I take a deep breath and let the Fool's energy surge inside me, filling me with that unshakeable sense of hope.

Then I take off at a run, knowing exactly where I must go. What I must do.

"Fight it, Stevie!" a voice echoes through the mist, but I don't pay it any mind.

"It isn't real," comes another. Sharper. Urgent. But again, I can't stop to listen. I'm on a path from which I can *not* turn.

My destination is much closer than I thought. In a matter of seconds, I reach the edge of the drop-off. Through the swirling mist, I can just make out the deep dark emptiness below, though I don't dare look for too long.

The Void.

I recall what Kirin told me my first day on campus.

L'Appel du Vide… Call of the Void… It's said that there are places in this world so deep, so dark, so… compelling… when you peer down into them, they literally beckon you to jump…

Lala's words come to me next, repeating the prophecy that allegedly foretold my death.

Thus her ache shall find no ease, so shall the daughter of The World surrender to the emptiness, to the void within and without. By her own hand, of her own volition, The Star shall fall, and take her eternal breath in utter darkness…

Lala warned me we would suffer great losses, and we have.

She warned me the unbearable pain would drive this prophecy to completion, and it will.

She said my mother foresaw my death, and I swore to myself it was impossible.

And on that note, *I* was right. My mother's prophecy? It wasn't a prediction of doom.

It was a clue.

She didn't see me jumping to my death. She saw me jumping into a new beginning—the Fool's Journey. A reckoning that would end one phase and begin another.

She saw me jumping for life.

For love.

Leap, and the net will appear.

All the sadness and grief and fear leaves me in an instant, washed away by a deep sense of peace and a knowing so clear, it shines through the blackness in my heart.

The Magician can't have me. I refuse to give him what he wants.

Taking a deep breath, I peer fully into the Void.

It's terrifying and beautiful, like nothing I've ever seen.

The call is impossible to ignore. I've never wanted anything as much as I want to jump.

I kick off my shoes and stand on the very edge, wrapping my toes around it. Cool mud squishes between them.

Starla Eve... the mist whispers, wrapping me up in its sweet invitation.

"Don't you dare!" comes a warning through the mist. I look over my shoulder to find The Dark Magician charging toward me, arms waving, eyes wild. "Foolish girl, what are you doing?"

"Being my own fucking light, asshole."

I spread my arms, and Jareth's energy bursts from inside me, a light so bright it knocks the Magician flat on his back. My body is on fire with magick, the black satin gown melting away, the braids loosening to unleash my crazy curls, my arms turning to wings that stretch across the mists.

I let out a primal scream, and the whole world trembles in fear.

Then I gaze back down into the Void, take one last breath, and answer its call with a spectacular leap into the unknown.

TWENTY-FOUR

CASS

They say in the final moments before a man's death, his life flashes before his eyes.

The best parts.

The worst parts.

All the tiny slivers of hope and love and betrayal and kindness and pain and elation and fear and ecstasy, all condensed into a milliseconds-long film.

I wouldn't know it for sure. My life was spared, along with the lives of Casey and her partner. Baz and Kirin are still breathing as well. As is Ani, returned to us with his soul intact, healed by the love of the woman whose torment we're now being forced to watch.

Taken prisoner and bound by dark magick, forced onto our knees just outside the caves, my brothers and I have front-row seats to the Dark Arcana's cruelest games.

Paralyzed, we watched helplessly as the Magician lured her here. Watched helplessly as he paraded her before us in her sacrificial gown, and then as he paraded *us* before *her*, using the Chalice's inherent emotional magick to invade her mind and heart.

Everything he showed her was a lie. His last great deceit —and I'm sure he couldn't have been more elated.

Until our beloved Star—our beautifully wicked witch— pulled off a deception of her own.

The Magician needs her blood. Even with all the Arcana objects in his possession, he can't complete the ritual—can't fully claim magick—without it.

So she's taking it away from him.

I would smile with abject pride if not for the consequences of her decision.

Instead, I'm shouting in horror, screaming at her to stop. To hear us. To see through the filthy lies.

But it's too late. I can't reach her. None of us can. Whatever lies they fed to her, they must've been so terrible that she truly believes there's no other choice.

The Dark Arcana chase after her, but they're too late as well.

Stevie has made her choice.

They say in the final moments before a man's death, his life flashes before his eyes, and I've always believed that saying to be true.

Now, I *know* it to be true.

Only… the life playing out before my eyes isn't my own at all.

It's hers.

My beautiful Star…

In the film version, I see her in that prison the first day we met, her orange jumpsuit covered in filth, her blue eyes bright behind the grime. I see the gorgeous smile on her face when she walked out of Lala's house and into the sunlit backyard, the golden afternoon rays lighting her up like a goddess.

I hear her too—the soft sighs of pleasure as she ate the tacos we made. The steely determination in her voice when she accepted my offer to attend Arcana Academy, her demands. The sass in her tone as she argued with me in class.

I remember her fetish for snacks, her skill at the kettle, the off-key songs she sang for Ani. I remember the way she fought for her brothers and friends.

I see her in my arms. Recall the taste of her kiss, the sounds of her sweet moans the first time I made love to her. The feel of her skin beneath my rough palms. The echo of her words to me back in Red Sands Canyon before the Black Sun took me. *I love you, Cassius Devane. Do you understand? I claimed you, remember? I love you, and I'm not letting you go...* The taste of her divine kiss when she saved me earlier, healing my wounds with her magick. With her touch. With her light.

And then, with a swiftness that nearly breaks me, I see her jump into the Void, those wild curls sailing up behind her like a cape, the echo of her scream a death knell for everything I once held dear.

She's gone.

I blink once. Twice. She's really fucking gone.

And now, all I see is red.

The Magician leaps in after her, so desperate for her blood that he'll chase her across the realms if he has to. Chariot quickly follows her master.

The moment the Dark One is gone, the Arcana objects vanish, and the magick holding us finally breaks.

But Judgment is heading back for us, as if his anger alone can save him.

Maybe it could have, once.

But that time is gone.

I look from Kirin to Baz to Ani, tears streaking their cheeks. I feel the same wetness on my own skin, pooling in my collar, leaving a cold trail in its wake. But inside me, everything burns with a furious fire bent on one thing and one thing alone.

"I promised you I would kill him, Ani," I say, soft and low and menacing, my voice a tremor in the mist. "I have no intentions of breaking that promise."

"We're all with you, brother," he says, and the others nod, their jaws set with grim determination.

"She's not gone," I say, needing the assurance as much as I need to assure them.

"No fucking way," Baz agrees.

Behind us, the discarded pack Judgment took from Kirin lies spilled on the ground. I grab a dagger and make a quick slice on each palm, passing it to the others to do the same.

They do it without question, knowing exactly what I'm about to propose. Sharing our magick—combining it— might give us a shot at overpowering Judgment.

We clasp hands, forming an unbroken circle before the spiral cave. Magick courses through us, hot and crackling, alive with our shared Arcana power. Never have I felt so connected to my brothers, so united in purpose and passion.

Judgment emerges from the holly thicket, momentarily taken aback by our formation.

"What do you think you're doing, unworthy filth?" he demands.

Ignoring him, I say my piece, rage fueling my words:

> *I am the Moon, the pull of the tides*
> *Fierce as the ocean, our power collides*

Baz is next, his red-brown eyes fiery with intention:

> *I am the Devil, the horned god of old*
> *Fierce as the darkness, our power is bold*

When Kirin speaks, his body trembles with the force of his conviction:

> *I am the Tower, the clash of the storms*
> *Fierce as the thunder, our power reforms*

Ani goes last, his inner fire shining bright in the gray haze:

> *I am the Sun, the flames in the pyre*

Fierce as creation, our power is fire

"Your little chants won't help you," Judgment says. He raises his hands, calling up a path of raging fire that barrels toward us. But it's too late for him. The magick is already rushing through us, strengthening us, amplifying our natural gifts.

As one, we recite our final spell:

> *Called to protect, to serve, and to fight*
> *By flood or by fire, by storm or by might*
> *We are the magick, the power reclaimed*
> *We are the mages, Arcana untamed*

A surge of power courses through my blood, mingling with the rage and grief and desperation, all of it making me feel strong and alive and utterly fucking unstoppable. Judgment's flames finally reach us, fizzling out at our feet as if we'd just doused them with water.

Enraged, he raises his hands again. "All of you are unfit to carry such power. Worthless. Shameful. You allowed your precious Star to sacrifice herself for you like cowards. All of you will burn!"

The mention of Stevie's sacrifice only emboldens us. Heat races up and down my arms, making my skin tingle, my hands itch. The magick inside me is quickly gathering strength, eager for an outlet.

Judgment stares at us with wide eyes, a hint of terror flashing in their dark depths.

Again, he attempts to call forth the fire, but this time it doesn't work. His magick is failing him. He put so much of himself into the Wand; without it, he's impotent.

"My father," I say, taking a step toward him, "spent the better part of his life trying to convince me I was nothing but a cruel, worthless monster. You will not have that opportunity."

"Bold words for a mage who just lost the only person in this world who professed to love him. You should've protected her, Cassius Devane, but you didn't. You couldn't. You are nothing but poison."

His words cut through my heart with the pain of a rusty blade, just as he intended. I feel them trying to take root inside me, blackening my soul like the very poison he speaks of. It's the same tactic he used on me the night Stevie and I discovered the Chalice. The night he showed me a vision of my dead brother, Xavier.

That night, it was almost enough to destroy me.

But now, it only reminds me of Stevie. Of her words the morning after we retrieved the Chalice. *I'm not naïve enough to say love can totally counter that kind of hate—not when people in power decide their personal beliefs are carte blanche for the murder and imprisonment of others. But I do believe love is where we start.*

Yes, love is where we start. And love is where *this* ends.

"You are nothing but *poison*," Judgment taunts again, sealing his fate.

I don't have a spell jar. Don't have a single ingredient.

The last of our potions from Professor Broome were spent on campus.

All I have now is my fury.

My determination.

And my undying love for a woman whose light I fucking *refuse* to believe is out.

Right now, that's *more* than enough.

"You're right—I *am* poison," I grind out. "A poison you're about to taste."

Amplified by the shared magick of my brothers, I close my eyes and call on the energy of the dark Moon.

My words fall as easily as a breath.

> *Black rider, void of light*
> *I call upon the Mare of Night*
> *Unleash the darkness in his mind*
> *For evil sown is reaped in kind*

Black smoke rises off my palms, curling in my hands as if my skin is mere seconds away from igniting. There's no heat in this magick, though. Only ice. Only darkness.

Judgment laughs. "Your illusions won't work on me, Cassius."

With little remaining magick at his command, he goes for blunt force instead, slamming his fist into my chest. It flames to life at the contact, but fizzles out once again.

There is no pain he can inflict on me now. No punishment to rival the sight of my fallen Star.

I hold up my hands before me, palms out. The black smoke thickens, sensing a fresh victim.

I see the change come over Dark Judgment in an instant. He knows he's staring into the face of death. He knows there will be no mercy and no escape.

His eyes widen with fear. "But that's... that's impossible. You don't have the ingredients. You're just... It's impossible!"

"Not impossible. Magick." In a blink, I grab the back of his head and cover his mouth with my hand, unleashing the full power of my wrath.

He screams beneath my hold, fighting me hard, but I don't relent.

I fucking *choke* him with it.

All my rage, all the anger, all the black and bitter hatred I've carried for decades—they're his now. I give him the worst memories of my father. I give him my fears, my nightmares, my pain.

I give him what he did to Ani, all the tortures he inflicted upon him, all the lives he forced Ani to take at the behest of the Black Sun.

I give him the shame that haunted Baz for years.

I give him Kirin's guilt.

I give him the seared flesh of my brothers' skin, the smell of it, the rot.

I give him the screams of battle, the blood running down the red stone paths on campus, the crumbling buildings of the place I've called home for longer than I can remember.

I give him every terror, every darkness, every demon he's ever used to torture the people I love. The people I would die for. The people I would *kill* for.

And then I give him the worst of it—the dark, soulless pit left behind in the wake of Stevie's sacrifice. The yawning emptiness of a possible world without her.

All of it pours from my heart like a million shards of glass, shredding me as it leaves, carving me up inside.

Judgment falls to his knees. Still holding him in my clutches, I follow him down. The pain is nearly unbearable as the vile poison empties from my body and flows into his, but I hold on until I'm certain I've released every last shard of glass.

After an eternity, his body stills. I no longer feel his breath. No longer hear his muffled cries of anguish.

And just like that, Dark Judgment turns to ash in my arms.

"All who are deemed unworthy shall burn," I whisper.

A soft breeze blows through the mists, carrying away his remains along with the very last of my shame and guilt. The very last of my poison.

Slowly, I get to my feet. Dust off my hands. Take a breath of fresh air. The world feels different now. Cleaner. Full of possibilities. Even crazy ones.

Especially crazy ones.

Stevie's voice comes back to me again, this time from the night we drove out to the desert to take the Chalice to the Fool's Grave. *It's called hope… And right now, I'll take that over freaking out like a little bitch any day…*

My brothers stand behind me. Even in their awed silence, I feel their presence. Their loyalty. Their love.

I turn to them, a smile stretching across my lips.

And a little flame sparks to life inside my chest.

Yes, my Star. I know. It's called hope.

Kirin lifts his eyebrows.

Baz cocks his head.

Ani returns my smile, a bit of that contagious hope shining in his eyes, too. "Feeling better, then?"

"Like a new mage," I reply honestly.

Baz blows out a breath. "That was... pretty epic, Cass. Fucking terrifying, but pretty epic."

"Cosigned," Kirin says. "But... what the hell do we do now?"

"Now?" I clamp a hand over his shoulder, another over Ani's. "Now we go get our woman."

Kirin lowers his gaze. "But she's—"

"Kirin?" I smack him lightly on the cheek. "To quote a very wise woman, it's called hope. And right now—"

"I'll take that over freaking out like a little bitch any day," Baz finishes up with a laugh of his own. She'd been talking to *him* that night—of course he remembers. Still smiling, he shakes his head and says, "All right, professor badass. You win. Let's go get our woman."

"Ah, one more thing." I shoot him a glare that all but eradicates his smile. "That's *doctor* badass to you."

TWENTY-FIVE

STEVIE

I wake up in darkness, my entire body burning with a pain so intense, it can only be magickal. Worse than any snake bite or scorpion sting, it feels like fire ants have invaded my bloodstream.

There's no way I'm dead, though part of me wishes that was the case.

I'm lying on a hard slab, my arms and legs bound. The only sound is a dripping noise, like rain splashing into a bucket through a leaky roof.

Plonk... plonk... plonk...

I blink rapidly, desperate to get a read on something—anything—but there's only blackness.

What the fuck happened?

I close my eyes again and take a deep breath, forcing my memories back to the surface.

Judgment... The Magician... incinerating my men...

It wasn't real. So I jumped into the Void.

But… this isn't the Void. Is it? Where is Jareth? Who the hell tied me down?

As soon as the thought enters my mind, some sort of window opens above me, letting in a swath of moonlight. Then, it starts to rain.

Tarot cards. Hundreds of them. They fall on me, landing on my body, on the stone slab around me, on the floor.

And they're all the same.

The Magician.

"Come out and face me, you fucking coward!" I shout into the darkness. "You want my blood so badly, come and take it!"

I'm met only by my own voice, the echo like a mockery.

Come and take it… take it… take it…

The window overhead opens wider, letting in more light.

Slowly, the chamber comes into view. I'm in a cave, but it looks like someone lives here. There are animal skin rugs on the floor, crude shelves lined with old books, a small kitchen off to the side.

I see now that I'm dressed in another gothic gown—pure white, this time. On the shelves closest to me, black dahlias bloom in clay pots.

The scent of blood prickles the back of my nose. It smells near—*very* near. I turn my head, trying to track the source of it.

From the corner of my eye, I spot a copper bowl on the

floor to my right. The dripping sound comes into sharp relief, along with a piercing pain in my wrists.

It's *my* blood I'm smelling. He's draining me. It's spilling from two deep puncture wounds in my wrists, collecting in a series of channels carved into the stone slab, ultimately spilling into the bowl beneath me.

"I hope your sacrificial altar is comfortable," the monster says, finally stepping out from the shadows. He's standing beside a low table that holds each one of the Arcana objects. "The dress isn't my favorite, but you've ruined all the others."

I suck in a cold breath. After all the illusions and games, *this* feels real. A sense of deep, unwavering dread pools in my stomach.

"How did you get here?" I ask, fighting to keep the fear from my voice.

"Same as you, child. Of course, I didn't do it in such a dramatic fashion, but the entry is the same for anyone who chooses to pass through this realm."

"And what realm is that, specifically?"

"The Void of Mist and Spirit. One of my favorite destinations. Your final one, unfortunately."

The Void of Mist and Spirit... like my mother's book, *Journey Through the Void of Mist and Spirit.*

"It's a realm?" I ask, both curious and stalling for time. My eyes dart around the room, searching for something—a weapon, a potion, anything...

"Of course," he says, busying himself at the table. In addition to the objects, he's also got a stack of books and a few vials of liquid, one of them glowing bright silver. "Though not so easily accessible to most witches and mages. Many who've attempted to enter have died— including my Chariot, unfortunately. Hasty woman. Prone to rash decisions. Not her best moment."

"Chariot's dead?" I ask.

"Yes. Judgment too. But not you. No, never you, little Star. You were meant for greater things than death."

"Oh yeah?" I ask, trying to hide my elation over the deaths of his dark companions. "Then why are you trying to kill me?"

"I'm not trying to kill you. That's just an unfortunate side effect—a necessary evil, if you will."

"So I'm going to die here?"

"I'm afraid so."

"How is that possible? I'm an Arcana witch. This is a magickal realm."

"This is the *most* magickal realm," he says. "The place that's in between the in-between. All things are possible here, including our deaths. But fear not—you still have a few hours left on the clock. We haven't even begun the ceremony yet."

He says this with so much glee, you'd think he was talking about a wedding.

I tug on my bonds. No dice.

"So, how does this whole thing work, anyway?" I ask, still casting about for an escape. Unfortunately, the only things in my immediate vicinity are this awful dress and the copper bowl full of my blood. Even if I could reach it, though, the only thing I could do with it is bash him over the head.

Somehow, I don't think that will stop him. This asshole is on a mission.

"It works as it did the first time," he says calmly, as if he's explaining it to a child. "Actually, allow me to read it to you—the authors are much more eloquent than I." He grabs one of the books and flips to the page he's looking for, then reads, "As part of the sacrifice, he gave his bones to create the first pentacle, representing earth magick; his skull for the first chalice, and his blood and tears to fill it, both representing water; his last breath to stoke the flames that forged the first sword, representing air; and the energy of his final ecstasy through forced ceremonial orgasm, representing fire. From there, these ancient artifacts were said to channel all elemental magick, and the man's spirit became the ultimate essence of that magick, known thereafter as the First Fool from which all magick flows, et cetera, et cetera."

He slams the book shut and turns to me with a wide grin, his eyes dancing with manic light.

I know that passage. He just read from the same text that Kirin and I discovered when we were first digging into Mom's prophecies and learning about the origins of magick.

"I hope that answers your questions," he says.

I swallow hard, desperate to quiet the sudden frantic pounding of my heart. With every wild beat, more blood leaks into the copper bowl.

He's not going to kill me—at least not right away.

He's going to perform the same ritual on me as the elemental beings performed on his father, the First Fool.

A slow, torturous death.

And I'm trapped here, locked in a cave with this psycho, no weapons, no magick, no... *wait.*

What am I talking about? I still have my magick, don't I?

I close my eyes, forcing myself to calm the fuck down. With a deep breath, I send a pulse of healing energy to my left wrist—the one that's farthest from the Magician's view. Slowly, the pain begins to recede. Not completely, and it's still bleeding, but it's something. A start.

Stay focused, girl. You can do this. Keep him talking and distracted.

"So what happens after all that?" I ask. "You get your magick back, you've got the Arcana objects... What's next on your vision board?"

He considers the question as though it's a serious conversation between friends. "Well, the next logical step is to take care of the remaining Arcana. I may have to wait a few years to track down your next incarnation, but the others are easy enough to find."

"What do you need them for?"

"To join me, of course. In darkness." He says it so matter-of-factly, as if it's just a forgone conclusion that all the Arcana—my Arcana—will jump on his fucked-up little dark side bandwagon.

The smugness and audacity in his tone turn my stomach. More than his torture plans, more than his past cruelty, it's this smugness—this entitlement—that finally gets my blood boiling.

"You'll *never* turn them," I spit. "They would rather die than they join you."

He clucks his tongue at me. "You say that with such confidence. Yet look how easily I was able to strip the Sun of his light."

"I brought him back, though," I say with a little smugness of my own. "I banished the darkness from him and called the light back."

He looks at me with a cocky grin. "Did you? Are you *certain*?"

The words have the intended effect, piercing holes in my confidence. All around me, fresh dahlias bloom in the pots, and the moonlight overhead dims.

"The darkness exists in *all* the Arcana," he says. "Light and shadow—that is our interplay. One cannot exist without the other. Some of you might cling to the light a bit more stringently than others, but ultimately, everyone has their price. Everyone is but one tragedy away from giving in to the darkness. Even *you*, little Star."

I open my mouth to unleash a string of curses and denials, but quickly clamp it shut.

Maybe he's right about that. Maybe there *is* a darkness inside me, despite Kirin's belief that my Star Arcana power is pure goodness and light.

But he's wrong about one thing.

I will *never* join him—not in this iteration or any other.

He can torture me, he can spill my blood, he can ultimately kill me, but I will never go dark for him.

If there's darkness inside of me, it belongs to me. Mine to claim. Mine to call upon. Mine to use as I see fit.

I close my eyes, and a new message appears—another Tarot card.

It's the Moon again, bringing with it another conversation I had with Doc, this time in my first mental magicks class.

How and when did you learn to dreamcast? he asked.

Dreamcast? I've never even heard of it.

Well, you just did it. Dreamcasting is when you conjure a dream or vision for yourself, then pull your target into it by casting it into his mind. Hold him there long enough, and eventually, the target will have no idea that the vision is coming from another person. It's powerful, complex magick, highly unethical, and advanced beyond even our graduate teachings... A person could literally go insane from magick like that.

It's a long shot, but if magick is all I've got, then I'll find a way to make it work.

Because I'm not going to die here. Screw that.

Keeping my eyes closed, I dig into the fear I'm feeling, the desperation, the hopelessness, trying to channel it into some kind of mental spell I can use against the Magician. But I know right away it's not enough—I need to dig deeper.

Though it nearly shreds my heart to do so, I force myself to go back to the spiral cave in my memory, picturing the guys turning to ash. The image brings a spark of dark magick to life inside me, stronger than before, but still—I need more.

I go back to the battle on campus. The dead bodies. The blood.

Again, the darkness inside me flickers. Brighter this time. Stronger.

More, it whispers. *More.*

I go back to prison, to the abuse I suffered at the hands of the other inmates and guards. I go back to the crime scene photos of Luke's murder. I go back to the top of El Búho Grande, where the dark mage possessed my friend and nearly killed me. I go back to my arrest, the very last time I saw my beloved Kettle Black.

And then I go back to the worst memory, calling it up in such vivid detail my chest constricts with the weight of fresh grief, sharp and devastating, stealing my breath.

My parents' death. I hear their screams as the water rushes through the canyons. I feel my father's hands on me as he shoves me into the cave, saving my life. I see them vanish in the rushing water.

I feel the loss of them as if it just happened. And in this moment—this brutal, terrible moment—I know that this is a pain the Magician and I share.

It's also the way I break him.

Deep inside me, the dark flame turns into an inferno, pushing its black magick through my veins, consuming me with the need for one thing and one thing only: vengeance.

Drawing on the power of the reversed Moon card, I

whisper the spell that comes to mind, so softly he can't hear it.

But I can.

> *Darkest moon, darkest night*
> *Now I set these wrongs to right*
> *What darkness festers in my heart*
> *Upon his evil mind impart*
> *By blood and flame and breath and bone*
> *These terrors become his alone*

And then I call upon the one man whose presence—real or imagined—still has the power to bring the Dark One to his knees.

The First Fool.

Leap, and the net will appear…

"Your father must be so disappointed in you," I say. "Disgusted, actually. He died to bring magick into this world—he made you the Arcana Magician—and *this* is how you use that gift? You're *pathetic*. It's probably a good thing he died, because if he saw you now… Goddess, I can only imagine."

And that's all it takes. The mention of his father fills his memory with the man's image, sending him back through time.

And my dark magick does the rest, taking hold of his fears and his anger, his resentment at his father for leaving the family, his deep sense of abandonment and magnifying them, making him doubt his own feelings and memories.

"*Pathetic!*" I call out again, filling my voice with rage, unleashing all my darkness and fury at once. I sense it the moment the magick takes true hold. His breath hitches, and he falls to his knees, just as I intended, driven there by awe and resentment and fear and confusion. Every one of his feelings radiates through the room, washing over me. I feel dirty and disgusting for using his father's death in this way, but I don't dare stop.

The darkness inside me flares hot.

My bonds weaken, then break.

Across the room, the Magician clutches his head and lets out a cry of agony so intense it makes me shudder.

For the briefest of moments, I understand his pain. Understand *him*.

But trauma—no matter how terrible, no matter how deep its scars may run—does *not* give him a free pass to inflict violence and brutality on others.

Free from my bonds, my wounds healing, I climb down from the altar and rush for the table, grabbing the Sword of Breath and Blade.

"Get up," I command, but the crumpled man at my feet doesn't obey. He's crying now, rocking back and forth, still holding his head as if he's trying to keep the memories at bay.

"Why?" he asks in a broken whisper. "Why, why, why, why, why?"

"Because you're a monster and you fucking deserve it!" I shout, my hands trembling as hard as my voice. Vengeance. That's all I want now. One more step. That's all it would take. One more step, a quick jab, and I could end him.

He said it himself—all things are possible here, even our deaths.

"Get up!" I shout, kicking his foot.

Still, he doesn't move.

I touch the tip of the sword to his chin, forcing him to look up at me. I want my face to be the very last thing he sees before he dies.

"You will never darken our realm or any other again," I tell him. "I will end—"

"That's enough, Starla," a soft voice calls from the shadows. A woman.

"Take a step back," another woman calls. Both of them sound familiar. Comforting.

I hesitate, blinking into the darkness. The flame inside me sputters.

"That's it," the first woman says, stepping into the light. "Back away. Put down the blade. You don't need to do this."

"Lala?" I gasp. Tears fill my eyes, her presence overwhelming me with love and light. At her warm smile, the dark flame inside me finally dims.

I take a step back and lower my sword.

Anna Trello comes to stand beside Lala. Her face is drawn tight, but her eyes hold only warmth and compassion. "Let it go, Starla. You have much work to do back in our realm. Don't dim your light with this act."

I close my eyes, trying to reconcile what they're asking

me to do with the burning need inside me. "How can I walk away from him after everything he's done?"

Lala comes to stand beside me, placing a warm hand on my cheek. "Because you, my dear, know that true power—true magick—comes not from darkness, but from the bonds of trust and friendship. From love."

"He will face Justice," Trello says, nodding toward the Magician. "But it is not your job to serve it. It's mine."

She holds out her own sword, touching it to the Magician's shoulder. The act seems to shake him from his grief and stupor, and he looks up suddenly, his eyes alight with new fire.

New hatred.

Trello and Lala exchange a glance, the air crackling with magick and meaning.

He climbs to his feet and backs up against the wall. Trello is still holding the sword, but he's not concerned with her.

Right now, he only has eyes for our High Priestess.

"Eulala," he says. His voice is ice cold, but his eyes flicker with warmth and familiarity. With longing, even.

It's only now that I remember their long-lost connection. Lala once described him as her beloved. *In a former iteration... Well, he was actually a she then. And she was my beloved, Starla. Not in this body or time, but in another, many centuries ago.*

"It is time to end this, beloved," she says now, her tone sad and soft. Goddess, I can't even imagine how much pain she's in.

"You call me beloved as if you still honor our bond," he scoffs. "As if you didn't turn your back on me the moment I reincarnated into a form you didn't like."

Lala shakes her head, her patience unwavering. In her eyes, I see a thousand years of heartbreak. "I will love and honor you for eternity, no matter whose form you inhabit, no matter what color your eyes are as you gaze upon me, no matter the shade of your skin or the shape of your body. But I will *not* stand by and let you destroy magick. Destroy life."

The Magician lowers his head, shame coloring his tear-stained cheeks.

For a minute, I almost feel sorry for him. I almost wish I could help him.

Almost.

"It's over," Trello says softly, lowering her sword. "You have broken our laws, and you must be held accountable for your—"

"She's mine!" he bellows, and in a blur, he leaps away from the wall, both hands raised, his eyes fixed on me, full of hatred and death. The flash of a curved, palm-sized blade is the last thing I see.

Before I can even raise my Sword to defend myself, Anna jumps in front of me, shielding me from the blow.

His blade slices through her neck in an instant.

A scream rips through the darkness as she falls to the floor, but it's not Anna's voice.

It's mine.

I drop to my knees and scoop her into my arms, but it's

too late. I can feel her life force leaving, her blood soaking my hands.

Seconds later, she vanishes, leaving only a dark pool of blood behind.

"Put down the blade," Lala says to the Dark Magician, her tone firm. Her horror washes over me, but she's focused on her former beloved now, desperate to diffuse him before he kills another one of us.

But for him, it's like she's not even there.

"I told you to come back with a better offer, Starla," he sneers, his blade dripping with Anna's blood.

She saved me. Anna Trello—Justice, my parents' oldest friend, the woman who promised my mother she'd keep me safe at all costs—took the death blow that was meant for me.

"I told you I'd be waiting for you," he says.

I nod. Take a deep breath. Nod again.

Inside me, the dark fire surges back to life. Consuming. Demanding.

The Sword is on the ground at my side, and I grip it tight, relishing in the power that surges up my arm.

"You did," I say. Then, with everything I've got left, I jump to my feet and shove the blade into his chest. "And I told you, *fuckface*, wait for your death."

Lala sucks in a sharp breath of surprise, but she makes no move to pull me away now. No utterances about love and light.

I reach out for her energy, expecting to feel shame and disappointment. Anger, even.

But I find only acceptance. And there, shimmering just beneath it, a hint of pride.

"Light and shadow," I whisper, parroting the Dark Magician's words. "That is our interplay."

He sucks in a wet, pained breath and stumbles backward into the wall, but I'm not letting him get away so easily. The darkness rages inside me, and I welcome it now. I follow him, twisting the blade deeper.

"For my parents," I say, my voice unwavering. "Connor and Melissa Milan." Another twist. "For Luke Hernandez, and the pain his death has caused his mother, Rita." One more, this time with a swift jerk upward, making him sputter. "For Anna Trello, Justice Arcana, Trump Eleven and Headmistress of Arcana Academy." Another twist, and the flame inside me grows brighter. Hotter. "For *all* the witches and mages you sacrificed. Their deaths were not in vain. And unlike you, they *will* be remembered, honored, and cherished."

"But…" he wheezes, his eyes going glassy. "I… I… I—"

"*I* am the Star," I say, loud and clear, my earlier helplessness evaporating. "Trump Seventeen of the Major Arcana of the sacred Tarot." I jerk the blade free from his chest and watch him fall to the ground. "And your days of darkening the realms are over."

"But I am…" he pants again, refusing to give up. "I am the One… the Magician… I am…"

"*You* are already forgotten." I toss my Sword onto the table and turn on my heel as he sucks in his last ragged breath.

The dark flame inside me surges once more, then fades, finally sputtering out.

Lala nods solemnly and holds out her hand.

I take it gladly, gratefully, and together we walk out into the light of a better place.

TWENTY-SIX

STEVIE

We walk down a long corridor glowing with tiny lights that look like stars. The walls are such a deep black it feels as though we're walking through outer space.

"Where are you taking me?" I whisper, afraid to speak any louder. Somehow, this place feels sacred—more than any house of worship I've ever been in.

"There's someone I'd like you to see," she says cryptically. "Not much farther now, child."

Nodding, I continue to keep pace, though my limbs are begging me for a hot bath and a long sleep.

It seems like hours before we finally reach our destination—a red door at the end of another starlit corridor. Before she opens it, she turns to me and smiles, her eyes full of sadness and love and ancient wisdom I can't even begin to comprehend.

"Thank you," I say. "For finding me. For helping me. I wasn't sure I'd see you again after Harvest Eve. You told me not all Arcana were meant to fight. I thought…" I trail off, my words tangling into nonsense.

"I did say that," she replies. "But I changed my perspective. As much as you've learned from me, it seems I've learned from you as well."

"What could you possibly learn from me?"

She reaches up and tucks a lock of hair behind my ear, her eyes sparkling. "When the world falls into darkness, we have but two choices. Exist in the darkness, or find a light."

"Or become your own damn light," I add.

"Well… yes! Maybe I should write that one down." Lala laughs, but then her smile fades, her eyes glimmering with new emotion. "Existing in darkness allows darkness to exist. To *persist*. But you… You have been a light to so many, Starla. You helped me realize I still have some light to shine as well."

"More than you realize," I say.

Lala winks, then opens the red door, gesturing for me to go on without her. "It's time."

"Will I see you again?" I ask.

She touches my face and smiles. "Most definitely."

With that, I step over the threshold into another dark room, closing the door behind me. This time, the darkness is so deep and all-encompassing it feels like I'm underwater, shadows pressing in on all sides.

But the air is clear and crisp. And when I take a deep breath, the familiar scent of roses and vanilla mint tea fills me, making my heart squeeze.

"Mom?" I whisper.

Soft, warm hands close over mine, and light fills the room all at once, illuminating a small but well-appointed apartment and the woman standing before me.

"Hello, my Starlight." My mother beams at me, beautiful and whole and perfect.

"Holy shitcakes," I breathe, and we both laugh as we wrap each other in a fierce hug.

When we finally pull back, she looks at me through shining eyes and says, "A wise woman once said, 'there's no problem a proper cup of tea can't fix.' Something tells me you could use a cup."

I nod, struck mute all over again by the sight of her. The feel of her. She's here. Not rambling in incoherent prophecies, but as the mother I remember.

I have no idea how much time we've got, but I'm grateful for even a minute to see her again. To share a cup of tea. To hold her. To tell her all the things I never got to say.

So as she leads me into a small kitchen and puts on the kettle, I do just that.

* * *

"I am so sorry, Stevie," she says, shaking her head over the rim of her teacup. "I never wanted you to see such horrors. But even if I'd seen this unfolding before I had the chance to bring you into this world, I'm afraid I would've made the same choices." She smiles, then drops her gaze. "Selfish. I know. But I fell in love with you long before I ever brought you into this world. And love like that…"

I reach for her hand across the table, squeezing tight. "I know, Mom. I understand."

And I do. Because of my mother, I was born a spirit-blessed Arcana witch with a destiny that led me to the Academy. To the men who cracked my heart open and filled it with so much love, I feel like I can accomplish anything. Do anything. *Be* anything.

She gives me an all-knowing mom smile, and in the warmth that follows, I finally ask the question I've been afraid to ask since I first stepped over that threshold.

"Mom? Where's Dad? Why isn't he here with you?"

A soft sigh escapes. "Your father has actually chosen to return."

"Return? As in, reincarnate?"

Mom nods.

"But… where is he? *Who* is he? Why hasn't he tried to get in touch, or… Does he not remember me?"

She rises from the table and clears away the teacups, setting them in the sink. "I can't answer those questions for you, Stevie. I wish I could, but some mysteries are just too vast to comprehend, even for me."

I bite back a disappointed grumble. "And here I thought my fortune-telling mom knew everything," I tease.

"*Almost* everything." At this, her smile brightens once again. "Come on. There's something I want to show you."

We head back out through the red door and into the endless corridor system. But this time, we reach our destination quickly. It's another red door, which Mom opens without preamble, stepping aside to let me in first.

"A library?" I suck in a sharp breath at the sight that reveals itself before me.

Yes, it's a library, but it's so much more than that.

It's open in the center, not unlike our Academy library. But here, there are so many levels, I can't even see all the way to the very top. Shelves upon shelves stretch up toward the sky, with gleaming golden staircases spiraling up to each one. All around us, witches and mages scurry about, pulling down books and artifacts and ancient scrolls that look like they must hold the secrets of the entire world.

And every few seconds, the entire library seems to expand, rearranging itself.

"This is the sacred Hall of Mist and Spirit," Mom says. "An ever-growing, ever-changing library and living monument to magick and all who study, honor, and protect it."

"But... but this place is *massive*. I can't believe there's so much stuff written about Tarot."

"Oh, this isn't just for Tarot magick. The Hall of Mist and Spirit holds the records of every magickal system known to witch- and mage-kind, across the boundaries of all time."

I don't even know what to say to that. It's so beautiful, so incredible, my eyes fill with tears, just like they did the first time I saw the library at the Academy.

"Kirin would love this place," I whisper.

"Perhaps you'll show him one day."

I grin at the thought of seeing his Genius Boy eyes light

up. "I'm not sure I'd ever get him to leave. But… how did you even find this place? Is this, like, some kind of Arcana nirvana?"

"I discovered it in a dream," she explains, her voice breathy and full of wonder. "And I was never the same again. I taught myself how to lucid dream just so I could return. On one visit, I discovered the book."

"Journey Through the Void of Mist and Spirit," I say without hesitation, and Mom nods. "I had a feeling that book wasn't from our world."

"It was and it wasn't," she says. "Think of it as a repository of sacred knowledge. This library is a living, breathing entity. There are no librarians to keep its shelves, no authors to write its books. The knowledge here… it just *arrives*. The magick itself decides what is kept and what is not, what is revealed and to whom, when it must fade into the recesses of memory or legend."

"So the library itself… the magick… it decided to let you take the book out of your dream and into our realm?"

"After many, many visits with it here in the library, yes. It finally allowed itself to accompany me back to our realm."

"But what about the other book?" I ask. "The one Kelly Maddox gave me?"

Mom runs a hand over my hair. "*That* one was always meant for you."

She leads me to a shelf on the first floor and plucks out a book. The moment she hands it over, I know it's the exact same book as the one Kelly gave me.

"But... how?" I ask.

"Everything that exists here will always exist here. But because I brought it out, it also exists in the material realm. It's hard to explain, but it's a bit like the realms themselves."

"Like soap bubbles," I say. "Overlapping."

"Exactly." She flashes that knowing smirk again. "I find its best not to overthink such things. Too much knowledge dulls the mystery."

"Okay, but *some* knowledge might be good." I run my fingers over the book's spine. "I mean, you say this is meant for me, but I can't even read it. It's like a foreign language."

"You *couldn't* read it," she says. "But I suspect you'll find that's no longer the case."

At her prompting, I flip through the pages, shocked to see the passages coming to life at my touch. Words scroll across the page in bright, golden fire, then settle into the parchment in black, as clear as any textbook or novel I've read.

It's magickal gibberish, but at least it's in English. The individual words make sense, which means eventually, I've got a shot at cracking the code.

"I feel like I've just leveled up," I say.

"This book, once you've learned to decipher its mysteries, will teach you how to access the Hall of Mist and Spirit through your own dreams. I won't always be here when you visit, but there's a good chance we'll cross paths again."

I clutch the book to my chest, its magick radiating right

through me. "I can't believe I have so much power. It scares me, Mom. It really does."

Her brows knit, and she considers me for a long moment before speaking again. When she finally does, her voice is hushed and reverent. "Yes, you have power, Stevie. More than any of us ever thought possible—even the Dark Magician himself. But you also have a decision to make— one that will set the course of your entire existence as the Star Arcana."

I close my eyes, sensing what comes next.

"Will you remain here as I have done, dedicating your existence to exploring the mysteries of life and magick? Or will you return to your realm and your Arcana brothers, dedicating yourself to protecting this sacred magick and setting the world to rights again?"

I close my eyes, the choices weighing heavy on my heart. I feel like I just got my mother back, and staying here with her would be an honor and a dream come true.

But I can't imagine life without my Arcana mages. The love I feel for them... no. Leaving them is not an option. And beyond that, I *want* to make the world a better place. To shine that light. To help others find their own lights.

I remember Anna Trello's words from the night she told me about my magickal origins.

You can unite the Arcana objects and reclaim magick for the witches and mages who seek to honor it. You have the power to unite the Light Arcana in the battle against the coming darkness. And when the rest of the world wants to give up, to lay down their arms and walk away from this fight, you have the power to inspire hope. To give us all a reason to keep living. To keep loving. To keep fighting, no matter what the cost.

She was right. And even though we defeated the Dark Arcana and their undead army, the world still isn't safe for us. Not with groups like the Soldiers of Light running rampant and the human authorities looking for any excuse to lock us up—or worse.

Goddess, there is still so much work to be done.

I open my eyes and look at my kind, compassionate, beautiful mother, knowing what has to come next.

Mom knows it too.

"I have a good life, Mom," I assure her, sensing she needs to hear it. "You made sure of that."

My mother's eyes fill with tears, but a calm acceptance settles over her, smoothing the lines around her mouth, lifting the invisible weight from her shoulders.

For so many years, her soul was restless, chasing after prophecies even in death, trying to outrun the future she set in motion when she made the deal with the Dark Magician to give me life.

Now, the World can finally close this chapter. She can finally find her peace.

"I guess that leaves only one question," I say, my stomach filling with butterflies at the thought of seeing my mages again. Goddess, it feels like an eternity since I last held them in my arms, and suddenly I can't wait to get home. "How the hell do I get out of here?"

* * *

Clasping my mother's hands above the silver candle at her kitchen table, I let out a grateful sigh. "I've been dreaming about this day since the moment I first learned you were a witch."

"What day?" she teases. "Meeting my ghost in an other-worldly realm after killing the Dark Magician bent on the complete destruction of witch-kind?"

"Um… no." I roll my eyes. "Casting a spell with you, Mom."

Mom laughs. Goddess, how I missed the sound of it.

"Me too, love. Me too." With one last deep, cleansing breath, she squeezes my hands and says, "Let's get to it, then."

She closes her eyes, and I follow suit, sending her my magick, my love, my light.

"Oh, Starlight," she whispers. "My sweet girl. I couldn't be more proud."

Then, in a soft, melodic chant, my mother weaves her spell.

The World brings an end, a journey complete
And thus begins another
The light of the Star will carry you home
Returning you to your brothers

Through love and joy and light you'll lead
To help them through their pain
And in your heart you'll keep me close
Until we meet again

She chants the spell three times, her voice growing quieter and quieter until I can barely hear the breath of her words. On the last recitation, she repeats the final line over and over until her voice fades away.

Until we meet again. Until we meet again. Until we meet again...

Her touch leaves my hands.

Her scent leaves my awareness.

The darkness envelops me once again.

When consciousness finally dawns, I'm shivering in the mud, and a familiar voice echoes across the mist, setting my heart on fire.

"Cass!" Baz cries out. "Here! She's here!"

TWENTY-SEVEN

BAZ

We find her face down in the mud at the top of the cliff, right at the edge of the Void, shivering in a hideous white dress.

Anna Trello's lifeless body lies next to her, blood soaking her clothes.

All four Arcana objects are scattered on the ground between them.

I can't even begin to understand what happened.

Crouching down next to Stevie, I run my hands over her body, checking for injuries. Other than a few minor scrapes and cuts, she seems unharmed.

"Baz," she breathes, stirring to life at my touch.

I damn near break down into a hot mess of tears. I've never been so fucking relieved to hear my name.

"I got you, Little Bird." I scoop her into my arms and get to my feet. "I got you."

Cass kneels beside Anna, his face pale and gaunt. After a long moment, he says, "She deserved better."

None of us can argue with that. For all Anna Trello's faults, in the end, she was an ally—maybe even a friend. That much is obvious.

Without another word, Cass picks her up. Kirin and Ani gather up the Arcana objects, securing everything in the pack.

And then it's finally time to leave this place.

I'm about to portal us out when a soft murmur against my chest stops me. "The Arcana objects," Stevie says, so quiet I have to strain to hear her.

"Already packed up," I assure her. "Kirin's got—"

"No," she says. "We can't take them."

"So what do we do?" I ask. "Toss them back into the Void? Take them back to the Fool's Grave?"

She reaches up and touches my face, fixing me with a determined, don't-fuck-with-me stare that would have a lesser man pissing his pants.

Then, in a voice much stronger than it was only seconds ago, she says, "We have to destroy them."

* * *

Standing in a circle back at the spiral caves, the five of us stare down at the objects assembled between us. Each one pulses with blue light.

The Sword of Breath and Blade.

The Wand of Flame and Fury.

The Chalice of Blood and Sorrow.

The Pentacle of Iron and Bone.

For millennia, they were hunted, chased all over the globe by so many people on so many wasted expeditions, eventually they faded into legend.

But we found them. The most powerful, most magickal, most valuable artifacts our kind has ever known.

And now she wants to obliterate them.

"Stevie," Cass says for the hundredth time, "are you sure about this?"

She nods emphatically. Wrapped in Kirin's hoodie, trail mix dotting the front of it from her hasty meal, she looks much healthier now than when we found her. It's almost as if this mission has given her new life.

I've never seen her so adamant.

"The magick of the Arcana was a gift from the original elemental beings," she says. "It belongs to *all* witches and mages. We lost sight of that over time, but the truth is, these objects are just that—objects. And as long as they exist, they'll always be hunted, and so will we."

Ani sighs, casting a longing glance at the Wand. "But their power—"

"It's symbolic, guys," she insists. "That's all. They're powerful because the First Fool and the Elemental Beings made them so. But that power? That magick? It's the same exact stuff that runs through the veins of every witch and mage in existence. It doesn't belong solely to the Light Arcana any more than it did the Dark. It belongs to *all* witches and mages—to anyone who wishes to understand it. And we don't need these symbols to make it so."

Her blue eyes shine bright in her mud-streaked face, her voice firm and clear. A soft white light seems to glow from within her, illuminating her.

Whatever happened in the Void, it changed her.

My heart thuds against my ribs. My love for her is damn near overpowering.

"I agree," I say. "Stevie's right. These things are relics. It's time to let them go."

She beams at me across the circle.

I beam back.

Goddess, I fucking *adore* that woman.

After only a moment's hesitation, the other mages finally agree.

We pass an athame around, slicing our palms and spilling our blood onto the ground. Then, clasping hands, we recite the words that have come to mean more to me than any promise I've ever made, any vow I've ever sworn.

"Who gathers here as bonded brothers?" Cass asks, his voice a clarion call through the mist.

The rest of us respond as one: "We, the Keepers of the Grave."

"Who spills his blood as a symbol of our commitment to one another and in the service and protection of the First?"

"We, the Keepers of the Grave."

"Who vows, by his life or his death, by his silence or his words, in this and all incarnations henceforth, to protect the one true source?"

"We, the Keepers of the Grave."

"We, the Keepers of the Grave," he says, his last word echoing.

Gazing down at the objects, we call upon our magick once more, our shared power coursing through us, our intention set.

Suddenly, the objects begin to glow brighter, vibrating against the earth with a deep hum.

"Now!" Cass shouts, and together we recite the spell.

> *By Star, Sun, and Moon, by Devil and Tower*
> *Now is the end of your limitless power*
> *What magick first made, what magick first bound*
> *Return to the earth, by magick unwound*

An explosion of heat and pure, golden light bursts forth, knocking us all onto our asses.

By the time the light fades away and we scramble back to our feet, the once-revered Arcana objects are gone.

We stare at the blackened patch of earth for a long moment, no one speaking. No one moving.

After what feels like an entire day, Stevie finally breaks the silence.

"Okay, then. Done and done." With a bright grin and a cute shrug, she dusts off her hands and tosses her hair over her shoulder. "Now there's just one thing left to do."

I haul her into my arms, pinning her in a tight hug. She's my fucking queen, and there's nothing I won't do for her. I don't have to ask to know my brothers feel the same.

"Name it, Little Bird. Whatever you ask, it's already yours."

She lays her head on my chest, her ear pressed to my heart, and lets out a sigh of deep contentment. "Take me the *fuck* home."

TWENTY-EIGHT

STEVIE

One month later...

We've just returned to the house at Red Sands after our thirty-ninth on-campus funeral, and there are still so many more to come. So many more lives to honor and remember. So many more tears to shed.

They're calling it the Battle for Arcana Academy, and it stole the lives of one hundred and seven of our Academy witches and mages.

One hundred and seven. It's a number that will live on in our hearts forever.

One hundred and seven lives. One hundred and seven students and faculty. Staff. Best friends and sisters and cousins, sons and daughters, mentors, lovers.

All of them are heroes who died fighting by our side, sacrificing themselves to end the Dark Arcana's brief but brutal reign in a war many of them hadn't even heard about. One minute, it was just an outlandish rumor. The next, it was bashing down their doors, forcing them to take up magickal arms against impossibly strong enemies.

The Academy wasn't the only place to suffer casualties, either. Though we were the only ones directly attacked by the Dark Arcana and the undead armies, the Soldiers of Light were busy wreaking havoc in cities and towns across the globe. While none of them unleashed an attack as widespread and devastating as the one in Ani's hometown, *no* witches and mages were safe from their cruelty.

As of now, the death toll outside our boundaries is still unknown, largely because the authorities are loath to admit their failings in protecting their own citizens. But when that number comes through, it will live on in our hearts with the others.

They will live on.

In the wake of the devastating attacks, we find solace in this accounting. This remembrance. It's up to us now—the survivors—to carry on the legacy of the dead, ensuring that the lives of *all* witches and mages will somehow be better.

It's a tall order. And most days, I'm still not sure we can see it through.

But we have to try.

In the Hall of Remembrance, we've lit an eternal flame of witchfire to honor the fallen—a silver flame that calls us back for every funeral and reminds us of our implicit promise—that no matter how difficult it seems, *yes*, we have to try.

Most of the dead were returned to their families—a

small kindness in the midst of their endless despair. But we buried Anna Trello on the grounds of the Academy she so loved—the place she gave up everything to protect.

I visit her grave every Friday, bringing her a bouquet of yellow roses from Mom and keeping her up to date on our progress here—the rebuilding efforts. The healing. The new friendships and bonds formed over the darkest days, ushering us into the light. Whenever I'm with her, I think of Mom's prophecy—the one I now know was meant for Anna.

> *Fear not the evasive Queen of Air*
> *Though her manner is coarse, her outcome is fair*
> *By thought or by deed, by word or by blade*
> *Her sacrifice can't be unmade*

The last two lines are carved into her headstone.

Dozens of students are still in the infirmary, the healing mages and witches of the Academy working tirelessly to care for them. I try to help out when I can, recreating different forms of the healing spell I performed on Doc in the caves. It's an imperfect science, but I'm getting stronger every day.

Thanks to Professor Broome and several other potions and healing arts teachers, they finally crafted an effective spell to return the siphoned magick to its original owners. Unfortunately, the same dark magick Professor Phaines used to steal it in the first place was also deployed else-where, neutering thousands of mages and witches world-wide. APOA is working on locating the missing essences, but it's very likely a lot of them were destroyed in the Soldiers of Light attacks.

We may never know the true cost of this war.

I'm told that in the ensuing chaos after the fall of the undead army—after Ani returned to himself and the Black Sun vanished, no longer calling them to rise—Eastman and his mages were quickly captured. Many of the mages chose to end their own lives rather than face justice, but Eastman was taken alive. Casey and Quintana escorted him back to APOA headquarters in London, where he's currently facing charges of sedition, domestic terrorism, and murder, among other things.

He's maintaining his innocence, sticking to the story that he really *was* trying to protect us, but the evidence is pretty damning. In the days that followed, we found most of the material stolen from the archives in his possession, including my mother's research and his own conspiracy-theory, rabbit-hole findings about magick causing the downfall of society as we know it.

Personally, I hope he rots in hell. Or in prison, with Janelle Kirkpatrick. I heard she's not loving life these days either.

Despite the capture of Eastman and many of the mages following his lead, the outside world is still not safe for witches and mages. APOA has contracted Kirin to help draft legislation that would eradicate the registry of magickal humans and categorize all crimes against witches and mages as hate crimes punishable to the fullest extent of the law.

But as challenging as it is to change legislation, it's even more difficult to change hearts and minds. Eastman and the Soldiers of Light lit the fuse on a powder keg of hatred and anti-magick violence that dates back centuries.

Millennia.

Yes, we defeated the enemy, and in some ways, justice will be served.

But the work of defeating their ideology is just beginning.

As for the Dark Arcana, we believe we've defeated them as well. But even with the Arcana objects destroyed, we have no idea whether the Dark One will rise again some-day, reincarnated and ready to champion some other terrible cause.

Will it happen in our lifetime?

There are no answers. No timelines. No guarantees.

But the day after that brutal battle, when the first rays of a new dawn illuminated the sky, that was it for us. Day one in a brand-new world. And every day since then, we've been doing what we can to bring the Academy back to life. Through a mix of magick, hard work, and a deep commit-ment to honor the fallen, we're rebuilding the classrooms and dorms and offices. Repaving the pathways. Replanting the trees and flowers. Breathing life into the shadow of death.

When I first enrolled at the Academy, they said I'd be alternating houses, living in different dorms in accordance

SARAH PIPER

with my magickal affinities so I could learn from other students. But the rules have changed now, the old traditions making way for the new. I fully intend to embrace and strengthen *all* my magickal gifts, taking extra classes, reading all the books, immersing myself in this world I've only just begun to explore.

But as for the place I call home? The guys and I have permanently moved to the house at Red Sands Canyon—the place that's felt more like home than any other since I left the trailer I once shared with Jessa. After everything we've been through together, there's no way we're splitting up now. My love for them is... *Goddess*, the words to describe the depths of my feelings don't even exist. And their loyalty toward one another? Forget it—*no* one's coming between those boys.

It's the same for Carly and her hot-girl squad. She's moved into the house next door with Nat and Isla. Emory and Blue—the other Claires—are slowly coming back into the fold too, and the girls are considering inviting them to move into the house.

It seems the horrors of war have changed a lot of people's perspectives, softening some once-sharp edges.

Still, despite our deepening bonds, Ani has been harder to reach. He crashed after the battle, all the euphoria at our survival quickly evaporating in the wake of his own pain. He's distant now, still reeling from everything Dark Judgment put him through.

Physically, he's dealing with some latent effects from his dream-potion overdose—headaches, mostly, and difficulty concentrating. But it's the emotional toll I'm more worried about now—all the guilt and shame over what the Black Sun did.

In the pale hours before dawn, that endless stretch they call the witching hour, I often find him in his bed, thrashing from some new nightmare. Each time it happens, I crawl beneath the blankets and hold him close, rubbing his back and singing softly until he falls back asleep.

The first few times, he was so embarrassed and uncomfortable in the mornings, I could literally feel his shame. Now I leave before the sun rises, sparing him the awkwardness of talking about it.

Outside of those dark, silent nights in his bed, me holding him while he trembles and heaves, we haven't spent any time alone together. Haven't held each other's gaze for more than a brief smile as we pass each other in the hallway or take turns doing dishes after one of the girls' epic gourmet feasts.

The darkness in his energy is nearly enough to drown out everything else. He doesn't want to hurt me. Doesn't want to see his own shame reflected in my eyes. He thinks it's better to avoid me altogether than to face the rejection he's so certain I'll give him.

There's a gulf a thousand miles wide between us, and I know he's not going to be the one to cross it. If I want him back, it has to be me.

And so it comes to this day, exactly one month after the Battle for Arcana Academy, exactly one hour after our thirty-ninth funeral, that I finally extend an invitation. I don't give him any advance notice. Just waltz into his bedroom and offer him a headlamp, a backpack full of camping gear, a travel mug full of his favorite Sex with a Caramel brew, and a soft smile.

"Please come," I whisper.

Ani doesn't say yes—he doesn't say a word, actually—and in the aching silence that stretches between us, my heart falters. My brain races to try to find the right thing to say—the thing that will take away the obvious discomfort brewing in his eyes.

I hate that I'm causing him more pain.

I hate that I don't know how to reach him.

I hate that he didn't say yes.

Don't worry about it. It was just an idea. The weather probably won't be that great tonight anyway. Raincheck?

But before I can utter a single stupid word, he's slinging the pack over his shoulder and reaching for my hand, the softest glimmer of that old smile peeking out like the sunrise scattering the fog.

TWENTY-NINE

STEVIE

"I'm glad you came," I say. "I felt like we haven't hung out at all since…"

Since the world nearly ended.

Since the monsters almost took you away from me.

Since I last saw the light in your beautiful, melted-caramel eyes…

"I know." Ani lets out a deep sigh. "I'm sorry. I just…"

His voice is thick with emotion, and after a few more failed attempts at finding the right words, he gives up, turning his attention back to the trail ahead.

We walk on in silence, taking our time as we plod up toward the top of the Cauldron of Flame and Fury.

The first time we made this hike, we were still in the friend zone, and over a picnic lunch of Chinese food, I begged Ani for advice about my dueling feelings for Kirin and Baz.

Not long after that, we got the email from Anna Trello about Danika Lewis's televised execution.

Goddess, so much has changed since then.

I shake away the old thoughts, realizing I've fallen behind on the trail.

"You don't have to say anything, Ani," I say, jogging to catch up. "I'm just happy to spend time with you. I can talk enough for both of us. Or sing. Or…" The breath leaves me in a nervous rush. "Or I could just zip it and give you a little peace and quiet. Goddess, you'd think I'd learn how to read the room by now, what with my empathic gifts and all. I'm sorry. I'm just—"

"Stevie." He grabs my hand and stops, turning to me with the barest of smiles. "I like it when you talk. I missed it."

"Yeah?"

"Your voice was the soundtrack that got me through some of the darkest days of my life. I will *never* get tired of it. Never. In fact, I'd really love it if you'd just keep talking. About anything. Just… anything."

I take a deep breath, basking in the glow of his smile, however faint. "Okay, I can do that. How about I tell you everything you never wanted to know about brewing tea?"

"I would *love* for you to tell me everything I never wanted to know about brewing tea." He presses a kiss to my cheek, his energy washing through me.

Gratitude. Love. Shame. Fear. All of it.

But one thing is certain. He really *does* want me to talk. Maybe he just needs the distraction, but that's fine. Like I said, as long as we're together, I don't care who's doing the talking.

So I start in on the tea. And slowly, step by step, we make our way.

I've just transitioned from black teas to greens when we spot a familiar sight drifting overhead.

"Looks like we've got a hitchhiker," Ani says.

I wave at Jareth, but he seems content to ignore us for now.

"He's just making sure we're okay," I say. "My little guardian owl. He's quite protective."

Ani surprises me by dropping my hand and putting his arm around me instead. "Relatable."

"Yeah?"

"Yeah."

The trail turns steeper, and by the time we reach the top, we're both huffing and puffing.

"Remind me again why you didn't want to take the air bikes up?" he says.

I flash him a wide grin. "Because pushing ourselves to the brink of exhaustion is all part of the experience."

"I'm going to remember you said that," he teases, this time kissing me on the lips. It's short and sweet, but still. Progress.

"You get us set up," he says. "I'll find some wood for the fire."

Half an hour later, the blankets and sleeping bags are set up, and we're sitting on them side by side before a small campfire, the wood hissing and popping.

The sun has set, casting the top of the Cauldron in shadow. It's a near moonless night, and overhead, the stars are just beginning to peek out.

The silence is stretching between us again. I've run out of tea topics.

And I've got nothing left to say but what really matters.

I reach for his hand, holding it tight. "I love you, Ani. I need you to know that. I love you so much that just being with you makes my heart feel full and whole in a way I never thought possible before I met you."

I feel the pulse of his love, but he doesn't speak. Not for a long, long while.

By the time he utters a word, the fire has dimmed to glowing embers.

I'm still holding his hand when he whispers, "Why?"

He turns to me and holds my gaze, his own heavy with sadness, and I know he's not fishing for compliments. It's like he truly doesn't understand why I care about him so much.

"You were my friend first and foremost," I say. "One of the first friends I made on campus. You pushed me out of my comfort zone in the best way. You made me feel cared for and safe. And above all, you always made me laugh. From the very start, you had me cracking up at a time when I didn't have all that much to smile about."

I smile at him now, but it doesn't seem to penetrate his sadness.

In a dark, heavy tone, he says, "I really wish I could be that guy for you again, Stevie. The one who cracks jokes and pulls off pranks and puts that sparkle in your eyes with no more than a witty comeback." He brushes his fingers across my cheek and smiles, but his eyes are full of pain. When he speaks again, his voice is a broken whisper. "More than *anything*, I wish I could be him. But that guy is dead. *I'm* dead. That's how it feels when you tell me these things. It's like you're talking about someone else—someone I barely even remember."

"No," I say, my heart breaking for him. "You asked me why I love you, but the truth is, I can't put it into words like a list. It goes beyond words. Beyond anything I can consciously express. Those things I mentioned? They're just facets of you, Ani. A handful of so many, many things that make you who you are."

"Who *am* I, though? I don't even know anymore."

His pain is strong enough to make me ache.

"Ani. *Ansel*." I take his face between my hands, still holding his gaze. "You're the man I fell in love with. The man I want to build a life with. You're my family. *Our* family."

He doesn't believe me. I can feel it in his energy. He's so closed off and ashamed, there's no room inside him for this truth.

Breaking away from my touch, he glances out across the rim. Other than the soft glow cast by our dwindling fire, there's no light on the rocks. Only darkness.

"There was a time when I could give you the sunrise," he says. "And now—"

"And now I'm giving *you* the stars." I take his hand and

lean back onto the blankets, tugging him down with me. He doesn't resist.

When we're both settled on our backs, we look up at the night sky. It's a riot of stars, an explosion that glitters from here to eternity.

"Wow," he breathes.

"Told you." I nudge his arm, and a tiny laugh escapes his lips.

I lace our fingers together and let the silence drift between us again. There's so much more I need to say—so much more he needs to know.

Goddess, why is this so hard?

I close my eyes, feeling the weight of the dead on my chest.

"I need to tell you something," I say softly, knowing I can't put it off any longer. "It's about what happened in California."

He stiffens beside me, but I feel the curiosity in his energy.

I swallow through the knot in my throat, forcing myself to say the words, because no matter how painful this is, Ani deserves to know. "Casey was able to access the list of… the names. The people who died. Your mother and your… The man who raised you… they're dead, Ani. It's been confirmed."

The air rushes from his lungs. "And my—"

"No," I say, already knowing what he's going to ask. I turn onto my hip, placing my hand over his heart. Beneath it, I hold the small card Casey gave me. There's a phone number written on one side, an address on the other. "Your sister wasn't in California at the time of the attack. She was visiting a friend in New York, and she's staying there now." I slip the card into his shirt pocket. "You can get in touch with her if you want to. Or not—it's totally up to you. I just wanted you to know she's alive, and you have a choice."

"Thank you," he whispers. "I—"

It's all he can get out before his throat closes up. He turns away from me and rolls onto his side. Soft sobs wrack his body. It reminds me of the nightmares.

There are no words to make this better for him, to take away his pain, and I've never felt so helpless.

Worse? I know this is just the beginning. There will be more nights like this one. More nightmares. More guilt. More trauma revisited. More pain.

We spend our lives running from ghosts—not because we can actually escape them, but because it makes us feel like we're doing something in the face of utter helplessness. But running, no matter how hard it feels, is actually the easy part.

It's when the ghosts finally catch up to you—and they always do—and you've got no choice but to face them head on. That's when the real work starts.

"What should I do?" Ani whispers, his shoulders still shaking.

"I can't answer that for you. But whatever you decide? That'll be the right answer, Ani. And I've got your back."

"How can I face her, though? I murdered her parents. I murdered a *lot* of people's parents. So many innocents and... Goddess, how do I move on from this? How do I justify getting out of bed every day, knowing thousands of people *can't*, because I killed them? Or because I killed the people they loved, and now they don't think life is worth living?" He turns over to face me again, his eyes shining in the darkness. "All of that is on me. All of it. I don't know how to live with it. And you... Goddess, Stevie." He cups my face. "I hate that I hurt you. Every time I look into your eyes, I remember that night in Red Sands—the things I said to you. The things I did to you. And I hate myself for it."

He's talking about the night we—well, the Black Sun and I—slept together.

Every last reassurance rushes to the tip of my tongue, but I know they won't do a damned bit of good. In the face of so much pain, those words sound like mere platitudes.

"I won't tell you it wasn't you," I say softly. "I know you've heard that enough times these past few weeks. But if there's just one thing I can say to you—one thing to hold on to—know this: You are *loved*, Ani. Cherished. And you deserve every bit of that love. Mine, Kirin's, Baz's, Doc's, and the love of all our friends. You mean everything to us, and we're not letting you go."

"But... why? How can you say that after everything I've done?"

"I told you—we're family now. And our family doesn't work without you. It just doesn't. So you take as long as you need—take time, space, whatever. Just know that we're here. Always. And nothing is going to change that."

He closes his eyes and draws me close, his lips brushing

mine in the softest, sweetest kiss. After a minute, he deepens it, his tongue coaxing my lips apart, sliding inside my mouth with a soft moan.

My toes curl, my insides heating up. I missed him so much. His touch. His kiss. All of it.

His kiss turns more passionate, slowly moving down my jaw to my throat. Silently, he undoes the buttons on my flannel, his mouth trailing behind his fingers, leaving hot kisses on my bared flesh.

It's not long before we're both tearing each other's clothes off, suddenly desperate to get closer.

As close as we possibly can.

Naked on top of our blankets, we snuggle together, my leg draped over his hip, his cock pressing hard against my belly.

"Are you okay?" he whispers, and I nod, nipping at his lower lip.

"As long as you keep kissing me, I'm more than okay," I say.

He leans in close, pulling me in for another deep kiss.

For a minute, it seems like he might be relaxing. Enjoying himself, even. But then he stops, his whole body going still. Hand gripping my bare hip, he says, "Our first time together... It should've been different."

A shudder claims him, a wave of his regret rushing hot and prickly over my skin.

"That wasn't our first time, Ani. *This* is." I reach for his cock, stroking him gently, kissing his neck until I feel him relax again. "And I wouldn't have it any other way."

"No?" he breathes.

"No. It's already perfect."

He pulls back again, but this time it's with a smile. Cradling my face in his hands, he whispers, *"You're perfect."*

He rolls me onto my back and climbs on top, pinning me with his body, enveloping me in his warmth.

Everything about this moment is different from that night at Red Sands. It's just me and my Sun, exactly as he should be. Pure and real. Broken, imperfect, lost—but still holding a little spark of that thing that connects us all, heart to heart, soul to soul, magick to magick.

Hope.

Propped up on his elbows, he reaches for my face, holding it like he still can't believe I'm real. I part my thighs, and he slides between them, filling me.

The moment he's inside me, a sense of utter rightness falls between us. I feel the shift in his emotions, a subtle unwinding as he takes a deep breath and lets it out slow. I start to arch my hips, eager to bring him in deeper, but Ani shakes his head.

"Not yet," he whispers against my lips. "Just... just let me hold you for a minute."

"Anything," I breathe.

"I need to say something." He kisses me once, then pulls back, his gaze sweeping my face, settling on my eyes. "You brought me back. You fought for me when I didn't even have the strength to fight for myself, and you brought me back."

"It was never even a question. I told you—you're my family. I'll always bring you back."

Ani smiles, his eyes shining with wonder. "I love you. With everything I have and everything I am, I *love* you, Stevie."

Nodding, I reach up and cup his tear-streaked face, feeling the warmth of that love flooding through me.

His hips roll, and he slides in deeper. He holds my gaze, never once looking away. Not even when we're both panting. Not even when the fire dies completely and the chill sets in. Not even when the tingling starts in my core, a spark that ignites into a flame, slowly working its way through my limbs.

"Ani," I breathe, still locked in his fierce gaze. But the night sky wavers above me, making way for a new vision.

I'm used to getting glimpses of their essences when we're together—Doc's moonlit ocean, Baz's forbidden meadow, the storm-ravaged landscape of Kirin's tower.

But tonight, the vision I see with Ani isn't just *his* Arcana essence.

It's ours.

Together, we wade into the lake before my standing stones, but rather than the stars overhead, it's the sun that graces our bare skin.

He crashes against me in another bruising kiss, sliding in faster and harder. Deeper.

The orgasm finally takes hold, that flame exploding into a sudden inferno. My body clenches around him, driving him over the final edge. He moans into my mouth, and I dig my nails into his back, riding out the waves of pleasure. Of heat. Of love.

The vision finally recedes, leaving us back on the rim of the Cauldron beneath a blanket of endless stars.

Ani smiles at me, and I gaze up into his melted-caramel eyes and I know. I just know.

Nothing will ever break this bond.

THIRTY

STEVIE

The sun rises over the canyon in a brilliant blaze, illuminating the far side of the rim in a dazzling light show of reds and golds. It's so beautiful, it almost hurts to look at.

But I indulge anyway. Life's too short not to appreciate nature's beauty, right?

Ani's already packing up camp, his jaw set in a firm line as he repacks the bags. For a minute I worry he might be freaked out about last night, but when he notices me stirring, his eyes turn soft and warm, his smile almost as bright as the sun.

Now that's *a sight so beautiful it almost hurts to look at...*

"And there she is, ladies and gentleman," he says, sounding more like his old self than I've heard in a long time. "Rivaling the very dawn with her smile."

"Funny, I was just thinking the same thing about you."

He pretends to preen. "Must be my new whitening toothpaste."

"Yeah, that's it."

Bending down to steal a kiss, he says, "How did you sleep?"

"For the first time in forever, I can honestly say I slept like…" I pat the rock beneath me, my smile stretching ear to ear.

"Any dreams?"

"Not a single one. And let me tell you… It was *glorious*."

He helps me to my feet, then hands over the travel mug. "I made you some tea. It's *probably* not as good as yours, but I wanted to get back on the trail as soon as possible."

I take a cautious sip, grateful it's at least passable. "What's the rush? I thought we'd hike around to the other side of the rim—take the long way home."

"No can do, Stevie Boo Boo." He taps me on the nose and winks. "I promised Cass I'd have you back before breakfast."

"Hmm. Are the girls cooking again? Because if so, we may want to grab some to-go stuff from Broken Yolks. Last weekend, the so-called Hot Girl Squad drank all the mimosas before they even started cooking, passed out with the bacon sizzling on the stove, and damn near burned the house down."

Ani laughs. "No, the girls aren't cooking. This is… something else."

I narrow my eyes at him. "What are you plotting, Gingersnap? I'm not sure I like the sound of this."

"I've said too much already." He presses a final kiss to

my lips, then shoos me back toward the blankets. "Get those packed up. No time to waste."

Not wanting to miss a moment of a smile whose absence I've endured for far too long, I obey.

* * *

The air bikes are right where we left them at the bottom of the canyon, and we hop on and make our way back through campus. But rather than turning toward the portals that will take us back to Red Sands Canyon and the epic breakfast I've now set my heart on regardless of who's cooking it, Ani swings left, leading us toward the Promenade shopping center.

"So we're picking up takeout after all?" I laugh as we pull to a stop and park the bikes. "Ani, I don't think any of the shops are even open yet."

The Promenade sustained less damage in the attack than the main areas of campus, but it still needed a lot of repairs and rebuilding. Last I heard, they were planning a grand re-opening in a few weeks, coinciding with the start of classes.

"One shop is open," he says cryptically, eyebrows wagging. "Rather, it will be soon. Come on."

A nervous giggle erupts from my chest as he leads me toward a nondescript storefront, brown paper covering the glass doors. He pulls one open and nods for me to head inside.

To my surprise and delight, my friends and family are waiting for me just inside the entryway—Doc, Baz, and

Kirin, of course. Carly, Isla, and Nat. Professor Broome and Professor Maddox.

Every last one of them is wearing a mischievous grin.

Ducking my suspicious glares, the group suddenly parts, and Ani ushers me to the center of the shop.

"So?" He spreads his arms wide, turning in a slow circle. "What do you think?"

I follow his gaze, glancing around at the space. It's one of the shops that had to be completely remodeled, so everything is new and shiny, the air carrying the scent of fresh-cut wood.

Low café tables line one side, with a couple of smaller tables positioned near the papered-up windows. Counter seating takes up most of the opposite side, leading back into a kitchen. Tarot artwork graces the walls—the Arcana drinking from teacups and eating pastries.

"Wait!" The scent of fresh-baked scones hits me, and I bounce on my toes, my stomach turning as fizzy as Carly's pineapple mimosas. "Is this a new tea café? Oh my Goddess, it looks amazing! I've been dying for them to put in a tea café! Why should coffee get all the love, right? Guys, this is *amazing*!"

"Isn't it though?" Ani asks.

Still beaming, I turn to look at the rest of the gang. "So, who bought the place? One of the faculty? Someone from outside? Wait, don't tell me it's a franchise. Is it? I mean, as long as they know how to brew tea, I guess I can't complain, but..." I pop my hands on my hips and roll my eyes. "Okay. Let me in on the joke, because I don't get it.

What's so damn funny about someone opening a tea café?"

"Nothing," Baz says, covering his mouth to hide the smile. Next to him, Kirin turns his obvious laughter into a very fake cough. When I turn my gaze on Ani, he stares up at the ceiling and whistles.

"What's so *funny*, Miss Milan," Doc says, finally coming to my rescue, "is that this is, in fact, a tea café, yet the owner hasn't opened for business, despite having a full shop of eager customers."

"Customers?" I glance around the place, wondering where they're all hiding.

At my obvious confusion, the laughter everyone was trying so hard to hold back finally erupts in earnest.

Somewhere in the back of my mind, a little bell chimes, but I have no idea what it's trying to tell me.

There's something I'm not getting here.

Brow furrowed in concentration, I take another deep whiff of scone-scented air.

Wait, not scones. Are those… cinnamon buns?

My heart—that telltale little beast—kicks in to high gear. My mouth goes dry, my hands and feet start tingling, and everything inside me goes absolutely haywire.

"What is this place?" I whisper, afraid of what the answer might be. Afraid of what it might *not* be. Afraid and elated and overjoyed and overwhelmed in the best possible way…

No. It can't be. It *can't* be. They wouldn't do something so crazy.

Would they?

Did they?

I close my eyes, hope rising inside me like a balloon.

Warm hands land on my shoulders from behind, and a glimpse of Doc's moonlit ocean flickers through my mind.

"It's yours, my Star," he says softly, breath tickling my ear. "Fully stocked, paid in full."

"Mine?" With a gasp, I open my eyes and find Kirin standing before me.

He cups my face, his green eyes calming the storm inside me. "We wanted to give you something you love. Something that's just yours. Something no one can take away from you."

"You can change it up if you want," Ani says. "Get different artwork, paint the walls, move around the tables, get different supplies. Personally, I'm holding out for a karaoke stage at the back, but... We just wanted to give you a starting point."

"And if you don't like it or decide you'd rather pursue something else," Doc continues, "that's okay too."

"You guys... You... You did this for me?" They bought me a café. I'm hyperventilating. Holy balls, they bought me a café.

"You're our Star," Baz says with a shrug. "There's nothing we won't do for you."

"I... I... I... I'm stammering like an idiot because I have no idea what to say."

"Say you love it," Ani says, the hope in his eyes on full display.

"Of *course* I love it!" I choke out, my stammering quickly turning into sobs. Seriously, this is a code-red situation. We are fast approaching ugly-cry territory. "It's the most thoughtful, incredible, generous thing anyone has ever done for me!"

"Then why are you crying?" he asks.

"Because I'm so happy!"

At that, my ridiculous crying turns into laughter, and *that* turns into a very emotional, very dramatic group hug.

"Next time, let's skip the drama and get to the tea," Carly says, trying to play off her own tears. "I told you she'd love it. It was foreseen."

"Don't think this excuses you from your studies," Professor Maddox says sternly, but her eyes are warm and teasing too. "We've got big plans for your academic career, Miss Milan. So you'll need to find a way to juggle both."

"I can do that," I say on another bubble of laughter. "Goddess, I would *love* to do that."

I take another look around, my mind already racing with ideas for new blends, new techniques, new sales, new everything. I love the decor though—I won't change a thing in that regard. My mages picked it out, and no one knows me better. It's perfect.

Still half in shock, I walk up and down the space, exploring every inch. When I get back to the front, I notice the shelves behind the counter.

They're full, stacked with colorful teacups and saucers from my parents' collection.

My eyes blur with tears, my heart threatening to burst.

The last time I saw those teacups was the last time I stood inside Kettle Black—the last time I set foot in Tres Búhos. Jessa told me she'd boxed them up for me, but I assumed she kept them with her in Mexico.

"Where did you get those?" I breathe.

"Oh, they were hand-delivered late last night," Doc says. A wave of mischief and giddiness flows through his energy.

I narrow my eyes, still trying to puzzle this all out. "But I thought Jessa had them? And—"

"Yeah, I heard this place might need a baker, so I decided to throw my hat into the ring."

I spin around toward the sound of that sweet, familiar voice, daring to hope for one more miracle on a day that's already bursting with them…

And there, standing in the alcove between the counter and the kitchen, with perfect winged eyeliner and a fiery red lip that sets off her glossy black hair, my best friend Jessa beams at me.

I practically vault over the counter to get to her, tackling her in a hug and kissing her face until she has to physically shove me away.

"So, does this mean I got the job?" she asks.

I cock an eyebrow and give her the once-over. "That depends. You still know how to make a scone?"

"*And* cinnamon buns," she teases. Then, leaning in close and dropping her voice to a whisper, "I don't suppose any of your hot mages have a hot brother? Or two or three?"

"I'm sure you'll find plenty of inspiration on campus," I say. "Wait, you *are* staying, right?"

"Moving into the apartment upstairs, as a matter of fact."

"How did this even happen?"

"Given the situation outside, we felt it would be safer for Jessa at the Academy," Doc says. "And when I told her about our plans here, she leaped at the chance."

The waterworks are starting up again, but I quickly dash away the tears. I've never felt so happy. So excited about the future.

"Thank you," I say. "All of you. This is... Thank you."

Sparing me from a lengthy speech I'd certainly bungle, Doc claps once and says, "It seems to me there's only one way to properly christen the new space."

I flash him a flirty smirk, lowering my voice to a whisper only he can hear. "Agreed, but you're not into sharing, so a proper christening is *definitely* not on the menu today."

"Um, standing right here, hello!" Carly tosses her hands into the air.

So much for only Doc hearing my little innuendos.

"Goddess, we know you're all in love," she says, "but must you be so adorable and disgusting about it all the time?"

"Don't blame me," I say. "Doc's the one who brought up the christening."

His eyes blaze a fresh warning. Goddess, how I've missed that.

"*Tea*, Miss Milan," he says firmly. "I'm talking about the inaugural pot of tea."

I hold his gaze another beat, basking in the heat gathering between us, loving the way I can still make my controlling, commanding professor blush.

But he's right. The inaugural pot of tea is important. It has to be just right—it'll set the tone for the entire venture.

Isla takes a seat at the counter and hits the little silver bell.

When I shoot her a faux glare, she shrugs and says, "I told you that night in Red Sands I was going to be your first paying customer. Well, here we are." She plucks a credit card out of her pocket. "I'll take one cup of whatever you think I need."

"Same," Nat says, taking the seat next to her. Carly nods vigorously too. Behind them, the professors raise their hands.

"We'll need some as well," Professor Maddox says.

"All right." I grab an apron from a hook beside the counter and tie it around my waist. "Why don't you *all* have a seat? Give me a second to get the lay of the land, then I'll fix everyone something awesome to go with whatever Jessa's baking back there."

As they all find their tables, I scoot into the kitchen to explore the shelves.

Jessa follows me, heading for the ovens as I put the water on to boil.

"What are you brewing up?" she asks, sliding out a hot tray of cinnamon buns and another with chocolate banana scones. The smell is heavenly. "Vanilla Cherry Bomb? Lemon Lavender Luxury? Classic Black with a whisper of almond?"

"No. I'm feeling called to try something totally new. I'm just not sure *what*." Scanning the shelves, I pick out a few options, slowly getting my mojo back.

Black tea for the base. Cinnamon. Cardamom—yes, extra cardamom. A bit of chili powder. A splash of carnelian essence. A hint of this, a dash of that, one more sprinkling of this, and… *yes*.

That's it.

Grabbing the water from the stovetop, I pour a cup over the brew and let it steep. After just the right amount of time, I strain it and hand the mug to Jessa.

"Taste this," I demand. "Honest opinion."

"Wow. You're giving me the first sip of the first new brew?"

"Of course! There's no one I'd rather give the honor."

Her eyes shine with love and happiness. "I missed you, ya know."

"I missed you too." I tug on a lock of her hair. "Now take a sip. I'm dying here."

"Fine, fine." She closes her eyes and brings the mug to her face, inhaling the scent before taking a single sip. Then another. Then one more.

"Well?" I press. "What do you think?"

"I think… I think… I think I need to sit down." She presses a hand to her forehead. "Holy shit, girl. I'm having a hot flash. Or an orgasm. I can't tell. All I know is this tea is making me rethink everything I thought I knew about sex."

I crack up. Goddess, I really *did* miss her. "Awesome. Guess I know what to call it, then. Spontaneous Orgasm it is."

"So scandalous!" Her eyes light up. "I love it. But… what about the professors? The potions prof seems a little old to appreciate your raunchy sense of humor."

"Professor Broome? Are you *kidding* me? Thanks to her, my sex life is…" I bite my lip, cutting myself off. Now is not the time for *that* conversation. "You know what? We have a *lot* of catching up to do."

"Um, apparently!" Flashing me one more wicked grin, Jessa takes a few more sips. Then, setting down her cup, she looks at me with soft eyes and says, "Will you call it Kettle Black, like before?"

Kettle Black…

The old name echoes through my memories, settling into my heart like a favorite song whose lyrics I'll never forget, but whose meaning has changed so much over time, it no longer feels the same.

I've always loved making tea—I can't imagine this *not* being a part of my life. But things are different now. I want to make tea, just like I did at Kettle Black, but I want to make magick too. To infuse everything I do with the gifts I was blessed with—no more holding back. No more running away. No more hiding.

I pour and steep the rest of the tea, then assemble the cups on a tray. When I get back to the dining area, happy murmurs and bouts of laughter float to my ears, and I'm struck by how blessed I am.

Of all the possible paths my life could have taken, the twisty, turny roads of fate brought me here.

Yes, so much has changed since my life in Tres Búhos. And so much *more* change awaits on the horizon—an invitation to all the new adventures yet to come.

This time, I'm more than ready for them.

As I set the tray onto the counter and hand Isla the first cup, the name comes to me—simple and perfect, as the best things in life so often do.

"Welcome," I say with a grin that warms me all the way to my toes, "to New Leaf Café."

* * *

Thank you so much for joining me on this long, winding, twisty, turny Tarot Academy adventure!

I can't believe we've come to the end.

But! You don't have to say goodbye just yet... I've got a special treat for you!

Sign up for my newsletter and you'll receive a sizzling hot bonus scene featuring our girl Stevie and her favorite naughty professor, Dr. Devane. It's the perfect after-book chaser—especially for those who like a little steam with their tea.

Grab your free bonus scene now! Can't see the link? Drop me a line at sarah@sarahpiperbooks.com and I'll be sure to send you your bonus scene!

* * *

What's next after Tarot Academy? If you're in the mood for more spicy, witchy, reverse harem romance, I've got you covered!

Check out **Claimed by Gargoyles**, a sizzling hot paranormal mafia romance featuring a witch coming into her powers and four fierce, brooding, insanely overprotective gargoyles teaming up to break an ancient curse and get revenge on the cruel dark mages bent on destroying her. If you enjoy dark, supernatural thrills and super spicy romance featuring... *ahem*... special equipment, sensitive wings, and oh-so-dominant dirty-talkers, this is the series for you. **Start with book one, Wicked Conjuring!**

Read on for an excerpt...

* * *

Are you a member of our private Facebook group, <u>Sarah Piper's Sassy Witches?</u> Pop in for sneak peeks, cover reveals, exclusive giveaways, book chats, and plenty of complete randomness! We've got a great community of readers and fans (and fellow Tarot lovers too!), and we'd love to see you there!

XOXO
Sarah

WICKED CONJURING EXCERPT

Chapter One
JUDE

This many centuries into my cursed immortal existence, only three things have the power to remind me I'm not dead: fucking, fighting, and killing. Give me the full monty on the same night? Stuff of wet dreams, that. Bloody brilliant.

But thanks to the mortal feds crawling up our arses after a botched hit job on a crooked judge—not *my* botched hit job, mind you—Drae's got us on a real tight leash. Been a whole twenty-seven days since I broke a bone or spilled so much as a drop of someone else's blood, and he's still sore at me over the last bloke I put in the ground.

Human. The bastard abso-fuckin'-lutely deserved it too, but I digress.

As for my *favorite* way to pass the time?

Well.

I flick the lighter and hold the flame to the tip of the joint, sucking in a deep drag of witchweed. Across a pitch-black dead-end street in Brooklyn's Park Slope neighborhood, a square of golden light spills from a third-story brownstone window at the end of the row. A dozen crows hang out on the eves just above it, flapping and tittering like old codgers fighting over dominoes.

Those fucking birds show up here every night, same as me.

Watching. Waiting.

I'm pretty sure the little scarecrow inside knows she has an audience, too. But she's a nice girl. Too polite to shoo us all away.

Lucky for us.

A shadow moves behind her sheer curtains, and I keep a close watch in anticipation of what's to come.

She's undressing for bed—my favorite part of the show.

Stripped down to her bra and panties, she saunters past the window, shaking out that gorgeous mane. Dark waves spill down over her soft shoulders and cover her perfect, oh-so-suckable tits.

It's the color of crow feathers, that hair. Shot through with a few silver locks that set off the brightest blue eyes you ever saw.

Unfortunately, I only ever got to see them up close the one time. I was heading back to the office from a late-night coffee run when I caught her feeding the crows in Madison Square Park. Some pervert was harassing her, but I chased him off real quick. After that, I chatted her up a bit. Offered her the fancy-arse almond-milk latte I'd bought for Auggie and made her laugh enough times to get the sound of it stuck in my head forever.

Before I knew it, I was half the fuck in love with her.

So a bit later, when she thanked me for the coffee and said she had to get home, I did what any self-respecting lovesick arsehole would do.

I followed her.

Never did get her name, but I've been showing up here like a goddamn stalker every night since, hiding out in the shadows across the way and hoping for a peek.

Who's the pervert now, right? Fuck it.

As for the fuckstain who tried to mess with her in the park… Would you believe it was *exactly* twenty-seven days ago and no one's heard from him since? The poor chap. Although, there *is* a human skull on my desk presently serving as a paperweight that bears a striking resemblance. Coincidence?

The curtains flutter and her silhouette glides past once more. Every graceful movement makes my dick hard as stone, aching to sink inside her wet little cunt and make her beg for all the filthy things she never even knew she wanted. Needed.

And oh, I *will* make her beg.

In the end, they always do.

Her light flicks off. I hold my breath, heart slamming against my ribs.

Please come back, love. Night's young yet and I've got so *many naughty, delicious plans for us…*

Seconds later, the gauzy curtains part and I try not to squeal like a tween boy who's just discovered the dark side of the internet. I take another hit of the witchweed, then flick the spent butt into the gutter, my attention lasering in on that window. Her face fills the glass, blue eyes luminescent in the dark.

Searching. Always searching.

Perhaps she's searching for her white knight from the park, wondering if I've finally come to claim her.

Fearing it, as she damn well should.

The thought of making her tremble sends a dark thrill straight to my balls, and my human glamour ripples with the ancient magic holding it together. The real me is eager to come out and play. Hungry for a taste.

Her neighborhood is quiet at this hour, all the happy little babies tucked into bed by their happy mums and dads, so fuck it. Keeping to the shadows, I give my surroundings a quick scan, then drop the glamour and let my true form stretch to fill the darkness.

If my little scarecrow saw me like this… Damn. I nearly bust a gut at the idea. If the seven feet of muscle and massive leathery wings didn't scare her right the fuck off, the horns and tail would certainly get the job done proper.

Gargoyles? We're not supposed to exist. Problem is, we do. What's left of us, anyway.

But my girl doesn't need to know that yet. All in due time.

These days, patience is a severely under-cultivated skill. Me? I'm old school. Reckless and impulsive most of the time, sure. But when something's worth the wait, my patience is damned legendary. Just ask any traitorous cunt who's had the pleasure of regaining consciousness after a beating, only to find himself chained up in my basement with his bodily fluids leaking out.

Death by a thousand cuts is the ultimate test of a killer's patience.

And this girl? Fuck. She's the reason patience is such a bloody virtue.

So as badly as I want to fly up there, smash through that window, and put her on her knees for me, I'll wait until she's ready. Until I'm sure she won't run off. Even if I have to show up here again and again, play our little game every night for another month. Six. Hell, I'd do it for a whole year if I had that much time left.

Drae doesn't think so. According to his calculations, unless we break the fucking curse, we've got about two months before it all goes to shit. And trust me when I say there are *plenty* of things worse than death for an immortal fucking monster.

Like being trapped in our statue forms for eternity—fully conscious—rather than just turning to stone while the sun's out.

Like being forced to watch our own kind get pulverized into dust, knowing there's not a damn thing we can do about it.

A rusty old ache stabs at my heart, but I don't have time for it.

Right now, there's only one rock-hard thing about me, and it's got *nothing* to do with some bullshit dark fae curse and *everything* to do with the girl upstairs.

Resting her forehead against the glass, my little scarecrow slides a hand down along her bare belly, hooking a thumb into the waistband of her panties. *Mmm.* White lace, this pair.

Back and forth her naughty little thumb glides, driving me wild with every stroke. Her eyes drift closed as she tips her head back and sighs, one hand pressed flat against the glass, the other working its way lower, her back arching just so.

I'd give just about anything for a glimpse of her thoughts. Does she know I'm out here? Does she get off on the idea of being watched?

Does she have any idea what she's fucking doing to me?

I swear to the fucking devil I can almost *feel* her touch. Her small hand wrapped around my dick, blue eyes wide and scandalized as I command her to get on her knees, open her mouth, and...

Just fucking take *it*...

Pulling my wings close around me, I fist my dick with a tight grip, my gaze never leaving that window. That fucking girl.

Her eyes have haunted my dreams all month. Not even the feds or Drae's worries about the curse can break the spell this girl's got me under, and I don't want them to. From the moment I laid eyes on her in the city, I wanted her. Knew I'd make her mine one way or the other.

Her fingers continue their quest, finally dipping inside the panties as her mouth parts on a soft little moan only a supernatural beast could hear at this distance.

Grateful for my highly attuned senses, I stroke myself harder, faster, still imagining the feel of her soft pink lips, her velvet-smooth tongue, the scrape of her teeth as I make her take me all the way in...

That's it, darling. Just like that. God, you're so fucking good...

I fight the urge to close my eyes, focusing entirely on her. On the fog of her breath against the glass. The smudge of a damp handprint. The pretty way her cheeks darken with lust.

And—most enticing of all—the desperate, wet sounds her greedy little cunt makes as she fucks herself for me, faster and more frenetic with every stroke, drawing back to circle her clit before diving deep inside once more...

Fucking hell.

A sheen of sweat glazes her upper lip. Suddenly, I want to lick her, and my mouth fills with the imagined taste of it —a mix of sweet and salty that has my balls tightening, heat racing through my veins, heart slamming in my chest as I fight to keep breathing, and then...

"Fuck!"

When I come for her, it's hard and fast and messy, and her answering gasp of pleasure echoes right through me, connecting us on a fucking *soul* level as she trembles behind the window and rides out the last waves of pleasure.

And then, just as quickly as it all began, it's over.

With a deep sigh, she presses her forehead to the glass and closes her eyes, removing her hand from the panties.

Again, I imagine the taste of her. The way she'll moan my name as I wrap a hand around her throat and make her watch me suck those fingers clean, one by delectable one.

Such a good girl…

Still gazing up at her beautifully flushed face, I grin.

For now, I'll let her rest. But tomorrow?

Maybe I'll bring her a ring. She won't be able to resist.

I'll make sure of it.

"Until tomorrow," I whisper, damn near giddy as the plan forms in my mind. "Sleep well, scarecrow."

Overhead, the old crows finally take flight, and I stretch out my wings, leap into the air, and chase them all the way back to Manhattan.

Ready for more? Jump in to the dangerous, red-hot world of Claimed by Gargoyles! **Grab your copy of Wicked Conjuring now!**

ABOUT SARAH PIPER

Sarah Piper is a witchy, Tarot-card-slinging paranormal romance and urban fantasy author. Through her signature brew of dark magic, heart-pounding suspense, and steamy romance, Sarah promises a sexy, supernatural escape into a world where the magic is real, the monsters are sinfully hot, and the witches always get their magically-ever-afters.

Readers have dubbed her work "super sexy," "imaginative and original," "off-the-walls good," and "delightfully wicked in the best ways," a quote Sarah hopes will appear on her tombstone.

Originally from New York, Sarah now makes her home in northern Colorado with her husband (though that changes frequently) (the location, not the husband), where she spends her days sleeping like a vampire and her nights writing books, casting spells, gazing at the moon, playing with her ever-expanding collection of Tarot cards, binge-watching Supernatural (Team Dean!), and obsessing over the best way to brew a cup of tea.

You can find her online at SarahPiperBooks.com, on TikTok at @sarahpiperbooks, and in her Facebook readers group at Sarah Piper's Sassy Witches! If you're sassy, or if you need a little *more* sass in your life, or if you need more Dean Winchester gifs in your life (who doesn't?), come hang out!

Made in the USA
Middletown, DE
06 March 2024